I0722334

LOSING JUNE

Coming of Age at the Foot of St. Helens

A Novel

Catherine Sanders Bodnar

Burlington, Vermont

Onion River Press
191 Bank Street
Burlington, VT 05401

ISBN: 978-1-957184-10-4

Library of Congress Control Number: 2022910317

Book design: Marian Willmott www.willmottstudios.com
Inside cover: Placemat by Mary Gillis, 1958
Cover photo: Catherine Maureen Sanders, 1959

For John

PROLOGUE

A song keeps repeating in her head, fading off just as she is about to grasp the words, but she can not remember all of them. They seem to be playing a game of hide and seek with her. I'm off to see the wizard.... But why? Where?

Not asleep, really, nor awake, she hurls through the sky in some in-between place, touching down once, twice, to earth. Her body feels cocooned as if swaddled in cloth. Seeing nothing, she can measure time only by the bats that, she knows, sleep in the day. She feels soothed by their soft rustling that reminds her of the cooing of doves back home.

Her surroundings seep continually with pungent moisture. Without her sight, she is teased by her other senses, and they give nothing but flimsy scraps of information: smells of dirt and pee, sounds of distant wolves howling and night owls whoo-whooing, warmth enfolding her, and the bitter taste of chocolates.

She recognizes his heavy footfall when he climbs up a creaky ladder to where she lies. She can feel his eyes on her even as she travels high in deep space. He smells musty.

Was it a cave? But she was in the mine before. Had someone moved her while she slept?

Safe in her floating dream, she isn't afraid. Maybe she should be. Because because because because because....

1

James released just enough bubbles to sink well below the surface of the glacial lake. He was counting seconds now with the accuracy of habit. Every morning during his school year back East he swam a half-mile at the pool, speed training. Each day at the end of his last lap — no matter what his time had been — he took his reward and, exhaling, let himself drop to the bottom.

Such peace, the way the noise stopped, the way gravity eased the weight off his body. It almost felt as if he could give up the tiresome compulsion of breathing. Maybe become aquatic. A bubble slipped from his lips and spiraled up. He continued to count. Seconds into minutes, into seconds. His heart rate slowed. How far could he push it?

At Spirit Lake, James could endure submersion longer than in the crowded, chlorinated pool. Here, gray-green water sparkled as he touched the pumice bottom under the diving tower. He waved his arms in transparent water, water clearer than air, letting himself lift and roll with the current.

His Timex read two minutes and fifty-five seconds, and James's lungs ached to break the surface, but he hung on. After some time, he glanced at it again. Three minutes five seconds. Not enough. It hadn't been enough the last time. Was he man enough to qualify for the next Ice-Man Competition in August? This year it was in Alaska, and James was desperate to go to Anchorage. It was the very spot where, ten years before, his mother took him from his father. Chances were good Dad was still in Anchorage. I'm in Washington now, James thought. So close.

Four minutes. Like a flash, his toes pushed off the bottom and he shot to the surface. He sucked in air, breathing in his hard-earned ration of air, and, treading water, continued to breathe in shallow mouthfuls. He swam lazily to the diving tower, climbed the wooden ladder to the lower level, and grabbed his towel and glasses. He stood and replaced the thick horn rims when his eyes suddenly fixed south.

During his swim, the fog had burned off around Mount St. Helens to reveal a classical golden triangle glistening in ice. Less than two miles away, James felt the volcano's gravitational pull as immediate and elemental, like leaning over the Empire State Building. He imagined the tallest pines seemed to lean into her.

Then he heard his mother's voice. His heart jumped. *Shit.*

"James? James! Here you are. I could have guessed. Have you even unpacked?"

He glanced at her. He recognized that call anywhere. And from great distances. God, he wanted to dive back into the deep water. His gaze shifted from her to the sublime mountain, careful not to let his disappointment show. His Mom had drawn on her eyebrows in high arches, giving her a surprised expression even when she was bored.

"Gloria baked blueberry muffins," she said, her eyes still on him.

"Thanks." He pulled his towel tighter around his neck. "I'll go inside and change."

———————◆———————

From the moment they parked their rattle-trap Plymouth wagon at the landing, James felt haunted. White fog hung like a shroud over the eerie landscape. A pinkish smear on the eastern sky was the only indication that the sun had risen on Spirit Lake. They had driven across the continent to the end of the world as if the thin ribbon of Highway 504 stopped at the very edge.

He unfolded himself from the shotgun seat and shook off sleep, but a dreaminess remained. Quiet lapping guided him down to the dock where he took hold of a worn railing and breathed in deeply. Air fresh as rain. He had big plans for the lake. It was two miles across and back, perfect training for a long-distance swimmer. It would build his endurance, maybe make a competitor of him, and he would probably add it to the list of things he would talk about with his father when he met him.

A wave rippled across the water, a trill of light on mottled gray. It reminded him of moonlight on a bald man's head. Why a wave? There were no boats, no wind, no reason for a wave but there it was, like a ghost calling him in.

His mom stepped to a post where she pulled a hand crank that carried a signal across the lake and buzzed in the kitchen of Harmony Falls Lodge to tell Aunt Marie to come and get them. "It'll be about ten minutes," she said, turning to James. Looking down, she smiled wearily. "Darn coffee-to-go. Spilled on my slacks."

June nearly fell out of the blanket-bunched back seat brushing Cheese Puffs off her shorts. As she stood up she widened her stance to release a wedgie. James rolled his eyes. What a goofball. She started in his direction. *Shit.* He wasn't ready for her chatter. After the five-day haul, he was hoping to find some time alone. The sound of the drone of a motor nearly made him smile. He inwardly thanked the heavens that they were finally going to move.

The old prow cruised through the mist as if floating on clouds. On board, James looped his thumbs tightly in his back jeans pockets, shrugging his shoulders close as if that might keep the wet Pacific chill from leaching into his Yankee bones. Too much pit-stop coffee had soured his mouth and made him grind his teeth.

———————————— ❦ ————————————

About ten minutes across the lake, maybe halfway, the boat rocked.

What the hell? James leaned over the rail, dampness settling on his forearms and eyeglasses like condensation on a windshield. An uncanny moan issued from the depths like a vibration he felt more than heard. Did the others feel it too? Unlikely. His aunt gabbed and giggled with his mom, ignoring a battery of questions from June. Aunt Marie steered the old lifeboat around what looked to be a broken-off tree growing in the water. She glanced back at James.

"Too bad you can't see St. Helens." She shrugged. "Fog swallows it nearly every morning." Laughing, she reached to squeeze his mom's hand. She air-kissed her back. Like jolly twins, those two.

Suddenly he shivered. Ahead of them, a make-shift raft slid hazily into view like an apparition. An old-timer in a bent western hat waved at them with a long, thin arm.

"Wait," he called, his voice raspy.

But Aunt Marie didn't slow. Neither did she spare him a glance.

Wait? "What does he want?" James turned to watch the guy's raft rock in their wake. Soon, he faded back into the fog.

"That's just Max," his aunt muttered frowning. "Old prospector. A recluse. Been around forever."

Had anyone ever stopped for him? James felt a chill down his spine. What if he needed help?

Gradually, the northern shore of Spirit Lake emerged in shades of gray. First an eerie tower, then some docks, and then, just like the picture postcard, an old lodge and ten cedar-shake cabins snuggled into a vast forest near the shore. James stared at it, marveling at everything in front of him. Through the mist James made out Uncle Hank standing tall and portly on the deck, his wide smile nearly overrun by a grizzled beard. To James's sleep-starved brain he looked like Gandalf lording over a hobbit village. Harmony Falls roared behind the lodge. James tilted his head back to behold clouds of spray pillowing under a deep green canopy of cloud-tall firs.

Aunt Marie eased the boat alongside the dock and then turned around to James and June. Her smile disappeared. "You kids pay attention. Around here we got bears. And all kinds of campers, too. It's a small lake, but it's public and it's popular." Strands of her brown hair blew into her face as their wake rocked the lifeboat gently against the old wooden dock.

Once his shoes touched the planks, his cousin Tess bounded down to the dock to relieve James of his duffle. Once he let go of the duffle, he flexed his arm and bent to carry the other heavy boxes up the cedar-slab steps. Ahead of him, his Mom carried only her purse and train case, with June close behind with her small suitcase.

"Hey, this way!" Tess pointed inside Harmony Falls Lodge, showing her sweet toothy smile. A good elder at nineteen, she took James in tow. He banged his way up a steep narrow staircase to one of the five bedrooms. How dark the 1920s logger's lodge was. Even the ceiling beams seemed blackened. At his door, he whispered thanks to Tess, thrilled to get a room of his own. They hugged and laughed. It was the size of his bathroom back East, but he surely didn't mind.

When she turned to help the others downstairs, James eased the door shut and put his over-stuffed duffle on the lower bunk of a metal bed. He turned to a yellowed mirror hanging from a nail above a small table holding an enameled washbasin and pitcher. Stooping, he gazed at a cracked version of himself with a few days' stubble and eyes that looked like they'd been to war and back. People often told him he looked either tired or depressed. He was tired now, but always chalked it up to a high I.Q. Not that he ever said that, though it was true. He was different, set apart at the very least by his preference for solitude.

He set down his glasses and dipped his hands into the poured icy water to scrub off the trip grime. He splashed the water on his forehead and cheeks, toweled off, and replaced his heavy glasses. Ahhhh... He could see again.

He dug out his trunks. Time for submersion.

———— ┆ ————

Aunt Marie and Uncle Hank managed Harmony Falls Lodge and, finding themselves short-handed that summer, had called James's mom. "Great idea," Kay said. James heard her. Long-distance calls were a big deal in his house. "It will be grand for the kids to experience nature." So, without consulting him or his sister, she left her husband Dan in Boston, packed up the Plymouth, and pointed west.

Now in dry clothes, James dug into his duffel to haul out his *Classic Comics, MADs,* and his required summer reading. He lined them up on the bunk: *Look Homeward Angel,* Poe's collected short stories, and his dog-eared copy of *Catcher in the Rye.* Lately, he'd been on a tear with Jack London. No contest, though. "To Build a Fire" was best. Depressing as hell, but excellent research for his covert plan.

He had told no one. He was still forming the plan. But he had the money, hoarded from mowing lawns, and he was ready. That summer was a perfect time. It would be *their* time, father and son. He had enough money to buy them both a ticket to the competition. His dad would see for himself what James could do. They'd head to the mountains to camp, and Dad would tell stories at a lazy campfire. Would James recognize him from the picture he swiped from his mom?

James credited his father for what little he knew of the wilderness. He had taught James his ABCs with picture books borrowed from the local library. James learned to name lakes and streams and trees and wild animals, too. In time, he taught him how to write all the names, until his mother took James to New York City. Just like that. The car was packed when she pulled him out of nursery school and never went home again.

The thought of his dad returning from work that day to an empty house, his boy gone, always choked James up. He had learned to swallow it, but still had no word for how it felt. He hadn't gotten to say goodbye. Can a five-year-old even remember such things? Since then James had learned to spell the Lithuanian words for 'little son': *mazai sunus.* It was such a private phrase that when he said it aloud, he could hear his father's voice precisely.

James never quit reading and tore through novels in days. But that was a habit, his mother often reminded him, that kept him from teenage pastimes such as dating.

"Get your head out of that book and go to a show or something," she'd say, which irked him. He was beginning his junior year with maybe two friends and no steady girl. Okay, no girl at all, which only seemed to confirm that he was not well-rounded. Worse than that, he was bored. So, when he was offered a free western vacation, he jumped at the chance to get his hands dirty and climb the volcano, maybe meet a girl, and escape his tedious stepfather, who was more interested in golf and litigation than his stepson's swim meets. "It's not even a team sport," Dan liked to say.

Here was surely the place to train for the Ice-Man Meet. From Harmony Falls across the lake to the Boy Scout camp was a mile. Or he could swim to Duck Bay for a two-mile drill one way. No roads ran around Spirit Lake. Good, James thought. It would keep him focused: he would swim daily, do chores, read and chop wood. He was cut off from the civilized world, from toilets and running water, from television and telephones, from all transportation except boats. Spirit Lake was so remote that the dining tables' placemats claimed Harmony Falls was "The Most Secluded Spot in the Pacific Northwest." So here I am, James thought. Swimming at the end of the world.

His stomach growled. The aroma of hot berry muffins wafted up like an invitation. As James headed down, his every step caused the old lodge to elicit a creak, a shriek, or a sigh. He came into a bright, busy inn-sized kitchen with linoleum countertops, white cabinets, and an industrial-sized blue-enameled cast-iron cook stove. As he walked in, everyone was talking at once, but the loudest voice belonged to the cook who stirred a cauldron of bubbling blueberries.

"Tess, bring me that quart of maple syrup." In her long, colorful skirt and an oversized sweater, Gloria seemed bohemian to James. Easily as tall as him, but a good bit rounder, she wore bright-orange wrist bangles that clacked as she stirred. His cousin suddenly stepped between them.

"James, get over here!" Tess dropped her knife, wiped her hands on her apron, and pulled him into a hug. She reached for the cook. "Gloria, this is Aunt Kay's son, James." Tess winked at him. "See? I told you he was cute."

James reddened and stared at the uneven wood floor, any place but at the two females.

Gloria turned to him. Her pale blonde hair peeked out of a headscarf and formed a fuzzy halo around her face. "Nice to meet you. But if you don't mind, please open those cans of tuna," she pointed to the table, "and drain them before emptying them into that metal bowl." James looked over at where she had pointed. There stood two cases of chum tuna, ten cans a case. "Then when you're done, I've got five more things for you to do, including adding in the mayo and relish." She smiled quickly. "We're officially open the day after tomorrow. Ten overfilled cabins." She paused as if remembering something. "Hope you like to work hard, Mr. James."

"It's James." But she was already halfway into the dining hall. He emptied six cans in two minutes into the huge bowl. Fourteen to go. His thumb and index finger would be blistered, but he played tough watching Tess cheerfully chop carrots, even with the twenty-pound bag of potatoes waiting to be cubed. James spun towards the door when he heard a voice as deep as Perry Mason's.

"What do you mean, reopen Sweden mine? That place never got more than scrap copper." A bear of a man nearly shouted at Uncle Hank as they approached the back kitchen door. "It'll poison the lake." The man looked up and stepped aside when he saw people gathered there. He let Hank walk in first.

His uncle grabbed James in a hug and announced, "Welcome to the New World." When he laughed, his voice sounded gruff and soft, like timber falling on thick moss. James returned Hank's embrace, but in an instant, his uncle pulled away to pat his friend's shoulder. "Here's my right-hand man, Ben Stwire."

A rough-hewn outdoorsman towered before James. His face was mapped with deep grooves and a scar that ran the length of his left cheek. James examined the scar, the skin, the black eyes. This guy was the real thing, a true man of the wilderness, someone like Davy Crockett or Kit Carson who, left to his own devices, would survive anything. The man nodded at James without expression and shifted from one foot to the other. James couldn't help but stare. A leather-sheathed Bowie hung from his belt, the blade of which had to be a foot long. James was fascinated.

"Nice to meet you, sir." James winced from the pressure of his grip. Ben nodded. James tried to smile.

"You'll be seeing Ben around plenty." Hank lightly punched Ben's arm and smiled. "Practically runs the place." His uncle poured them both mugs of steaming black coffee.

"Hank? Hank! Come help, please!" Aunt Marie hollered from the dining room. Hank grinned and said as he left, "And your aunt's the one who runs *us*."

"See you, kid." Ben turned to leave and stepped out the back door carefully balancing his scalding coffee.

Cheery when they'd arrived that morning, the lodge turned bleak in late-afternoon rain as if the sodden woods had swelled and tightened around them. After dinner, James dried dishes. He didn't mind. Then he joined the crew at the huge river-stone fireplace for hot cocoa. James's mother looked on blankly from an overstuffed chair, sipping chocolate, intermittently reading Frost, but she was miles away. Come on, James thought. How much Robert Frost could a person take? When June plopped down on her lap, his mother gently pushed her off.

"You're too big for that, Junie." She brushed invisible lint from her clean navy slacks and continued reading Frost. June rolled her eyes before she took a spot on the sofa. From his position, James could see the pout on her lips.

James slightly shook his head. No question about it, his mother was remote. It seemed like she was drifting farther from his sister and him. Later, on his way up to bed, dog-tired, James registered dully that the waterfall-powered generator must have stopped. The old lodge's lamps glowed amber with the dirty burn of kerosene.

2

JUNE

She was not the kind of girl to sleep in. By early morning she was already standing at the lakeshore in her bright pink swimsuit. She slid her toes in first and then jerked them back out immediately. She looked down at the icy water, concluding in her mind that it would take some getting used to. Beside her, she stuck Barbie in a narrow hole to stand upright while she immersed her toes in the water again, this time daring herself to keep them that way. Slowly she was up to her ankles and took a few steps. She smiled as little minnows darted in the clear water and nibbled at her legs.

Soon, she heard someone chopping wood. It was her uncle's friend, the big man with a scar on his face and a long knife on his belt. Why did he have to be here? Why did her mother bring them here anyway? And why didn't her father come? She felt lonely without his lap to sit on, to play cards with her. Cousin Tess was nice but too busy to play Old Maid. She was practically a grown-up. Maybe tomorrow there would be girls her age checking into camp. Maybe a girl with a Barbie!

3

When James woke, the first thing he remembered was there was no bathroom, just an outhouse. *Shit.* A shave would have to wait. He slid out of bed. Somebody's transistor blasted *Venus in Blue Jeans.* Boy, he hated that cheesy Avalon song. Play some Elvis, for crissake. By nine-thirty, it was gray out and too late for breakfast, but he just wanted coffee anyway. Spirit Lake sparkled out his small window, and he wanted more.

He was nearly out the front door when he practically collided with Uncle Hank. "You're just the one I want to see, James." This was never a good way to begin a conversation with grown-ups. James let him take him to the side of the lodge.

"Everybody has a job at Harmony Falls," he said, "and yours will be trash removal."

James just stared. *What?*

"You don't mind a little work, I hope?" His uncle put an arm around his shoulders and grinned.

"But couldn't you have found me a more sedentary, not to mention a sanitary job, Uncle Hank?" James smiled though he knew he sounded like an eastern prick. *But garbage? Give me a break!*

"Lucky for you, James, we already hired a local kid to run Buckets. You know what running Buckets means?" Uncle Hank met James's gaping jaw with a triumphant laugh. "That's the guy that empties the chamber pots every morning."

James wasn't laughing. Weren't they done here?

"That's not all, James. Tomorrow, the families arrive and you'll be as busy as the rest of us getting them all settled in their cabins, moving in their luggage, firewood, barrels of drinking water, and whatever else they want. Soon you'll have to learn to drive the boats. Plenty of work this summer, don't you worry about getting bored."

So began the humbling that knocked James off his high horse. Could he get any lower? Jeez, June only had to work the candy counter, but he'd be hauling trash every stinking morning, and starting *tomorrow*! Get this – up at six every day. He had less than twenty hours as a free-thinking, respectable member of society before he'd be a friggin' garbage collector! If his buddies back in Attleboro ever got wind of this, he'd never hear the end of it. *My life is about to go down the toilet — if only there was a toilet!*

By ten, Gloria's crew was filling the kitchen with song. Kay, James's mom, and his Aunt Marie started on their favorite harmonies to "Boogie Woogie Bugle Boy." When James ambled into this hen house, he felt like he was in a roomful of family, and it felt good. He poured himself coffee and took a seat.

Suddenly, Tess appeared in the doorway, saying she wanted to tell them about her strange dream. As soon as she got the word "dream" out of her mouth, Aunt Marie stopped Bugle Boy and shot a look at his mom, and asked on cue, "Did she say 'dream', Kay?"

And before you could say "jack rabbit," Aunt Marie and James's mom launched into their favorite Chordettes' tune, *"Mr. Sandman, send me a dream /bom bom bom bom/ make him the cutest that I've ever seen..."* and they didn't stop 'til they finished the whole damn song. Their harmony was first-rate, and it knocked James out the way they pushed their heads together and sang cheek to cheek as if a microphone stood right there in front of them.

The spectacle wasn't unusual for these sisters who, evidently coaxed by their stage-struck mother, sang together before James's mom could even say "Daddy," or so the legend went. They sang through the Depression: the boarding-house blues and wrong-side-of-the-track Broadway hits. They'd up and break into a song at any occasion, particularly ones like this, James noticed, where the audience was a captive one.

Problem was, the minute they sang their first notes, Tess turned and bolted from the kitchen. Those ladies didn't even *pause*, despite Tess's abrupt exit. James figured even an apocalypse wouldn't have cheated them out of their encore. His stomach lurched at their stupid act, how they ignored Tess. He followed Tess upstairs.

Christ! Why was he always trying to help? What was he, the friggin' catcher in the rye? *Not me.* Being out there catching the people who fell was enough for old Caulfield. That's all he figured he was any good at. James wasn't even good at *that*.

He chickened out arriving at Tess's closed door when he heard someone talking, but who could that be? Tess was alone in her room. *Good, let someone else help her.* He went into his room instead and pulled on his swim trunks to head to the lake. As he hefted open the massive front door, he breathed deeply the crisp, squeaky clean air, infused with red cedars and pines that towered overhead and marched like giants to the shore. He heard the burbling creek and birdsong overhead. Suddenly, James felt part of the vast emerald understory, just another heartbeat in this mossy thrumming forest.

———————————◆———————————

June's laughter skipped over the water where she twirled in the shallows. Farther out, boaters and skiers crisscrossed each other like water bugs. James had already swum to and from the Boy Scout camp and sat drying on the dock. He could barely hear it over the waterfall, but tinny transistor music drifted from the diving tower. There, a pretty girl peeked over the higher platform. She waved at him. James climbed up a twelve-foot ladder where, facing away from him, she lay on a small towel, her brown hair gathered in a high ponytail. Smelling of Coppertone, she hummed along with "Where the Boys Are."

"Hey." James waited. No answer. Miserably, his eyes dropped to his clinging-wet swim trunks and continued to his long legs, pale as the pumice shore. Who was he kidding?

Below, June frog-kicked to the ladder and hollered up at him. "Want to see me dive off the tower?" She was practically screaming. James's cheeks burned as the brunette girl finally turned around and glanced at him.

"Sure, Junie. I dare you," he yelled back. His kid sister would do anything on a dare.

"I'm Natalie." The girl smiled, sultry as a screen star.

As June hauled herself heavily up to the top platform, she unintentionally flicked a little water on Natalie.

"Good grief! What are you doing? It's like an ice cube." Natalie made a big show of toweling off her legs with a haughty shake of her ponytail as if she'd had about all she could stand.

"It was an accident!" June swiveled and jumped off the diving board while James looked on casually as if she were a stranger.

He lowered his voice and said, "Hi. I'm James."

Without answering, Natalie rolled back onto her stomach and resumed humming with her transistor, this time a Brylcreem jingle. "A Little Dab'll Do Ya!"

Forget about it, James thought. The scene on the diving tower was going nowhere so he made moves to leave. She didn't even turn around. After waving to him, for crissakes. It occurred to James then that maybe she had waved to someone else.

Back up again, June eyed Natalie suspiciously, maybe jealously. Preparing to dive off the tower, June stood her full 4'10" and tried to suck in her tummy. She muttered to herself, "spring up high and curl head down," as her lips moved slightly. "Now the most important rule – do not hesitate."

James watched how determined she was. Sure, she was pudgy, but she could become athletic with practice. Maybe. Big splash. June landed on her belly. Maybe not. He looked back at Natalie, still ignoring him. If that's the way it was, James set down his eyeglasses and towel on the bench and stepped to the end of the diving board. As he pushed off the stiff plank, he sucked in air and sailed out like a missile before tucking his chin and slicing smoothly into gray water. Once surfaced, James kept the momentum going with a strong crawl. He was already in the lead. That was what he liked to tell himself even though he always swam alone. His steady stroke did not indicate that with each second he counted, he cussed himself for being such a loser.

James dove down and with a strong breaststroke headed out to the swim platform, about a hundred yards. Three minutes. Time enough that she probably forgot he existed. James slowly ascended to the black square mass above him. He pulled himself up and lay on his stomach breathing deeply. He had reclaimed himself.

4

TESS

Behind her closed door she sat moaning, "It's not fair. It's just not fair." She wiped the tears from her eyes and cheeks. But really. How could she expect her mother to understand? Sure, she tried to comfort Tess when she cried out at night, but she didn't want to hear about the dreams. She wanted to put a big Band-Aid on the whole thing. "You're just different, Tessie," she'd say. "You have to accept that." But the truth was the dreams scared her mom. They were weird and they were getting worse. Tess used to be able to tell James about them when they were younger. But now? He'd think she was crazy. Maybe she was. That was the part that terrified Tess. Like the one last night.

Tess was riding on a carousel with three young girls, all on brightly colored horses. Suddenly, the horses came to life. Her palomino was pulling her to jump off the platform, but she reined him into his pose, head reared back, mouth open against the bit, mid-gallop. Tess knew horses, she'd worked at a stable as a kid, so she could manage him. But the other horses leaped off with their young riders. Then mid-stride, each beautiful horse was shot. Dead. The hunters yelled out, "Those are wild horses and they have to be shot!"

"No, No!" Tess screamed back at them. The little girls were hurt too, and their agonized shrieks crazed Tess. The calliope music slowed down to a nightmarish crawl. Sobbing, Tess didn't know how long she could keep her horse on the platform. The dream ended as her palomino soared off the merry-go-round as she clutched his neck with her arms, waiting for the next blast to rip them open. The little girls could still be heard under the platform. Where were they?

Tess woke up screaming and coughing. Her mother ran into her room and held her until she stopped.

Of course, others in the lodge had heard her. How could they not? She was so ashamed. Nineteen years old and still having childish night frights. Tess believed her mom was embarrassed. That was why she started Aunt Kay singing in the kitchen. To keep Tess from describing the dream. What must her aunt and June think?

And it wasn't just the dreams. She had started hearing voices. Voices like the little girls', and stranger deep voices that said *Beware*. Sometimes *Beware of the hunters,* or *beware of the volcano*. Where did the voices come from? What part of her brain would trick her like this? Would torment her?

Maybe she should move into Gloria's cabin. She could sleep on the couch. But Gloria would know she was crazy. Better Gloria than Aunt Kay who would certainly never understand. No Band-Aid was going to fix this.

5

Sparks crackled and hissed at the fire pit by the shore. Behind them, the waterfall sounded like high winds howling. A circle of faces glowed orange in the darkness. The camp was open. Families had been arriving that afternoon. Less than fifty feet from the lodge, a dozen campers splashed and swam in the jewel lake. Some just stood in the icy water, turning a bluish shade of pink. James loved the little frozen kids that jumped around spastically, jaws tight with clenched laughter.

For hours, James had transported luggage to cabins in a wheelbarrow. Along with Tess and Hank, they hauled more luggage than any of the families would need in a place like Harmony Falls. He was tired but eager to be a part of this place. He smiled seeing campers' faces light up as they opened the front door of their cabins, warmed by a wood-burning stove, cozy with braided rugs, patchwork quilts, and fresh linens folded on the beds. Delivering the campers' luggage didn't feel like work. James was one of the lucky ones: he could stay all season.

But he would have preferred to avoid campfires and sing-alongs altogether, a condition probably due to his embarrassing stint as a Cub Scout. The other scouts already knew how to start fires with flint stones, chop wood with hatchets and build shelters from scrap wood. James had had no father to teach him guy stuff so he felt left out of the scout master's circle of favorites, left to take the jabs of mean boys. The only good thing that came out of those few awkward months during second grade was his Scout pocketknife. He fingered the textured plastic case in the pocket of his blue jeans, warm from his leg. James always carried it when he wasn't in school because, really, you never knew, and besides, you could do everything with it. You could puncture a can with the ice pick, cut rope, open a pop bottle, repair a bike with the miniature screwdriver, or clean fish with both large and small blades. But James hadn't used any of those features, just the blades, mostly for whittling. Back home, his Scout knife had been more than he needed.

That was before he saw Ben's Bowie. Now, James's prized boyhood memento was like a Mattel toy. The lesson was loud and clear. Mountain men needed tools they could depend on. It could mean life or death. James would look into it.

James noticed how Ben stoked the fire with precision, drawing hot coals together to keep the heat, creating air passages between the logs. At Harmony Falls, campfire was a time-honored tradition that began last century when loggers' families summered at the old lodge. That was thirty years before legendary Jack Nelson retooled the lodge into a rustic resort for hikers and Portland families. With no electricity, they made their own entertainment. Many were singers, dancers, fiddlers, and poets – some quite good. The best storyteller was Jack Nelson himself. He knew every ghost story and tall tale in the Pacific Northwest. He and his wife Essie and sister Ruby ran the place until he died in 1955. The Portland families continued the campfire tradition of storytelling and singing as they rented out the cabins and hired managers to run the place. Among them, Aunt Marie, Uncle Hank, and daughter Tess kept the place going and sang at every campfire.

James walked around the group to the opposite side to sit nearer to Ben. He wanted some distance from his mother and June. The campfire offered visibility of maybe eight feet so James heard Natalie's footsteps before she emerged from darkness into light. She smiled radiantly as if everyone had come just to see her.

"Well, hey everybody. Ready for a tune?" Finished with the dinner shift, she strapped on her guitar. Standing with confidence beyond her seventeen years, she upstaged the dodgy moon. James held his breath until she began.

She started to strum quietly then began. "Way out here we have a name for wind and rain and fire." Natalie's voice was true and clear, but while she sang "They Call the Wind Maria," her mouth held a smile continually. She reminded James of a phony starlet. What was he thinking? He could never date a girl like Natalie anyway. His attention moved to Ben.

June, on the other hand, watched Natalie with wide eyes, her face gleaming as she stared, rapt with Natalie's performance. She mimicked the words of the song's refrain, learning as she went.

In the fire's pulsing glow, Ben's face looked lunar, a topography of craters and rivulets. His short hair had begun to gray, but James couldn't guess his age. Everyone quieted, waiting for the storytelling they'd come to expect at Harmony Falls.

"Some nights when the moon is full and the lake shimmers with light, I hear the drumming." Ben's gravelly voice cast a spell. He looked around at each face, taking his time. "They say that here, all around the Cascades, Indian spirits drum their history." Ben turned for another log though the fire was already blazing. "You can hear them in the waterfall, in the wind, and over the lake." He looked at James. "If you listen."

A cold wind stirred the boughs and shifted smoke into James's eyes. He blinked and swatted the air, then turned to see what Ben was staring at.

"Look how Spirit Lake sparkles in the moonlight," Ben said, pausing. "Yet, a hundred years ago the lake was feared. Indians believed it was spirit-haunted."

Some of the little kids got antsy, and their dads picked them up to return to the cabins. The adult group compressed around the fire. James listened attentively; his head was full of questions. Lake spirits? Suddenly, Spirit Lake turned spectral. James remembered their arrival: the fog, the strange wave, the ghostly old man. He shivered involuntarily, not from the cold but with thoughts of what the lake had yet to reveal.

"You've heard the moans in the lake?" Ben looked at each of them. James nodded vigorously. Of course, he had, everyone had. "Local Indians heard them too and named the lake for the spirits below. They believed the moans came from souls that died in the lake whose bodies were never found. They taught their children to stay clear of Spirit Lake lest they get snatched and drowned by the long arm of a demon."

James wondered. Was it safe to swim there? To swim deep? Was it bottomless? Should he try it and find out? He shook the thought out of his head.

"Their legends were not such tall tales, as it turned out." Ben paused for the effect. "You see, whenever anyone drowned here, and over the years there've been many, the bodies never surfaced. The lake seemed to swallow them whole." The collective intake of air from the audience was palpable.

"Eventually a scientific explanation emerged, at least about the missing bodies. Turns out, corpses sink straight to the bottom, due to very low oxygen levels and glacial temperature. They sink, yes, but they don't rot. Nor do their clothes."

James tried to picture it.

"Other scientists tell us the wailing in the lake comes from the wind whistling through the pass." Ben shook his head. "I prefer the Indians' version. Spirit-haunted. They respected the mysteries of Loowit." Ben spoke briefly about tribes, the Cowlitz and the Klickitat, who had lived in the region for centuries until the late 1800s. "They're all gone now, driven like cattle from this sacred land they loved, driven from the salmon runs that fed them, from their ancestors' graves. They were herded to the Yakama reservation far from here. Their women were made barren, their seed scattered to the four winds."

Ben stoked the fire and sighed, pausing before talking again as if feeling all that loss. "Some folks believe their spirits have remained here. I can't blame them. Nobody ever wants to leave Spirit Lake."

James remained quiet, his head full of thoughts of what would or could happen.

Ben continued, "Loowit. That's her real name."

"What does it mean?" James stared, too, now drawn in.

"Keeper of fire," Ben murmured.

"But isn't it dormant?"

Ben stepped closer to James. "Lots of tourists believe that, but not one is an Indian. Their ancestors witnessed a few of her eruptions." He shook his head and then gazed south. "They thought the mouth of the volcano was sacred ground. They never traveled above timberline." He paused. "That was probably smart."

Ben spread his arms wide. From where James sat it looked like his reach was as wide as the fire mountain as if he could embrace her, something Paul Bunyan might have done. Ben's quiet voice suggested a long-distance perspective.

"Sometimes, it feels like we're on a tiny mortal island in a vast sea of spirits."

James stared at Ben. He felt drawn to him, as if Ben knew things James could learn, should learn.

James began to count the ways he could die in this isolated place: falling into a crevasse or sliding off a glacier on Loowit, boiling in a volcanic eruption, or slowly suffocating in an avalanche. Or yanked miles down to a watery grave to sit at a table of clothed corpses like mannequins from a cowboy and Indian diorama at the bottom of a goddamn haunted lake. James made a mental note: don't black out holding your breath. *Demons? Really?*

Ben soon parted the logs to burn out and left for the boathouse. No one spoke in the space he left. As campers clicked on their flashlights, they found the paths back to their cabins. Staff drifted to the lodge.

Unexpectedly, Natalie brought her guitar to sit next to James. Shocked dumb, he couldn't shape a thought. He stared at her. His head was full of her dusky perfume, and his eyes were drawn to the smile on her lips as she easily strummed some chords. She strummed for a while before she came to a simple pattern and began to sing softly as if to herself, Elvis's "Blue Moon." Despite his fascination with Natalie, it didn't escape James that her beauty was probably shallow: uncomplicated by any self-doubt. He almost envied her thoughtless ease.

A thin line of sweat trickled down his lower back. He was hyperaware of his lack of experience with girls. Like with Cub Scouts, he'd had no father to teach him about such things. He ached to find him at last.

Natalie's last guitar chord echoed across the still water. He was caught in its echo and flinched when she leaned over and brushed her fingertips against the back of his hand. He wasn't prepared for his reaction, couldn't even look at her when she murmured, "Sweet dreams."

James remained alone at the pit. The once-mighty blaze had paled to pink embers.

6

GLORIA

She never made it to the campfires. As head cook, she rose promptly at four each morning to start the fire in the great cast iron stove. While it heated, she worked her dough. This was her time. The big kitchen, her domain; the dough, her solace.

In San Francisco, she'd learned to make sourdough and crusty French loaves. Of course, her specialty was pies, beautiful berry pies. By the time Marie joined her at 7:30, her loaves of bread and pies sat cooling on the wire racks, sending their delicious redolence throughout the lodge. Then she made lunch sandwiches and prepped dinner. She was done by four in the afternoon.

She rarely showed her face after that. There was no need, as the girls handled dinner and cleaned up. Gloria had her dark days, but she tried to keep them hidden. Marie would remind her if she got too crabby, sometimes encouraging her to leave a bit early.

At those times, the raised caterpillar-sized scars on the backs of her legs throbbed. Even still, after all this time. She knew it wasn't the scars themselves that hurt so much, but the cause of them. Scenes she tried like the devil to forget. When she couldn't, she retired early to her cozy little cabin. Apart from all the others, it stood on the opposite side of the boathouse where Ben had his room. Once there she washed up and went to bed. There was no more healing going to happen after fifteen years. What was done was done.

7

Late morning, they took the long way to the top of the waterfall. Tess, the hiker, insisted. James called his cousin "True Blue." Somewhat plain-faced with long wavy brown hair and bright twinkling eyes, she was an outdoorsy girl. She'd learned a lot from 4H Club, but not much from dating. Kind of like James, just minus the 4H.

Like him, she rarely sought company, but that morning she'd pulled him aside after their chores. He was not surprised that she did as it often signaled that she had something fun up her sleeves. But that was when they were younger. It was her dreams again, she said. James nodded. With only a thin wall between their beds, he had heard her crying. But he wouldn't have brought it up. He wished that she hadn't. Typically, James squirmed when forced to listen to private things like dreams or confessions, feeling like an eavesdropper. Or hearing his buddies trash talk back at school. Or accepting a compliment from anyone. It was a regular minefield.

If it hadn't been Tess who needed to talk, James might have turned down the hike. But he hadn't seen her in two summers. Now nineteen, she seemed to have bigger worries. Usually nervous around people, she was always calmed by helping animals. She often had something wild recuperating in a crate in her bedroom. During their few summers together at other inns where her parents worked, James had assisted her in the rescue and feeding of a variety of hurt creatures, mostly birds and squirrels. But this summer, Tess had no hard-luck cases to give her purpose. She seemed different, almost adrift.

The mist had lifted. They grabbed a canoe to row to Duck Bay, where they tied it and hiked up Trail 211 due north. Alone on the path, Tess pointed to a clump of Lady's Slippers. When James stooped to pick one of the dreamy hooded flowers, Tess pulled back his arm. "No," she said. "They're too beautiful."

They stopped at Donny Brook to watch a few sailboats bobbing in rough water. By the time James and Tess reached Cedar Creek, though, coal-dark roiling clouds had moved in and gobbled up the light. Boats dropped sail in hasty retreat.

A sudden gust set the vine maples dancing. Tess sped up, sensing the urgency, just as the dark forest burst with motion: swallows swooped for cover, butterflies pressed their orange wings together, and chipmunks dashed into holes hidden under spikey ferns. They both began to run but couldn't outrace the downpour. Raindrops plunked loudly on vine maple leaves as large as hands and set them waving 'so long' as they hurried past.

"Follow me!" Tess glanced back to see if James was close. She sprinted through the woods, lifting her legs high to clear gnarled tree roots and fallen trunks. James raced after her, chasing his breath to the mouth of a small cave, nearly hidden under curly moss that dripped off the rocks like black hair. Outcroppings of mushrooms swayed in the rain like tiny umbrellas. They eased into the dark space, then yelped as a flurry of bats whooshed out at them, their arms shooting up to block the bony wings. James and Tess flew out, too, grabbing each other's shoulders and laughing. When they caught their breath, both drenched, they popped back into the dark hole and sat down on smooth wet rocks.

James heard the cave seeping with a secret life and felt the wonder of nature's tranquility. He dried his eyeglass lenses on his shirttail, letting his eyes adjust, and touched the wet rock. Caves were nature's perfect shelter. He watched Tess as she struck a kitchen match to light up the dark cave. Suddenly, black walls wiggled with salamanders scrambling from the light. James's hand snapped back and he pulled in his shoulders.

Another nice day suddenly swamped. It was unbelievable how wet, how constantly moist the Northwest was. They sat in the mouth of the cave and waited patiently for the hard, sideways rain to thin out enough to race to the waterfall.

Tess began quietly, almost hesitant. "Last night was different from other dreams."

James had forgotten about the dream. Chilled, he remained silent, breathing the smell of wet leaves and black soil. She continued.

"Another merry-go-round dream where our horses were alive. But this dream was more peculiar. As the calliope music slowed down and became deeper and distorted, I threw my arms around my horse's neck and leaned down low. I heard voices, James." She looked at him. James met her eyes even though he didn't want to. "I heard little girls' voices below me, under the floor. Muffled, but I could hear them. More than one and they were crying like babies."

Tess's face contorted and shivered. "Where *were* they?" Tess asked James in a way that suggested he might know. Of course he didn't know. It was a dream! She was visibly trying to puzzle it out. After a moment she said, "Then I woke up."

James shook his head, feeling lost. He had no idea what to say. He didn't know where the kids were or why they were crying. The dream she described didn't match with what he'd heard last night. She'd been crying out, "No, No! Don't!" What was Tess not telling James?

"I felt sick when I awoke. The little girls…." Tess shook her head and wiped her eyes and cheeks with her sleeve. "They were scared. That's what I wanted to tell you. I've never dreamt about kids like that. Or voices."

A pall had settled on them as surely as a spring avalanche. Tapping, dripping, seeping, the cave never for a moment quieted.

"Do you have nights when you don't have bad dreams?" James struggled to find a light in this gloomy talk. *Was Tess going crazy?*

"Sure." Tess paused as if measuring her trust for him and finding her need to tell him greater. "It's when the loons sing." Her childish crooked grin appeared seconds after the tears. "That's when I have good dreams. Loons are rare in summer – most of them fly north." She paused. "You know, their songs kind of sound like babies crying." Tess edged out of the wet cave and stood tall. She turned her palms upward. "Hey, the rain has stopped. Let's head for the falls."

As they approached the top of the sun-dappled waterfall, their ears were deaf to all but the roar of a winter's worth of snowmelt exploding off the ledge like diamonds, stirring up clouds of steam that lifted James's shirttail. Surging down from warmed glaciers, the cataract dropped about fifteen feet into a green pool then spilled down another eighty-five feet, over mossy boulders and dead logs alive with bright-green lichen, into the creek, down to Spirit Lake.

Below them, water pounded into the pool, churning and splashing on feathery maidenhair ferns and yellow monkey flowers that lined the falls. Spray obscured some of James's view, but he saw rainbows shimmering there. Breathless, he wanted to do something crazy like jump down into the pool. It was so inviting but, as if reading his mind, Tess shook her head. "Don't even think about it." She wiggled her finger in front of her as she spoke, "It's only four and a half feet deep. Some kids go skinny-dipping there, but it's killer cold." James involuntarily shuddered.

There was no footbridge at the top of the waterfall. The trail ended at the east side of Harmony Creek and began again on the other side. Getting from one bank to the other required hopscotching across slippery rocks, clearly bad odds for James. Tess smiled. "Don't worry— I'll go first."

If James slid off a mossy rock, he'd be listing knee-deep in rushing water, that is, water rushing over a hundred-foot drop. He wanted to be a sport, but he was rigid with fear. Tess leaped across the rocks in a half minute. Great for a damn wood-sprite, but James wore a pair of beat-up Keds that let him down. He slid off into rushing water. Tess screamed something over the roar, reaching for him. With a slight bend in his knees, James spread his arms out for balance and crept carefully over the waffling creek bed. He jumped onto the bank as Tess pulled him towards her, both of them laughing that he had made it. Crossing over became a rite of passage, one that he'd never fail again.

Harmony Falls — another way to die.

8

Pacific North westerners measured their men by, among other things, how they split and stacked wood. James watched Uncle Hank and, by that yardstick, James was all kid. The next morning when he saw Hank at the woodpile, he said, "Hey, can I give it a try?"

"Sure, come here." Rather than hand James the twelve-pound axe, Hank kept the blade on the log and lined James up with the handle. It was smooth and warm from Hank's grip. The handle fit nicely in James's two hands. When he tried to lift it high, though, he could, but only with great effort and no precision. Using every one of his body's muscles, he tried again and raised the blade high enough, but came down beside the log. He tried again.

"Give it time. Aim for the block. It's in the stance," Hank said. "You go through the wood, but you aim for the block." He touched his fist against James's abs. "Tighten here. Then exhale on exertion." James nodded, sweat sliding down his temple. His uncle had made it look easy. Repetition with rhythm: Stand the log on the block, and split it; stand another log on the block and split it, continue until stacking. Then stand a log on the block and split it. Stand another log on the block. Same swing, same beat. James could feel the rhythm even before he got the skills.

James continued practicing after Hank left. He shaved the log twice before he hit it solid. One slice and a three-quarters piece toppled to the ground. "Crap." He picked up the larger piece and tried again. And again. After a half-hour, clenching his teeth until his jaw ached, he split the log through, though still not into halves.

After a time, Uncle Hank returned. "Hey, look at the woodsman!" He picked up the recently split pieces and examined them. "See how you've been correcting your aim? Look at the first ones, that splinter you shaved off? You've come a long way in an hour."

"Thanks." James beamed. For an instant, he saw himself beaming pitifully like a little boy. He stopped smiling and wondered how long since his stepdad had praised him.

"Yeah, well, I got work to do. Great job." Hank gave him a nod and turned to go into the boathouse.

Watching his uncle's broad back departing, James imagined his real father, trying to picture his face. He couldn't. Impulsively, he planted the axe in the woodblock, walked up to the lodge to his room, and closed the door. He sat down on a plain wood chair and reached into his wallet, carefully easing out a small sepia photograph from inside cloudy plastic. James's shoulders dropped as he exhaled. A new breath filled him, warmed him. They looked alike, his father and him. They belonged together. That calmed him, the thought of belonging to someone.

All James knew about his real father was his name and nationality, and that was only because he'd overheard his mother speaking to his aunt years ago as if it were a family secret. Since Dan had adopted him when he was six years old, James hadn't registered that his last name had been changed. His father's name, Ralph Soulis, was a kind of holy chant through James's private thoughts.

That spring, after ten years of silence from his mother on the subject, James had worked up the courage to ask her about his father. He would be sixteen the next day. Time for some answers. He had walked deliberately into the laundry room after school.

"Mom. Did you ever write my father after you left him?" James sat down and watched her fold laundry.

"Why would I do that?" His mother didn't miss a beat, lining up towels corner to corner, the pile of them tidy and inviting.

"I don't know … to tell him about me, things I've done maybe? Like my swim trophies?" James sat hunched into himself.

"No, I didn't want to hurt him any more than I already had. Besides, I lost track of him." She turned away to reach for another basket. "What?" she said. James was staring at her hard, searching her face for a shred of emotion.

There was waste in James's heart where a father should have been. Did his father feel that too? Would he be happy to see him? Would they bum around Alaska, camping and cooking the fish they'd catch in clear rivers? Yet James's memory of his father's face had long faded.

The day before they left to come out west, while he stood shaving in the family bathroom, James asked his mother, "Do I look like my father?"

His mother looked at him. "Hmmm. Yes, you do. He was quite handsome, you know." His mother smiled vaguely then hung the clean towels she had brought in.

"What was he like? Am I anything like him?" James had wanted to know, something, anything. He had followed his mother to her bedroom, his hands unconsciously clasped together in front of his chest.

"Oh, I don't know. He was a kind man." A moment passed as if she'd forgotten the question. "So, yes, you are somewhat like him. But you're smarter." She smiled again, seemingly taking full responsibility.

"Do you think he might like to meet me?" James's heart thumped wildly.

She shook her head slightly. "Back then, he loved us very much. It must have been hard." She slammed the suitcase shut, locked it, and turned back to the closet for another.

James waited. When she said nothing else, he asked, "Why did you leave him?" His heart raced ahead, bent on disaster.

"Why are you asking this? Do you want the truth? Well, do you?" She paused and looked at the door. "He couldn't support us." Her voice trailed off. "He didn't have the opportunities. He spoke broken English." She looked away.

What? James blinked. She left him because of a foreign accent? No, surely. Was she saying his father was stupid? So, she dropped him and found a smarter guy? Knowing his mother, it must have come down to his enlisted paycheck. He couldn't have been stupid. At Hamilton, they had said James's I.Q. was 146, so his dad must have had something upstairs. Maybe he was smarter in Lithuanian. He could have been a goddam genius in Lithuanian for all his mother knew.

"That's crap,"James murmured before leaving to watch TV. He ignored her as she yelled at his back for cussing. After she'd gone to bed, James riffled through her letters in the study. That's when he found the tiny photograph of his father, the only one he'd ever seen. Neatly pressed in his khaki uniform, he stood in front of a little house with two blue spruce trees. A tall man with an uncertain gaze, he held James's mother close with his arm around her waist.

Seeing the little photograph, James had instantly recalled a day when he'd tumbled off a jungle gym in a park. His father had picked him up and wiped his cut knees with a handkerchief, holding James on his lap and rubbing his back until he stopped bawling. James remembered the scent of his aftershave. He had called him Jimmy, a name rarely used since.

Though it was already bent, James had tucked the photograph into a protective plastic cover in his wallet, so his father would travel with him. He had imagined the moment he would find him a million times. James would knock on his door. (Yes, he would!) Even if he slammed the door in James's face, he would see his father at least for a second, and his father, whether he wanted to or not, would have to see James.

—————————— ✦ ——————————

As he lay in his bunk at Harmony Falls, more images of his dad filled his head, more hopes. The thoughts in his mind wouldn't let him sleep. He kept tossing around in his bed, restless. He needed answers. Specifically, he needed his father's address. Unable to bear it any longer, he got up and knocked on his mother's door across the hall. She was still up. Standing before a small mirror, she had twisted her hair into a thousand pin curls. Without her full head of blond waves, she looked to James less like a beauty queen than a carnival pinhead. He sat down on her bunk and without waiting, said, "I'm taking a bus to Anchorage in August for the Ice-Man competition. And I need my dad's address."

His mother began shaking her head from side to side, saying, "No, no, you will do no such thing. No." She frowned at herself in the mirror as if testing the expression.

"I can be back before we leave for Attleboro." James said, "Please."

She leaned in towards the mirror, squeezed her eyes shut, and kept shaking her head.

"I *have* to see him." James pleaded, turning her around by her shoulders. "I need to see where I came from, Mom. Can't you understand that?"

She averted her eyes. James took her face in his two hands and made her look at him. When her eyes met his, they were wet. James backed away yelling. "Why keep me away from him? I have a right to see my father, goddammit!"

"Stop, James. Just stop." She put her head in her hands for a full minute. "Oh honey, I'm so sorry." She took a long breath. "I guess I should have told you."

"Told me what?"

She sighed loudly. "Oh, God." A sob stuttered out.

"What? What? Tell me, dammit."

"Your … father died four years ago."

Something like lava filled his lungs, rose to his throat, and choked off his breath. He clasped his hands to keep from shoving her. "No, Mom. You're lying. You just don't want me to see him. Come on! Give me his address!"

"Oh James. I had no idea you'd ever want to know. You were so young."

"Of course, I'd want to know! I've always wanted to know!" James squeezed his fists tighter.

His mother tried to hug him, but he blocked her arms and, not meaning to, almost knocked her over.

"Stop it!" she said. "I'm sorry. But it's the truth. He's not in Alaska anymore. He's not *anywhere*. He's gone." As the realization hit her, James saw it was true.

June poked her head over the edge of the top bunk. James glimpsed her from the corner of his eye, but he didn't care. He began to advance on his mother.

"You lied to me. You told me he'd moved. That was a fucking lie. He'd already been dead for years!" James stopped himself, brakes squealing in his head, and he spun around stifling a scream. He marched back to his room, slamming both doors. The whole lodge shook. James collapsed on his bunk, muffling his sobs in a pillow. After about fifteen minutes his mother opened his door, started to speak. But before she made any stupid excuses, James spat, "Go away! Leave me alone."

And without a word, she did.

9

KAY

She'd hoped it would never come to this. It felt like ancient history to her, but apparently not to James. There was just never a right time to bring it up. Why tell him his father had died if he didn't even remember him? Kay couldn't even recall the date he died.

James had never asked questions, so Kay assumed he'd forgotten him, like she had. Alaska was a bad dream that she was happy to forget. There was nothing in Anchorage for her except Marie and Hank. That was the only reason she moved there. She settled on the first handsome man who'd have her, regardless of his ancestry. Kay was barely eighteen when James had been delivered in a primitive clinic with no anesthesia. He was a big baby. She screamed the whole time.

Ralph was a sweet man. He loved his little son, but they were dirt poor. Life was so hard there. When a high school girlfriend wrote Kay to come to New York saying there were plenty of jobs, she thought wow, Manhattan! Her mother met Kay there to watch Jimmy so she could model. She got a job with a famous designer, Adele Simpson. She frequented El Morocco, The Stork Club and private parties in Long Island. She changed Jimmy's name to James and her professional name to Maureen Mitchell. Life had officially begun.

10

James groaned as if he'd slept only a minute. He thrashed around most of the night beating a dank pillow. When sleep eluded him, he sat on the edge of the metal bed, head in his hands, his eyes dully fixed on his bare feet, toes curling to grip the floor. He must have passed out finally, but not long before dawn. When the soft knock tapped on his door, he glanced out his window. It was barely gray and still drizzling. He pulled on his Levis and lurched to the door. Yanking it open, he mumbled, "What? Oh."

Ben filled the doorframe. His raised eyebrow said he wasn't in the habit of being disrespected. "Hank asked me to show you your summer job." Ben handed James some gear and turned to go back downstairs. Over his shoulder he said, "You're collecting trash from the cabins each morning."

Collecting trash? Shit. Remembering his manners, James called after him, "Thanks, Ben." He pulled on the rubbery yellow slicker. Everyone at Harmony Falls had a job — he knew that was part of the "free" vacation. But garbage? Ben stood outside, loading burlap sacks on the trash cart. James pushed open the kitchen door with churning dread, remembering his argument with his mother, trying like the devil to forget the whole thing.

As light rain fell on his tired face, James smelled wafts of pine and fir, scents that swept him back to at least a dozen Christmases. His spirit lifted. James breathed in the moist air and stood taller. Maybe this Pacific air was just what he needed. As he and Ben headed toward the farthest cabin, brown pine needles crunched under their shoes and crushed at a lower pitch under the cart's wheels. Ben explained James's duties.

"The trash haul is easy, I'll help you out," he began. "Dump the contents of each cabin's trash bin into one of these burlap bags. When the cart is full, wheel it to the boathouse where you off-load the bags in the storeroom. Hank and I will take it from there." James squirmed under Ben's black eyes.

"Be sure to put the chains back on the cans. We got bears."

"Here? By the cabins?" This was something else entirely.

"Sometimes, the campers get lazy or forget." Ben shook his head and said, "No, sir. You don't want to watch a family of bears make a ruckus and tear up the property. Worse yet, you don't want to be the one to have to stop them. Bears can kill you with a swipe of their paw."

Ben led the way back from the farthest cabin, Eagle's Roost, while James added bears to his lengthening tally. Ben stopped at one of two wood bridges crossing Harmony Creek. He crouched by the rushing brook to cup water in his hands. James bent down and did the same, gulping the sweet water in suddenly thirsty mouthfuls, his fingers numbed with the chunks of ice spinning down the creek. Crystal clear, the glacial water tasted fresh, as if there in the Cascade Mountains the earth was brand new.

"This land is new," Ben said, as if hearing James's thoughts. "The volcano forges new ground whenever she erupts." Ben stood and gazed at Loowit, still half-shrouded in pale-dawn mist. "She made Spirit Lake, too." He stared for a minute, breathing deep, filling his lungs as if imbibing her power. Then he elbowed James and chuckled.

"Hank said you want to climb Loowit this summer." He looked in James's unfocused eyes. "Let's get down to work, guy."

James gave him a thumbs-up.

"We'll hike the back country," said Ben. "St. Helens Lake, Ghost Lake, and then Mount Margaret."

"I'm in, and thanks for reminding me." James would have to focus. He had to be fit to climb a 9,600-foot volcano. He wasn't. Not nearly, but he had many weeks to sweat, to swim the lake and to train with Ben's regimen of Charles Atlas exercises.

------------------------◆------------------------

Ben threw their packs into a shore boat after ten the next day for a half-day hike to St. Helens Lake. Ordinarily, they would hike around Spirit Lake, he said, but he had to get back by late afternoon. "We'll take that other route next time, when we hike up Margaret." They motored to the South Shore Landing, James tied the boat up, and they walked west. Trail 207 was known as the Mount Margaret Trail. "We'll only go halfway up it today."

St. Helens Lake was the easiest of the three hikes, about three miles, up fifteen-hundred feet. "It's also the prettiest," Ben said. James took in the clear sunny sky, the trail cool and shaded by dense fir and hemlock. He felt sheltered. Suddenly, Ben grabbed James's shoulder, pulling him backwards. *What the hell?*

"Mind that devil's club!" Ben pointed to a six-foot shrub with gigantic flat leaves that James was an inch from stepping on. He stepped away from it. "Touch the leaves or stems, and the thorns will poison you."

"Okay. That's good to know." James continued his death tally. Even the flora here was deadly. James stooped to examine the devil's club. Its wide leaves were hairy on the underside with tiny thorns, each thorn loaded with toxin. Since it spread wildly in creek beds and since the trail wound past creek after creek, devil's club became their companion: adorned in bright-red berries yet poison to touch.

"Just like women," Ben muttered. James nodded. His mother came to mind.

Emerging from the dark forest, the trail broke into a clearing where huckleberry bushes glistened in the sunlight. James looked to Ben, "Are they safe to eat?" He nodded, barely, so James set about filling his bandanna. When he stood, he wiped his hands on his Levis, but his fingers were stained dark. Far in the distance was Spirit Lake, shaped like a butterfly. James lingered there with no idea why he'd stopped. Longing stirred deep in him before he even realized its import.

One switchback led to another, and James breathed heavily on the steady incline. After three miles up, the path briefly descended toward the east shore of St. Helens Lake. Blades of blue-green water shimmered through the towering trees. James quickened his pace.

St. Helens Lake was a forgotten gem sunk in an ancient forest, though they found ready seats at a picnic table, one of two tables, both smooth with years of wear. Ben and James were alone in a silent place, but for a few twittering goldfinches and the occasional splash of a trout. High overhead, conifers leaned with the wind this way and that, a dance of giants. Everything out west was grander, riskier, prettier, and just plain wilder than any other place in the world. James was sure of that.

"I made many of these tables," Ben said, surprising James with a rare detail about his past. "Back twenty-five years ago when I worked for the Civilian Conservation Corps. We built hundreds of them all around the Northwest. Those were good days. Everybody had jobs." Gnarled and calloused, Ben's hands told the story. The man had evidently whittled back the wilderness one table at a time.

James ran his thumb along the satin edge of silvered wood. With no warning, his gut clenched. *Mazai sunus.* Never again. James's head dropped onto his arms on the table. His shoulders shook as he gulped back sobs. Snot ran from his nose. Ben placed his hand gently on James's shoulder and left it there without words. After a few minutes, James peered up, wiping his nose on his cuff, his red eyes locking on Ben's.

"My father is dead. I just found out. Died four fucking years ago."

Ben's face lost its ruddy color. "What? Oh man. That's rough." His arm stretched around James's back and pulled him a little closer.

"Yeah. And my mom didn't even tell me. 'Till now." James shook his head. "I was going to see him this summer."

James's gut seized again, pulling him over. He lay his right cheek down on the table, as if the old wood might absorb his loss.

11

The next night, a gibbous moon shone on June's pale hair while she spun her pink hula-hoop around her thick waist. Walking and hooping, she circled the campfire in a kind of waddle, far enough from others to avoid collision. Among eight kids at the fire were toddlers popping up like bubbles, seven-year-old girls that giggled at boys who thwacked rocks with stick bats. At ten, June was too old for the young kids and too young for the teens. Shorter than average, she had a teddy-bear shape. As she held her arms straight over her head, the hollow plastic hoop twirled around her torso like a bright ribbon.

June often glanced over her shoulder at three boys, but she couldn't catch their eyes. She had James's attention, though. With a laugh she edged toward him and exaggerated the walk like a crane, still hooping. "Look! I can go up and down… and back up."

One of the boys laughed, too, but whether with her or at her, James couldn't tell. The kid glanced at his buddies and stepped toward June. She smiled at him. With no warning he hit the Hula Hoop with a stick. It fell and wobbled on the ground.

"Hey, I'm practicing," June said. Then sticking out her tongue at the boy, she picked up her hoop. James saw it, saw her face squeezing back tears, but decided not to interfere. The kid hadn't hurt her, just teased her. James had to admit there was a meanness in boys, old and young. He recalled himself a few years back, how he thought it was hysterical to tease June endlessly. When he learned the new word, he started calling June "the obese one" in a mock horror-movie voice. His mom made him stop when she checked Webster's. Now James couldn't remember why he'd thought it was funny.

Kay arrived at the campfire and, with surprised eyebrows and a wide red smile, she made a big deal about how "expert" June was hooping. "That's fantastic!" She didn't acknowledge James. He got up and moved from the hot flames to a log behind Ben.

Ben poked the wood and the fire crackled and spat. More folks from the cabins drifted down to the circle, settling close to the others, whispering, lighting cigarettes. Tess strolled down with her guitar. "Hey, why's it so quiet?" Her gold-green eyes flashed with firelight as she laughed. "Looks like I'll have to sing!"

Tess's version of "Roll On, Columbia" got them all humming and tapping — even James clapped along, surprising himself. It felt good to join. After a rousing applause, all eyes moved from her to Ben, who stood holding his long fire pole like a river boatman.

Ben, the storyteller. It was a talent he'd forged at countless fire pits around the country, picking up local tales and spinning his own. Uncle Hank said that after forty years of hard living, Ben's tales could take a dark turn. He'd seen too much dying in the war, Uncle Hank said, too much senseless cruelty as a medic in trenches and makeshift hospitals. Even when he couldn't save them, Ben had sat with soldiers as they died.

When James had asked Ben why he stayed, he said, "I wouldn't want to be left alone." Some wanted to talk. At their sides Ben heard deathbed confessions, and with a squeeze of his hand offered peace. He learned bits of sacred knowledge, as a disproportionate number of the soldiers were Indians. In the war, Ben learned the language of suffering, Uncle Hank said, and somehow he survived to tell the tale.

Ben pushed the red logs together with his pole. "I've searched for ghosts all over the Pacific Northwest. You hear things, you go looking, and ghosts show themselves. They take shape, they take names, and maybe they tell you their stories. Truth is, there're more ghosts in Portland than anywhere else I've traveled. The city might look normal, but it's about as normal as a Sunday morning in Hell. It has always been a rough seaport.

Kay said to June, "I'm tired, honey. Let's head up to bed." For once, June didn't argue. Other parents whispered to each other and herded their children to their cabins. Ben waited for them to leave before continuing.

"I remember Nina," he said. "She'd been a young waitress at Old Town Pizza on Davis Street. I experienced Nina's ghost myself. I know she was there."

James believed Ben. "Nina was sold into prostitution young. When a couple of street missionaries convinced her to share information about her pimp in exchange for her freedom, she trusted them and cooperated. A few days later Nina's body lay at the bottom of the Old Town elevator shaft. No one was ever charged."

Was this a ghost story or *Sister Carrie*?

Ben grabbed a thick log and balanced it on the pyre. "When I was at the Old Town years ago, I saw, quite distinctly, the face of a girl in a mirror, but when I turned around I was alone in the lobby. I walked down to their tunnel door. All the downtown taverns and restaurants had basement doors to the maze of tunnels that ran under the city to the ports. I opened the door. Oh man. That's where you really hear ghosts holler."

James scrutinized Ben's face. Was this true? It wasn't the kind of ghost stories James remembered from Scouts. Those were made-up. The ghosts or spirits were never real. Just scary. But Ben's stories seemed to be about real people who lived there. That would mean Nina was once a girl like June.

"Thing is, when I went into the tunnel, in a near-by alcove I saw Nina's name scratched into a brick, crudely but clearly. I touched the cold imprint, and in the same instant, I smelled lilacs." Ben closed his eyes and he smiled as if transported. "Unmistakable. She was there. She was definitely there."

James's jaw dropped open. Ben lowered his voice. "You've never heard about sex trafficking back East?" James shook his head. "Out here it's called white slavery. Girls sold into prostitution."

This was no ghost story.

Gloria stood to leave, noisily clacking and swishing. She mumbled something about beating the rooster at four to no one in particular, then drew her shawl tightly around her shoulders and left. James looked around at three others, surprised at being included.

"There's bad news from Portland today," Uncle Hank said, then looked at James and paused, maybe unsure if he should continue. James's face surely showed how he felt: Yes, tell me the worst of it. Tell me all of it.

"A fifteen-year old working girl was found dead yesterday in Portland in a downtown apartment, overdosed on brown heroin, the sheriff said." His uncle reached over to take Tess's hand, his whole face fallen as if the victim could have been her. "The girl had dropped out of school and was lured into the trade, part of a ring."

This was much worse than James had imagined. He wanted to be grown up, part of the group, but he wasn't. Why hadn't he left earlier with the other kids?

Nodding, Tess whispered to James, "I heard of a girl who was kidnapped and sold. She was only twelve." To James's stark frown she said, "It's true."

Ben took a seat on a log to be closer to James. "That's a fact. Those Portland tunnels move more than dry goods and liquor." He paused, glancing in the direction of the cabins. "It sometimes happens to guys visiting from out of town, or maybe a girl from the local high school. Anyone young and unaware is fair game. Some are dropped into the tunnels through a trapdoor in a tavern. Some are taken into the tunnels by force. They're isolated in one of the maze's tiny rooms built to break them in. After that, they can be moved like sacks of grain onto cargo ships or into brothels."

Tess rubbed a stone hard against a boulder to draw a spark. "Ask me, that girl's death was no accident. I had a dream early this morning. The cottonwood branches scratched on my window. It sounded like sharp fingernails. Like someone in trouble, trying to get in."

James eyed his cousin. What did she mean? How did her dream relate to this story?

Ben nodded his head. Agreeing with her. "A warning is in the wind."

Unmoored, James looked at Ben, then to Tess, and on to Uncle Hank. He shook his head dully. Nothing at Hamilton Prep, or anywhere, had prepared him for Spirit Lake, for such crimes and conversations. Sex slavery? A prostitute younger than him? Dead from heroin? What circle of hell were they in?

Hank hacked off strips of kindling with his Buck, his unkempt beard shuddering with each impact. "These young girls don't have a clue what a cursed life they're falling into." Hank stood tall, a big man, and stared across the water. He turned back to James.

"Thing is, Portland's just a crow's fly from here."

12

June whimpered loud enough for James to stop in his tracks. He stood in the dark hallway beside the slightly opened door of the room she shared with their mother. Inching a bit closer to the door, he peered in. June had become quieter since being here. She hadn't made friends. She either swam or played with her Barbie, but seemed happiest whenever she was with an audience, like at the campfire. Certainly their mother had noticed June's loneliness, but she seemed to notice less when she was with Aunt Marie. Like twins, the two sisters completed each other, playing to the other's cards, no matter the game, adding a punch line or harmonizing on songs.

With a plank wall between rooms, Harmony Falls had few secrets. James stepped closer. June sat beside Kay on the lower bunk staring at the rolled-up pile of dirty linens at her feet.

"I'm sorry, Mommy." June's breath caught with a sob. "I don't know what happens. I'm sorry!" Her expression shifted, now her brow furrowed angrily. "I hate that awful outhouse! It scares me."

"Well, June, that's why we use the chamber pot under the bed for number one."

James exhaled deeply, watching his mom pull June into a full hug. "I know, Junie. It's okay." She smoothed her fine light hair. Then she tilted her head. "Tell me, has your brother been teasing you?"

The words "what the hell?" formed on James's lips. He was about to push open the door but stopped when June spoke.

"No. I hardly even see him." She wiped her wet nose and lips with the back of her hand. "I miss Daddy," she said, taking the tissue from her mother. Fresh tears rushed down her round cheeks. "When is he coming to see us?" June blew hard into the Kleenex. She was likely the only one missing her father. Kay hadn't spoken of Dan since they left Massachusetts, at least not around James.

Now, she raised June's chin so she was looking into her eyes. "Daddy has some very important cases this summer. I guess he can't take the time to leave."

"But he said he'd come, remember?" June sat up straighter on the bed. In fact, he had promised them. James had doubted it then, the man worked ten-hour days. And he sure didn't believe it now.

"I thought he would, too," her mother said vaguely. "Maybe he will — it's early."

James knew it was a lie. Dan wasn't coming. Turning around, he hurried back to his bedroom, annoyed. Maybe lying down would calm him, maybe sleep would take him.

But an hour later he was chewing the inside of his cheek. Seemed like they were always waiting for Dan. June could keep waiting, but James had long stopped hoping his stepfather would take any interest in him. After a decade with Dan, James still couldn't call him Dad.

Admittedly, he'd stacked the deck against Dan. By keeping his real father so close to his heart, there was no room for Dan. In the end it hadn't mattered. Dan wasn't the kind of man who cared about going to his stepson's swim meets or long distance competitions. James stopped asking long ago. Instead, he stoked the dream of a fantasy father who, given the fresh facts, could never, ever be. His mother had left him in Alaska in the most absolute way: she never looked back.

James didn't give a damn if Dan came out west or not. What pissed him off was how he was hurting June.

13

A week at Harmony Falls and already James's summer days had taken on the rhythm of routine, lake-paced, weather-based, days structured by his chores. That morning, he was downstairs before everyone but Gloria. As he had done each day, he headed down to the dock to witness the morning's emerging landscape. The Merganser paddled by with her five, funny ducklings. Farther out, a big rainbow trout shot up out of the water, froze for a long second at the top of its arc, and fell back on its side with a splash. James had become part of nature here, keeping the same time. Every morning he awoke before six, walked onto the dock and stretched. Then he dove off and swam across the lake to the Boy Scout Camp and back. His daily routine.

After his trash run, James stood drinking a Hires on the wood deck fronting the lodge. Uncle Hank jogged up the slab steps, more fit than his graying beard suggested. He winked at his nephew then pivoted to the south with an uptick of his chin.

"Look at St. Helens over there, glazed with butter-cream glaciers, so pretty you want to put a cherry on top." Hank laughed, nodding at her as if he knew her, and sat on the bench. "Got a minute?" He patted the space next to him. Hank looked at the lake, its blue even bluer in his pale blue eyes. "I don't know why some Portlanders put on airs when they come here. We're just folks at Harmony Falls. With all the boys and girls camps on Spirit Lake, we get rich kids, poor kids, nice campers and some not so nice."

James wondered which category he fell into. Sure, he was one of the kids who would return to private school in September. Like them, he had brought along some attitude. He'd arrived fresh from a promising first year at Hamilton Prep and thought he knew it all. Who was he kidding? What James previously knew counted for nothing next to the vastness of the Pacific Northwest.

Each morning when James collected trash, Ben came along. He held the bag open while James tilted the cans and poured in the contents. Their talk roamed around the most peculiar places. That morning, Ben started randomly. "Hey, don't you think Alaska becoming a U.S. state this year has something to do with Russian missiles?" This time he emptied the contents of the bin into the bag while James held it open.

"Think about it. Alaska was always just territory – a lot of wilderness with a handful of frontier outposts. Now, suddenly it's annexed as a state. Property of U.S.A."

No doubt that was true, but James didn't want to talk about Alaska. Ever again. "I heard some of what you said to Uncle Hank about your base camp on the volcano, about the Cowlitz Indians. Can you tell me more?"

"What?" Ben was quick to react. "Kid, you shouldn't listen in on private conversations." He pushed the cart to the next cabin, not waiting for James to catch up.

"Wait." James hurried over to him. "What's wrong?"

Ben stopped by the trash cart. He watched James approach with a frown. "Conversations are personal, James. It's not your business."

"But you shared it with my uncle."

"That's my concern."

Despite Ben's arbitrary-seeming rules, James was intrigued with his and Uncle Hank's world, which was why most nights he carried his supper down to the fire pit to join Ben. Unless it was damn near pouring, Ben would be there, coaxing sparks from damp wood into high flames. They rarely talked. Ben liked to eat thoughtfully, with the gratitude that good food inspired in him. Ben lived simply, immaculately, in a small room in the boathouse. His few belongings were organized on a dresser. Most of those were books, among them one about carpentry, another about roofing and others that James couldn't make out from a distance.

One day while he and James were chopping and stacking firewood, Ben's attention turned upwards to the cottonwoods and firs where a minor racket was kicking up, a skirmish of squirrels. He turned back to James, catching him off guard with the answer to a question James had wanted to ask but hadn't known how.

"Your uncle helped me after I saved his life in the war. He made sure we worked together as a team on these jobs." Ben took his aim and halved the log perfectly, then grabbed another. James picked up the pieces and stacked them, staying quiet.

"Harmony Falls keeps me sound and straight." He stopped chopping. "I shore up the sagging beams, and I shave the cedar shingles, I ferry families around Spirit Lake, keep the boats clean and the fire burning. Hank and Marie and I do whatever it takes to hold together this shabby wonderful place. It's a good life, a good enough purpose for me."

"Let's go, James!" Tess hollered from the dock, already in her swimsuit. Today was the day: the drizzle had cleared and the lake was absolute glass. It was flat-out perfect for skiing. In Washington, weather never held for long, unless, of course, it was bad weather, and then you might as well just tuck into some dry place with *Moby Dick* or risk getting cajoled into a mind-numbing marathon of gin rummy with the kitchen crew. Aunt Marie chuckled her way into winning nearly every hand they played. James thought she might be cheating, but he never called her on it. They were guests at Harmony Falls. She could do whatever she wanted, the way he looked at it.

Next thing James knew, he was standing one-legged in the shallows tugging on the hard rubber foothold of one wood ski then the other. His hands were stiff with cold, but he was going to try to ski if it killed him. Ben expected that.

Tess and Ben cruised away, leaving James floating, knees bent, strapped into an orange life jacket. He gripped the wood bar with both hands and kept the ski rope between his knees, the tips of his skis just above the surface, as Ben had instructed. James waved one arm around to balance himself as he repeated the steps to himself: *wait for the slack to pull tight and bend my knees tight to my chest 'til the acceleration jacks me up. Slowly straighten legs. I can do this.*

Turned out, he couldn't. Not then. But by the afternoon, after a dozen more wipe-outs, James redeemed himself. Surprised as hell, he let the boat pull him up and he stayed up. He was hunched over like an old man holding on for dear life, but he held on. As soon as he could straighten up and risk looking at the boat, a blurry Tess, identifiable only by her blue bathing suit, held up two thumbs for a victory that lasted maybe a minute.

Ben had glanced back and seen Tess's thumbs-up. He thought she meant to speed up. He did. At that moment, Harry Newman zoomed by, impressing his inn guests in his fancy mahogany runabout, and threw up a huge wake. James's skis crossed one over the other and he shot airborne over the water. The rubber fittings ripped off of James's feet as he slapped down and tumbled over and over until lake water poured out of his nose and only his life jacket kept him afloat. But he signaled he was good.

Ben sped back to him and circled, then idled beside him. "Hey, guy, take a break." Out on the water Ben seemed younger, more alive, as if the icy spray renewed him. With one hand firm on the steering wheel, Ben pushed his fingers through his thick short hair. "Hey, you cold, guy?"

"Ben, you're killing me!" James's laugh stuttered with cold, "ha,ha,ha,ha," sounding robotic and silly. He pushed his skis up to Tess with some difficulty then with her help climbed up the back near the motor. James stood tall, took in a deep breath. He'd finally gone vertical, if only for a minute.

"Hey, it took me a whole summer to learn." Tess's good cheer boosted James's mood. "Let's just motor around the lake," she said.

They settled in for a slow ride close to the shore. At this speed, the inboard purred. Ahead, a flock of about a hundred cormorants flew over them, their wings stirring up a breeze. The boat coasted by an odd tree trunk sticking grotesquely out of the water.

"What the heck, Ben?"

"It's a snag. An ancient dead tree, some still attached to the lake bottom. You can see a few, but most hang below the surface. Every now and then a snag pops up out of the water, scaring the life out of folks, and sometimes even crashing down on them. Local Indians believed the snags are ghosts of Spirit Lake, the living dead. In a way it's true. Each one was a soldier of Loowit's many eruptions when the lake rose, boiling, filled with volcanic debris. These ancient firs died standing."

"When was the last eruption?"

Ben turned back from the wheel to look at James eye to eye. "1857. But it wasn't the last, James, just the most recent. Loowit is a young, active volcano. Vacationers forget that." Ben reached back and pushed James's shoulder, ribbing him.

"Come on, guys," Tess cut in. "Enough geology. Let's go check out Coe Creek."

Tess's favorite swim spot was a deep cul de sac where Coe Creek flowed into Spirit Lake. There, the pale green water was so clear that ten feet down looked like a yard. Even before Ben had cut the motor and dropped anchor, Tess climbed on the prow, probably anticipating the deep freeze, but that didn't stop her. She posed like a figurehead, laughing, and dove to the bottom. Bubbles rose in pulses above her as she swam a strong breaststroke along the bottom.

Ben pushed the boat to full throttle on the way back. Speeding over the smooth lake, his face wind-stung, James felt joy surge through every wrung-out muscle in his body. Frigid spray slapped him and raised goose bumps on his sunburned chest and arms. James smiled like a silly kid reliving the high. It wasn't pretty, but he'd gotten up on skis, as promised. Before Tess handed James his eyeglasses, he squinted to see Harmony Falls across the lake, but the horizon was a tatty ribbon of black.

14

MAX

High on a ledge above Spirit Lake, an old man cleaned out a square in the mine, big enough for his pallet. The digs were hardly glamorous: copper dust caked an inch deep, and salamanders slithering on cold stone walls. But he was used to stone walls, and he wouldn't be there long anyway. He had his own shack nearby. He came to the mine to hook up with his buddy, just out.

That's where he planned it. In the pen. Vince read up on that part of Washington so he knew the facts. They were a natural team, the man thought, with him a prospector and Vince with connections.

Vince said the Cascades was the land of plenty, the Golden Country, that's what he called it when he showed him a placemat from Harmony Falls, though how he came by it was anybody's guess. Vince read: "The most secluded spot in the Pacific Northwest." Perfect.

"It's God's country. Golden," Vince said. "There's gold in the mine, there's treasure in the waterfall and there's more lily-white girlies in the camps than you could shake your stick at."

Somehow, Vince won the rights to the mine in a poker game and when he got here, they'd find them silver and gold. Definitely copper. Hell, he could see that much. But gold's what he came for, of course. That's what everybody came for.

15

Root beer bubbles stung the back of James's throat, a bracing pleasure after his ski lesson. The white kitchen gleamed, clean, quiet, and empty. Gloria, gone by four, had been in the kitchen since four that morning, baking bread and prepping supper.

As James walked into the empty dining hall, he was startled at the sight of a lone man sitting at one of the tables.

"Too early?" The man asked him, then shrugged, as he looked around for other diners.

"A bit. Dinner isn't until six."

The man smiled at James disarmingly.

James smiled back but kept walking out the front door to sip his victory soda on the deck. Who was that guy? He wasn't staying at Harmony Falls, James was sure of that.

Anyway, James would've remembered a face like his. In fact, at first glance he would have sworn that Burt Lancaster had been sitting there. The fellow had Burt's famous grin, his blue eyes and thick brown hair. But as James stood out in the open air, he realized that the grin had been off-kilter, the blue eyes slightly watery, and the hair, uniformly dyed. He'd been friendly, though. James swigged the last of his Hires and returned to the kitchen to read.

When Natalie circled the tables to add condiments, she stole glances at Burt whenever she could. At ten of six, a herd of hungry campers filled the dining hall, scratching chairs on the floor and settling in. It didn't take a minute before their attention turned toward the stranger. Harmony Falls was a small place and everyone, even the campers who had just been there for some days already knew the usual faces. This man's face definitely wasn't a familiar one. Some of the campers stared at him, their expression obviously wondering who he was. Others just watched him disinterestedly. He seemed oblivious, content to study Aunt Marie's original Harmony Falls placemat. Her childish drawing of the resort depicted cartoon people frolicking around cabins that bore names like Harmony Fails and Malarkey.

"Hi there." Natalie said. He looked up at her and she pointed to the chalkboard for the specials. "Want some ice tea?"

He turned to look at it, though James was sure he already knew what he wanted. "Hello. Sure. Tea would really hit the spot." He cocked his head and grinned. "Not really. But fetch me a glass anyway." Natalie nodded and walked away. Everything about the man screamed that he didn't belong there. His creased trousers and a Banlon shirt set him apart from other campers at Spirit Lake.

James watched him from the hallway, kept looking at him, trying to make the parts of his face fit together like the celebrity's. Bored, he joined the others in the kitchen.

Natalie spoke up. "Marie. Look at that guy. Who is he?"

As she stirred a half-pound of butter into an enormous stainless bowl of hot lima beans, Aunt Marie sang the same tired song she sang to all teen girls, without even glancing up. "If you gals wouldn't wear those short shorts, the boys wouldn't ogle you."

"He's no boy. Look at him." Natalie watched him, and the corners of her lips tipped up. The kitchen crew craned to look.

"Yes. Alright." Marie smiled at him in case he was looking, which he was. "Hank'll find out who he is."

Throughout dinner, Natalie worked wide around the mystery man. When James left the lodge to join the campfire, the stranger still lounged in the dining hall tapping a spit-shined shoe on the old, warped floorboards.

———————————◆———————————

"The Burt Lancaster guy?" Hank said to James the next day at lunch, pausing over his cheese sandwich. "Well, I rode over to St. Helens Lodge this morning to find out. The owner Harry knows everything that goes on here at the lake. He said his name is Elias Craft. Says he's staying there at his lodge and coming here for his meals. 'Course Harry had to make a dig at me. 'It's not for your food,' he said. 'Ours is just as good. Hell no, it's for the pretty girls.'"

James didn't like the sound of that guy's remark though he'd never met him. It was crass referring to Natalie that way.

"Craft is the guy that applied for permits to reopen the Old Sweden Mine. He owns the mineral rights. Says he's got investors." Uncle Hank's brows furrowed like the idea was nuts, pointing at the side of his head with his index finger and circling it round and round. Crazy, maybe. But Hank wasn't laughing.

"That's dumb!" Ben's voice rose. "The old mine never made anything but scrap copper. You know that." When Ben got mad, one eye opened wider than the other. He hated people spoiling the wilderness, and often said he'd hunt down anyone who did.

"That's what I said, but he's got a lease on a new-fangled air compressor. And permission from the Forest Service to tunnel deeper. He claims there's gold. Says the early miners never bored deep enough."

Hank was almost out the door when Ben yelled after him, "Not deep enough? Sweden Mine is twenty-two hundred feet deep!" Ben's scowl would have made a bear turn and run.

Gloria paced the width of the kitchen, back and forth, her skirt swishing. Suddenly she stopped. "My God. The copper seepage from drilling will foul Coe Creek. The Portland Y Camp's drinking water."

"It will foul all of Spirit Lake," whispered Aunt Marie.

———◆———

"Hi, I'm a little early," Natalie said the next afternoon, arriving in the kitchen.

"Great, hon," Aunt Marie pointed to the dining hall. "Go help James roll the silverware."

"Sure." James laughed. "I could use some help." Natalie joined him at a table and started sorting silverware. She was all thumbs, fumbling as she rolled a fork, spoon and knife in a paper napkin.

The rest of the crew was gathered in the kitchen. Marie's tinkly voice counterpointed Kay's deeper tones. From his seat in the dining hall, James could hear them talking. His mother's voice sounded conspiratorial, hushed. "... hasn't even written."

"Honey ... just busy. You'll see." Aunt Marie's face wore a rare seriousness. Usually she laughed at everything, even stuff that wasn't funny. Hearing them whisper, James had an inkling why his mom had herded them to Spirit Lake that summer. Sure, his uncle and aunt needed some extra hands. More likely, though, this vacation was about her leaving home again, like she left Alaska, fleeing whatever trouble brewed there.

When Elias Craft walked into Harmony Falls that evening, it was to the same small table where he'd sat the previous night. He hailed Natalie. "You going to be my waitress?" He gave her a wink.

"Sure, Mr. Craft." Natalie took his order and nearly skipped back to the kitchen.

Elias reached into his pants pocket and pulled out a small doeskin pouch. On the table, the soft felted skin fell open from the weight of five pea-sized gold nuggets. He picked one up and polished it with a scrap of flannel. Next time Natalie passed by, she slowed.

"Like those, little lady?" Elias said, grinning.

"Sure. Who wouldn't?" Popping her Juicy Fruit, Natalie flashed her best Hollywood smile. Other diners ambled by the table then stopped. When a group had gathered, Elias raised his voice, extending what seemed like good will to a swelling audience.

"We're on the verge of tapping a gold vein here at Spirit Lake," he said, as if announcing a scientific discovery. Men in the room stepped up closer. James imagined that Elias saw in their eyes an expression he would have known well. They tried to mask it, but Craft could apparently tell when a mark was ripe.

"I'm looking for investors in the famous Sweden Mine." Another announcement. He had the paper, creased and dirty on the table before him, a testament to his mineral rights. "I've got a prospector ready to start drilling with top-of-the-line equipment. My part is to make sure our wallet is deep enough to keep drilling to find more of these beauties." He fondled the nuggets, focusing on the gold, not their faces.

Elias was right about the people. Uncle Hank had told James that most newcomers to the Northwest dreamed of a big break. "This is the New World," he had heard them say to their young wives. "A land of plenty! Biggest timber in the world! Gold and silver runs right through the rocks!"

"Is this a sure thing?" asked the closest fellow.

Elias smiled. "Where do you think these nuggets came from?"

"Where *did* those nuggets come from, Mister … did you say Craft?" A nicely dressed gentleman eased up to the table and spoke like James did, with a Northeastern accent.

"From the mine, of course." Craft glanced at the rest of those gathered and cocked his head, sharing the joke.

"You already drilling? Or were those just laying around the abandoned mine?" The man moved in closer.

"What's your business, mister? Because if it ain't gettin' rich, then you should step aside and let these other fellas have a shot." Craft flashed his grin at them.

"Mind if I take a look at your paperwork?"

"Help yourself. Then move on. Don't stand in the way of gold," Craft said. "I can tell you're not from around here. Maybe you don't know about the fortunes folks have made." He raised his eyebrow at him. "You sure you don't want to invest, Mr. ah, what did you say?" he asked, looking him square in the eye.

James stood behind the checkout counter, fascinated with two men testing each other. Who was this guy?

"Name's Bill Haley, and you got me right. Boston. Just arrived. I'm not a gambling man, but thanks. Mind if I take a closer look at the nugget?"

"I'll put you on a short leash, but yeah, you can hold it."

Haley reached for it then hefted it in his palm. "Hmmm. Heavy piece." He chuckled. "I'm no expert. Here you go." And he dropped it back into Elias Craft's waiting hand. Turns out, it didn't matter what Bill Haley thought. Craft had found his fools.

Hank watched keenly from the kitchen door, Ben from the hallway where he sat and read. They acknowledged each other with a nod, but neither moved. James counted five men, probably in their twenties, ready to hand over fifty dollars for a two -hundred percent return as the gold "came in". No money would be exchanged in the dining hall, not under Hank and Marie's gaze. So, Craft took a small group down on the dock to view his Polaroids. Harmony Falls was one of Spirit Lake's three public resorts. Add them to the private camp owners, and that money could add up fast.

Ben watched the wives. James did too. The young women sat like steel rods ran down their backs. Their brows creased and their eyes darted around like they were hoping for a decent man to stop their husbands from throwing away their future. Ben looked away from them. No one would interfere, of course. It wasn't their place. And the wives knew this too.

Ben stayed where he was, watching the scene, likely one he'd witnessed since his boyhood. He told James later that day, the lust for gold made of men monsters and fools. Any lust, whether plain greed or lust for alcohol, seemed to repel Ben. He stood apart.

16

Later that night, James was too revved to sleep, so he pulled out a MAD from under the bed and tried to have a laugh with Alfred E. Newman. Soon, though, James set out on the too-long walk to the latrines. An outhouse, for crissakes. At eleven at night it was a creepy walk outside. Even with a flashlight, James imagined wild animals watching him edge past the back of the lodge and down an endless covered walkway to the side of the boathouse where the stink of lye announced a row of latrines. Understandably, most guests preferred to use the chamber pots in their room. Why hadn't James?

Returning from the outhouse, James walked through the living room. He stopped abruptly when he saw Natalie. She hung her head, her chestnut hair falling forward, hiding her face under an eave of bangs. When her eyes lifted up to see James, she shook her hair back. Natalie's small pink mouth turned down in a pout.

She could have been a cheerleader, James decided: her hair in a flip, her crisp navy shorts and tan camp shirt, her Keds and compact figure. At that moment, her legs were draped over the arm of an overstuffed chair and crossed at her ankles. She had been reading a letter by the light of an oil lamp, one with ornate, opaque glass that shone on Natalie a diffused, creamy glow. Softer than a kerosene flame, it cast her as a Vermeer portrait, all shadows and light.

"I couldn't sleep," she murmured. "This whole business about the girl dying in Portland scares me."

He shrugged and thought it best to remain silent. What if she cried? What would he do?

They lingered there. A chill whisked down the chimney, sucked into the void left by a dying fire. James shivered. He thought maybe Natalie was flirting with him.

"Hey, let's climb up the diving tower and look at the stars." James held his breath, not believing he had said it.

"Really? You like to do that?" Her face brightened.

"Sure. Why not?" James had actually spent many nights up on the tower, not all night, just an hour or two after everyone had gone to bed. He listened to creatures' sounds arc over the drone of the waterfall — the most amazing cries, coyotes, owls, and nightjars as they dive-bombed for insects around him. Usually James lay on his back and methodically located the constellations and planets, as bright in the Cascade Range as full moons. But tonight was different. Tonight he wasn't alone.

James grabbed a jacket from the closet under the stairs. They sneaked out, easing the heavy front door closed behind them, and ran down to the water. He wrapped his hands around the railing and climbed up the creaky ladder. Night tightened around them.

Natalie stooped down to sit, and then she stretched out. The cloud cover was partial. A waning moon found them lying straight as beans, touching shoulders, touching the backs of their hands and their thighs. Natalie's baby-blue angora sweater smelled smoky, and close.

Hearing noises, they rolled onto their stomachs. Footsteps crunched and a canoe scraped against the shore beneath them. It was another stranger. James's hipbones dug into the worn wood as he watched the man paddle toward Coe Creek, disappearing silently into fog.

After a while, Natalie stood. As James sat up she put her hand on his shoulder to brace herself. For one foolish instant James held his breath.

"'Night, James. Got to get to bed." She climbed carefully down the ladder, disappearing below the platform. As he lay back down on his back, James pressed himself against the warm soft wood. Had he said something wrong?

———◆———

The following afternoon, Natalie pulled James aside. Up the trail from the lodge, she said, was a meadow she wanted to show him. A narrow path led out of the dense forest to a sunny field of lupines and Indian paintbrush. As if released, they both ran amid lavender spikes and bright orange clusters, all crowded in that acre of sunlight. James pocketed his glasses and squeezed his eyes. The pastels bobbed and blurred into a fine painting. His fingers grazed the tips of blossoms as he ran by. They were laughing when they landed, crushing the cotton-tail tops of bear grass.

The chatter of crickets and crows surrounded them. Hot shards of sunlight sliced through them. Natalie pulled her jacket over their faces to block the sun, and they kissed, tented together. Well, she kissed him. Lulled, he began to kiss her fully and pulled her close.

Interrupted too soon, James heard branches breaking near them. Natalie nudged him. "C'mon! Crap! Someone's in the woods," she whispered.

They jumped up and James ran to the edge of the tall trees where, he was sure of it, he saw a figure departing.

17

As if at the bottom of a deep well, she feels too heavy to swim to the surface. When she tries to open her eyes, her lids stick closed by something tight around her head. Slowly moving each limb and finger, she runs down a delirious checklist and finds her body parts in order.

She has journeyed far in her sleep, flying through confetti clouds at the speed of light, soaring over the moon. Yet, she knows she hasn't moved from this hard pallet. All this is a dream anyway; it has to be. Her hands are tied with soft ribbons and she is trying to sit up when Max climbs up to her, heaving like an old man, saying, "Hey angel, I thought I heard you stir."

She flinches as his flat rough fingers graze her cheek and forehead. She can feel him smoothing her loose hairs out of her face. It feels nice, like when her mother does it.

"You sure are a pretty thing. Do you know that?" She feels his gaze and his light touch on her legs. She had thought it was salamanders, it was so light. His breath comes close and she can feel its damp warmth.

Then it moves away. "I'm sorry I have to keep you tied like this, honey. It's for your own safety. Hey, guess what? I've got some chocolates." She listens as he unwraps them and places one on her lips. She opens her mouth to accept it. " That's right, take 'em, one at a time."

When she bites into it, the center of the chocolate bursts with the bitterness of turned cranberries, kind of sticky, like caramel. Every bite releases sugary dark chocolate. She chews carefully, one at a time, slower and slower, heavier still as she gets to the third one. Then she slips off, tingling, her ship launching from some distant shore.

18

June's chore at Harmony Falls wouldn't have been the worst job in the world for a kid who wasn't addicted to chocolate. But working the candy counter during dinnertime was a sore temptation to the chubby girl and, truth be told, she snuck a few candy bars. Often. That evening, as she loved to do, June repeatedly opened and closed the drawer of a majestic silver cash register, sale or no sale. The old-time beauty was almost bigger than her. It rang out a bright *ca-ching* each time she closed the drawer, provoking her giggle and a dour look from Aunt Marie.

From his self-designated seat in the dining hall, Elias's laugh reminded everyone he was still around, working the crowd. Natalie hovered, but his attention was with June when she made the register sing. He mouthed something only she could see, and she beamed at what must have been a compliment. James watched from the hallway bench where he was reading.

Elias walked to the counter and bought a Hershey's bar. June happily opened the drawer and shut it after putting in his cash, and they both laughed at the drawer's closing tune. Then, big surprise, the grand gesture, Elias returned the chocolate to her, then winked at her, and turned to leave. Smiling almost wider than her face could bear, June opened the wrapper, broke off a section and popped it in her mouth.

As he headed for the front door, Elias nearly walked into Ben, who was standing in the hall, blocking his exit. Standing there together, their contrast was extreme: Elias was average height but tightly wound, real ropey. Ben, taller by a head and straight-backed, looked down on the man who minutes before had seemed larger standing beside June.

"Excuse me," Elias said. "I'll be on my way." He tried to loop around Ben, but Ben side-stepped him, blocking him and crossing his arms.

"Craft." Ben stared down at him. "Reopening your mine will ruin Spirit Lake. That's a crime." Ben noticed Elias wasn't looking at him so he moved closer, into Craft's line of vision. "So is taking good folks' money when you know the mine stinks."

"I don't answer to you, old man." He walked around Ben. This time Ben let him leave without saying another word. James wasn't sure which one came out ahead.

June was still chewing chocolate, giggling and grinning at the register when Aunt Marie walked up to her, her mouth uncharacteristically tight. "June. I know you've been eating the chocolate bars. I've seen you." June shook her head. Marie stared intently into June's blue eyes. "Just tell me this. Who's going to pay for all that candy? How many bars have you eaten that I haven't seen?"

June sniffled, barely holding back tears. She spit out, "None."

"That's a lie, June. I've seen you take them when you leave, too." Tapping her fingernails on the counter, Aunt Marie said, "You'll need to work it off. You do that and I won't tell your mother. Is that a deal?"

"No!"

June's tears spilled over as she bolted from behind the counter straight up the stairs to her room. James was mildly alarmed that his sister would steal, and from family! He followed her to check on her. As he stepped up the first stair, Natalie came from behind. "Hey, I had an early dinner hour." She turned toward the door. "How about a walk?"

"Sure." All thoughts of finding June vanished.

Out on the deck, James gasped. The sky was bruise-violet, graying at the edges, where a cup of spilled water might have bled it of primary colors. Natalie took his hand and led him towards the little bridge that arched over Harmony Creek. Dusk's lengthening shadows played games with James's eyes. He stumbled twice on tree roots on the steep hike winding up to a level ledge. James had to stoop to follow Natalie under the low hanging boughs of a giant fir tree. A bower enclosed them. Soft humus underfoot emanated warmth. Perhaps it had just been vacated by wild beasts. James imagined wolves or bears huddling together for warmth, steaming the hideout with their body heat and soft fur, protecting their young from human intrusion.

Being there, James was one of them, breathing in their rich odor, breathing out the human part of himself. He inhaled deeply the scented night air. "Do you think wild animals sleep here? Is this a wolf den?"

"Not a chance." Suddenly, Natalie looked at him quizzically. "All the wolves were shot decades ago. You didn't know?" She saw the look on James's face and rushed to divert him. "But plenty of humans have laid here!" Natalie's flirty grin teased him. She sat and patted the ground beside her.

Of course people came here to make out. But James didn't want to picture it.

He sat down on pine needle duff. He inhaled. Her hair smelled like roses. He liked it. When she lifted her face up to his, James leaned in to kiss her. As their lips touched, he felt Natalie's curl of a tongue darting against his own. He pulled her to him feeling warm as he did so. They kissed for a while, their tongues involved in their own sensual dance. Their hands roamed freely on each other's body. He pulled away suddenly; Natalie opened her eyes to look at him dazedly. He placed a finger to his lips, signaling her to keep quiet. Alert, he looked around and turned to the quick steps scuffing outside the bower. The lightning-bug flit of a swinging lantern stopped at the entrance. *Shit!*

"Who's that?" James lowered his voice an octave to scare off the intruder. He had learned somewhere that deep voices commanded respect. A shuffling of leaves, then June's face materialized above her lantern, ghoulish.

"James! What're *you* doing here?" Then she saw Natalie, and she frowned. Her voice dropped almost to a whisper. "Oh, hi?"

"No, what are *you* doing here?" James growled. "I thought you were in your room."

June had stepped inside the hideout, now crowding them, daring them to defy her. "I'm running away. Aunt Marie just called me a thief. She's going to tell Mom." June paused, her words failing to move him. "Besides, I come here all the time. This is my hideout." She stood, feet apart, claiming territory.

"You better find another hiding place." James heard the annoyance in his own voice. "You know?" He waited, but June didn't leave. She just stood there like she had nowhere to go. He could have wrung her little neck.

"Hey, your brother told you to scram," Natalie muttered. Even to James, her words sounded mean. June's shoulders rose around her ears to keep from crying.

"Hey, lay off her." James stood. "Let's go." They would need to find another trysting spot. He couldn't take this again. It wasn't June's fault, exactly, just another interruption. He softened his tone. "You can stay here, but if any teenagers come, you better go back to the lodge, okay? Keep the lantern on."

"Alright. Hey? Don't tell Mom I'm up here."

But June didn't need to worry about their mother missing her. When Natalie and James got to the front deck of the lodge, James ducked into the hall. His mother and Aunt Marie sat at a dining table playing gin and sipping Manhattans, red bandannas securing their pin curls. Elvis crooned "Love Me Tender" and they hummed along. Aunt Marie must have just snuck a Pall Mall because that cloying mix of tobacco and perfume hit James, like passing by a girl's high school bathroom when the door swung open. James walked in, took one look at those two clowns and marched right back outside, down to the dock, where he waited longer than he should have. But Natalie didn't return.

19

The next afternoon, Kay shouted to James from the lodge deck. He tried to ignore her. Lately, he couldn't do anything right with his mother. If Ben hadn't been standing there, he might not have answered her at all.

"What?"

"Could you look for the head of Junie's Barbie, please? It's missing. She's despondent." Her eyebrows shot up. "Come *on!*"

"Are you crazy?" James yelled. "Look for the head?" Oh boy. Another of his mother's treasure hunts. "Someone probably took it and left the body. That head's not just lying around under a bush." There was no use trying to reason with her. "Okay. If I see it, I'll grab it. Guess that's the least I can do." James walked up the steps towards her.

"Turns out, yes, it is the very least." Her voice was glacial. "You could jump in and help. You know, play with her once in a while?"

"Wait, Mom, you brought us out here to West Bejesus. There're no other kids her age around. Do you see any little friends? June and I have had to find our own way since you're busy in the kitchen or reading." James was careful not to say "or playing cards and drinking Manhattans."

When his mother pivoted and pushed through the front door, he followed her. He'd had it with her nasty moods. He speeded up to her near the stairs and, when she refused to stop, he yelled.

"You're the problem, Mom. You're the reason June's fat!" James was sorry the instant the words left his mouth.

Her face went white. "How dare you.… "

"Mom, remember? You put her on all those lousy diets, like grapefruit and cottage cheese? Who would eat that crap?"

"Stop it! She asks for my help!" Kay sat, her eyes wide with fury.

"And then you pick at her, pick at the way she dresses, pick at the way she talks. Does she ask for that, too?"

Kay jumped up and lunged at James to grab his shirt, but he stepped backwards and she tripped on a chair, hitting her knee. "Dammit to hell!" She screamed and clutched her leg. James turned away quickly, his face down, red. He hadn't meant for her to fall.

"You're grounded, buster!" Kay turned around and limped up the stairs. *Damn it.* He followed his mother up the stairs and down the dark hall, talking all the while.

"You should just buy her a new Barbie. It's going to be a long trip home, and she needs a Barbie with a head."

"Mr. Moneybags, huh? We're on a tight budget and a new Barbie's not on it. I got her the hula-hoop, didn't I?" She started to close the bedroom door.

"Yeah. Thank God for the hoop." Then a thought occurred to James. He pushed her door open an inch more. "Hey, why are we on such a tight budget anyway? Dan makes plenty of money."

"That's *his* money." She practically spat out the words. "And that's not your business." The door closed.

James stood there for a moment. What the hell? He and his mother used to have great times. Now he couldn't remember the last time she'd gotten a kick out of his off-beat humor. She was sure having a goddam ball with his Aunt Marie. The two of them could wind it up, especially with a few highballs. With Aunt Marie, his mother practically forgot about her kids. That was fine with him, but who was watching June?

20

Her other senses sharpen as she anticipates his visit. She can distinguish his steps now and the way he sits in the silence with her. She feels his touch, that slight caress against her skin, soothing her, and keeping her quiet. Call me Max, he had said, and so she does, ever since he ripped off the tape. She tries to imagine a face to go with his gruff voice and smoker's breath, and she pictures an old, old man. He is a hermit, he said, and a free man.

Max tells her stories when he sits beside her, lots of stories about gold and what it was like to find a ton of it, how the nuggets shimmered underwater or trembled in your pan. Those were golden days, he says, when he was young and followed the crowd out West. He had a wife then and a daughter named Suzy. It was for them he had stashed a load of nuggets, insurance for their future. But when the wife died in childbirth and the baby, too, Max had to give up six-year-old Suzy to an orphanage. "A miner's life is no life for a little girl," he says. His voice grows faint as if he is disappearing, but she can still feel his presence.

"Are you still there, Max?

He takes a while before he replies. "You look like her, dang it. You could have been her sister! That's why I first noticed you up at the ledge behind the lodge: how much you were like my little girl. Oh, she was a pearl of a girl, that's what I called her, Pearl." She can hear the sadness in his voice, the deep hollow it leaves in the space between them.

"Please take this stupid blindfold off!" She loses her patience and pulls it down with her ribbon-tied hands. He is a shadow in the dark, skinnier than she thought. His long hair and beard gleams white as snow but sticks out all over like Clara-belle's.

"What are you doing?" Max yells at her. "You're not supposed to see me!" He scrambles to pull the scarf back up over her eyes. "There."

She lets him do it. Whatever he says will keep her safe. "But Max! Where am I? What happened to Elias? Where's Natalie?" Her voice rises with each word, her agitation mounting. She hears her answer in the rustle of the paper bag of chocolates. She loves the way the little candy balls smooth her fears. All her worries float away on pretty clouds.

21

Two days later when Ben had some time, James hiked with him to Ghost Lake, a trek that took the entire day. They picked up Trail 211 heading north, though it did not intersect with an actual trail to Ghost Lake. Evidently there was no trail, hence the name 'Ghost'. Hikers just followed Coe Creek to an obscure landmark then walked west on elks' trails. As they walked, Ben pointed out medicinal herbs like tansy, arnica and biscuit root. His deep voice was quietly authoritative when he talked about wild animals. He stopped to identify the scat of coyotes, bears, and foxes. Though Ben had once been a hunter, and a good one, Uncle Hank said, he now followed a conservationist's path.

"Show me some wolf scat." James had hoped to see packs of gray wolves out west. Not believing Natalie, he listened every night for howling. They had to be out there.

"No more wolves," Ben said flatly. "They were hunted down like the Indians were. Gray wolves were deliberately hunted to extinction. They killed the last breeding pair and strung 'em from a tree to rot like trash." Ben had the saddest far-away look that James had ever seen on a grown man. Ben just kept walking.

By noon a winded James was sweating and cursing Ben under his breath. Ben pretended not to notice. James had to buck up. This was rigorous cross-country hiking through Norway Pass.

Once they finally got to the Green River, they sat down on a wide felled trunk. James threw his head back in awe. This was the Valley of the Giants, Ben had said. So named for the old-growth firs looming hundreds of feet overhead. James imagined himself climbing up Jack's beanstalk, up and up, into the clouds, soaring with bald eagles. Ben brought him back.

"Hear that black-backed woodpecker? That soft *chic* call? There, over on that snag." Ben pointed at a black bird scaling the trunk, yellow head and white-striped wings. "They're rare." James watched it peck at the snag, but only for Ben's sake.

Where were the elks and mountain goats? The bears, the coyotes? They roamed at these higher elevations, but so far James had seen none.

"Hey, you going to use that fishing pole?" James asked, just noticing it.

"Well, yeah," Ben said, smiling at James's interest. "This little lake is famous for its rainbow trout. They say Ghost Lake has the biggest trout. But the worst mosquitos." Ben slapped the blood-sucker on his arm, leaving a tiny splat. "Come on, we're almost there."

They followed a footpath up a creek to Ghost Lake's rim. The doll-sized lake looked undiscovered, despite another old picnic table. James walked straight to the bench without stopping. He sat, brushed some leaves off the table and put his head down on it to rest. Near him, some Steller's jays and squirrels squawked. Farther out on the lake was the gathering rush of a large shorebird's takeoff. James heard it but was too tired to note the species.

Ben nudged him. "Let's catch us some fish, James." Ben opened his bait box and loaded the hook. They shared the pole back and forth, and an hour later they had five good-sized trout strung on their line in the shallows.

That evening Ben and James were alone at the fire pit. It was a night too cool and damp to interest the others. Watching Ben panfry the trout so expertly fascinated James, even though he wasn't keen on eating them. The only fish he'd eaten back home were Morton's frozen fish-sticks. But these trout weren't like anything he'd had before. Sure, there were a few little bones to watch out for, but the flavor was unique to James, like tasting fresh fruit for the first time. They ate in relaxed silence, savoring what had been swimming only hours before. The rainbow trout were, as Ben said, "killed with mercy and eaten with thanks."

22

James was perfectly capable of bagging the trash alone when Ben wasn't around. Monday was shopping day in Longview so Kay, Marie, Tess, Ben and Hank all left early to buy a truckload of supplies. James was up early with them, groggy and drinking coffee. As they left, he had already fetched the trash cart and bags and was making his rounds, starting with Paddle Inn.

As soon as he opened the first can, the stench of garbage stung his nose. Turning away, he pulled open the bag to stretch over the lip of the can and inverted the can, usually without pulling it apart and dumping the garbage on the ground. Otherwise there'd be a clank of bottles, soured BBQ, soiled baby diapers speckled with coffee grounds, and a clean-up that could take a half hour. Finally, securing the chains on each trash can couldn't be rushed. The reality of bears was ever present.

James had taken longer than usual to complete the chore that Monday. His reward was the two-mile swim to Duck's Bay and back. Setting out, his body resisted him at first, shoulders awkward and arms dragging for five or ten minutes. Then he found his reach, his own rhythm and ready strength. He could have kept swimming forever, no friction, all forward, with the ease of mindless repetition. His mind was already anticipating the peace of submersion.

After four minutes sitting on the lake floor deep under the diving board, James floated for a while on the surface. Later, when he returned to the lodge, he found the kitchen empty. Gloria was at the base of the waterfall, he guessed, up behind the lodge. As he approached, she came gradually into view, leaning over the icy creek. Big covered ceramic crocks were submerged in the creek, half empty. After the shopping trip there would be chilled fresh cream, cheese, raw chickens and pork, and at least ten pounds of butter. Once Gloria loaded the remaining ingredients for the night's dinner into a wood crate, she stood to lug the food back to the kitchen. Rays of dusty sunlight cut through the dense forest like golden glass and shone patterns on her headscarf and her skirt of many colors, though the hem now dragged in muddy moss.

"Hey Gloria, hang on. I'll give you a hand." James walked towards her quickly. He hoped she'd let him help. With her fierce independence, she often shrugged off friendly offers.

"Thanks," Gloria said, straightening to stretch her back. James easily hoisted the crate onto his shoulder, and they walked down to the kitchen. "Just put it in the walk-in. I'll deal with that stuff in a minute. Hey, grab a soda, I've got my tea." She nodded toward the kitchen table. "Let's take a break," she said, smiling, reaching for her teacup.

James opened a Hires and swallowed a huge gulp that sent a zillion tiny fireworks down his throat. He liked Gloria. Though they rarely had a chance to talk alone, he respected the way she ran her kitchen. James had hardly sat in the chair before he heard the twang of "Chantilly Lace". Over Gloria's shoulder, James partially glimpsed June in the foyer, practicing her hula-hooping while the Big Bopper belted it out. James saw flashes of the hoop as it spun below her waist. At least she had something to do.

Gloria pulled her tea ball up and let it sink slowly back down. Then she gave it a yank back up again and watched it submerge. "I love it here," she murmured. "The trees and birds are good for me. And Hank and Marie always make me feel welcomed, like I'm family." She gazed at James as if that meant they too were relatives.

He nodded, wondering what next?

"And Ben . . . .." Her voice trailed off, and a smile flickered for a moment across her lips. "Well, Ben is part of this land." As quickly as it came, the smile dropped and she pursed her lips, distracted. "You're sixteen, right?" James nodded. "That's the age of my son. You kind of look like him, I think. What I can remember. He was a newborn last time I saw him. The only time I saw him." Her voice trailed off.

"You have a son?" She didn't look old enough. James glanced over Gloria's shoulder again, seeing flashes of June's hips swinging the hot-pink hoop in time to the fast beat. Into his line of sight, then out again. In, then out. "Where is he?"

Gloria pulled out her pocketknife. "We're not together." She made little cuts in the paper placemat, short parallel lines. Her eyes, usually bright gray as if by some inner light, were dim. The Big Bopper yielded to Elvis when the radio jumped to "Blue Suede Shoes." James was trying to concentrate, trying to hear Gloria. Why had she asked him for a talk? His eyes kept drifting to the foyer. June had stepped forward and he could see her plainly. Perspiring, she was performing for someone out of the doorframe. He looked back at Gloria who'd been watching James, waiting for his full attention.

"I'm sorry to say that people's claims about Portland's sex trafficking are true."

Where was this coming from? James had no idea why Gloria was saying this. His foot tapped incessantly but not to music. More to the beat of his heightening anxiety.

June had swung the hoop up to her armpits, all the while exaggerating the undulation of her hips to keep the pink rim spinning around her body. James heard June emit a high-pitched giggle. He shook his head to clear out what sounded like Natalie's flirty laugh. Then someone was clapping. James and Gloria stared at each other, puzzled. A wave of nausea swamped him. *Christ*.

23

GLORIA

"James," she continued. "You're shaking your head like you don't believe me. Her tone was sharp. She was telling him something personal, and he was looking everywhere but at her. She followed James's eyes to the foyer though she could see only June.

"She loves that hoop." Gloria scrunched up her nose. "But it's sort of, hmm, suggestive. Don't you think?"

He looked at her sharply, "Hey, come on. That's my sister you're talking about."

Gloria blinked. Jeez, she hadn't meant to offend him. She had wanted to confide in him about trafficking, about how young girls can attract attention without meaning to. June was as innocent as she had been. Once.

June's moves were awkward — she was just a kid — and her polka-dot shorts made her tummy pop out over the tight waistband: hardly sexy. Nonetheless, Gloria was concerned for her.

What was she thinking? A 16-year-old boy was hardly one to confide in.

"I'm sorry, James." She pushed back her chair with a squeal on the old floor. She stood, her chin lifted. "I didn't mean to upset you."

"Forget it," James muttered.

She swept back into her kitchen.

24

As soon as she left, James marched to the living room. As he rounded the corner, there was Elias Craft sitting on the couch, hair oil shining, a wet curl bent over his brow. He scowled at James when their eyes met.

"June!" James yelled. She jumped, clearly too caught up to have noticed her brother approaching. The hula-hoop fell to her feet and wobbled noisily on the wood floor for what seemed a full minute.

"What?" She huffed and bent down to pick it up. It was slow motion for James: June bending down to grab it, her defiant retort, her defiant stare. "What?" She repeated, now standing with her hip thrust to the side. "Can't you see I'm practicing for Elias?"

"Come on!" James's voice hardened. "Practice is over." He clapped his hands twice to hurry her, but he felt like one of his P.E. teachers. "Let's go!" He grabbed June's arm and, when she tried to yank it away, he squeezed it harder and half-dragged her out of the lodge to the deck.

"Hey stop! You're hurting me," she said, but she went along.

"Now you listen, and you listen good," James said, sitting June down on a deck bench. "You need to stay away from him. He's a bad man. Okay?"

"That's not what Natalie thinks." June cut in, looking up at him as he hovered over her. "I saw her with him in the lake."

In the lake? "Were they swimming?" Another punch in the gut. James felt his authority, or any advantage he'd had, vanish.

"They were floating on inner tubes. Talking, I guess." June had the subdued smile of a girl who was holding all the cards.

What the hell was Natalie doing with Craft? He glanced back at the foyer, anger seething in his chest. James needed to think fast. "June, go sit in the dining hall and wait for me." She rolled her eyes and dragged herself to a far table. James heaved out a sigh and went out to the deck to gaze at Spirit Lake to cool down. With a few deep breaths he had gained composure, adjusted his attitude, and walked into the dining hall.

"Do you know how pretty you are?" Craft was laying it on thick.

Holy Christ! He was standing over June, bracing himself with his hand against the window frame above her.

"Are you a 'sweet sixteen'?" Craft leaned close to June.

Without pausing, James slammed towards him, his heart pounding wildly against his chest.

Of course, June was giggling. But when Craft put his hand on June's shoulder, she began trembling, still laughing, as if trying to shake off her shivers.

James surprised them both. "Aren't you supposed to be gone?" he said to Craft, who straightened to face him, the famous Burt Grin whittled to a broken line.

"You got a problem, kid?"

James was the only man at camp, a fact that gave him no comfort. Beads of sweat rolled down his lower spine. As Craft flashed his phony smile, bile rose in James's throat. He gulped it back and advanced on him, herding him out.

Hands up, Craft muttered, "I'm goin', I'm goin'. Just waitin' on my ride." He strolled over to the windows to look, to stall, to basically piss off James, who now wanted to cut his ropey throat. As James directed him out, behind him June waved goodbye with her fingers like the little girl she was. Craft ambled out of the dining hall, making sure James caught him tossing June a wink. She tried to wink back but could only blink with both eyes.

"June!" James snarled. How the hell does a ten-year-old girl know how to flirt with a man her father's age? "Come *on.*"

Craft paused in the doorway and looked at his buffed nails. "You're way out of your league, boy," he said.

"And my little sister is in *your* league?" James surprised himself with his boldness. Craft had opened his pocketknife and began to clean his nails.

"You're a pervert!" James yelled. At least James stood taller than the wiry con man, though it was hardly an advantage as the other held a ready weapon.

They all heard the motorboat idling at the same moment. Grinning, Craft sprang outside like a compressed coil. The runabout looked like one of Harry Newman's, but James couldn't be sure. He turned to June who sat pouting, picking at the ric rac on her shorts.

"He's gone, now, June. He won't be back." At first James believed he was reassuring her, but then he noticed how her hair shone, gathered with a blue ribbon into a ponytail, neatly brushed, very un-June. He left her sitting there. Out on the deck, James breathed in deeper and stood taller in the damp afternoon sunlight. He needed to spend some time with his sister. She was out of line batting her eyes at that creep. But James didn't want to lecture her. An idea hit. He walked back inside.

"Hey Sis, want to hike up to the falls?"

"Sure!" June popped up, grievances overruled.

It was a good day for a hike, with his mother and everybody gone. There was no one for June to play with. What the hell had his mother been thinking?

25

Drowsily aware of the light touch on her legs, she can tell that Max is leaning over her by his heat. She tries to sit up, but falls back over, boneless. Max sits her up properly and pulls the fresh tape off her mouth. "Shhhhhh, don't cry or make any noise, alright?"

She nods, woozy, her lips smarting from the rip of tape. She will be very quiet. "Yes sir," she whispers in a gravelly unused voice. "Where's Elias?"

"Oh, he's around. If you hear him, say nothing! Stay as still as a rock. Not a breath. He'll hurt you if he finds you."

"I don't believe you." Her voice sounds like it is scraped out of someone else's mouth. She wonders dully why she should hide from Elias? He is her friend, why would he want to hurt her? Max is lying to her so he can keep her here, tied up in a cave, all for himself. "Where is Natalie?

She hears her answer in the rustle of the paper bag of chocolates.

That isn't what she wants right now, but she will take them. They are the only things that can soothe her now.

Put a couple of these in your mouth, June, and chew them slowly."

She opens her mouth obediently.

26

Taking the footpath by the creek up to 201 gave them a chance to talk. The brook ran high and loud, splashing over mossy boulders, slicking parts of the path. When June hit a muddy patch, James reached for her but she didn't slip, nor did she complain about having to climb over fallen limbs as big as trash barrels.

"Look," James said. There's Dead Man's Lichen on that trunk."

June countered, "Did you know Mom and Aunt Marie dropped me off at YMCA Boys Camp to spend the night with the director and his wife?"

"Yeah." James had heard. Christ. Another of his mother's stunts. "How'd it go?"

"How do you think? Terrible. There weren't even any *girls* over there." June kicked an old snag, dislodging a purple fungus that she picked up. "I didn't want to be with all those boys. It was embarrassing. Why would Mother do that? Just to get rid of me for the night, that's why." June tossed the fungus away and walked ahead sullenly. James picked it up, examined it, got lost in its filigree pattern.

"That wasn't much fun, was it?" He muttered thoughtlessly.

"It was worse than that, James." She stopped as if unsure to continue.

James looked at her and said, "Tell me."

"The director and his wife made up a bed for me on their sofa. The whole thing was so weird, so uncomfortable. They were nice people, but I didn't know what I was doing there. When I woke in the morning, I was lying on wet cushions. I had peed on their sofa. A lot. It was gross. I was afraid they'd see it before I could leave so I pretended to be asleep. When they went into the kitchen, I balled up the bedding and hid it under a table. I stuck a throw pillow over the big pee spot. I don't think they saw it till after I was gone." She walked ahead alone.

How could his mother do that to June? James moved slowly, fungus velvety in his fingers. It was easy to blame his mother, but he hadn't been much better. He hadn't once offered to spend time with June or even tried to talk with her.

What had she been doing during July while he was hiking with Ben? James hadn't noticed. What did he know about her summer? She swam like a mermaid with her ankles tied together with rope, even in the rain. She took her Barbie swimming, too. She stole chocolate bars and hid Fritos and Lays in her bed, she read *Archie* and *Veronica* comics. She wet the bed fairly often, judging by the sheets rolled up inside her door. She hula-hooped when she had nothing else to do. She had made no friends.

They hiked up the path, both quieted by the thunder of the approaching falls. James wondered about her going up into the woods alone. Halfway up, he yelled, "June, you think the hideout's safe?"

"Yes, James." She screamed back. "I told you, it's my special place. Want to go?" He did. It was a short detour. Remembering the last time he'd seen her there, he realized he'd never asked June what happened that night. He figured she'd returned, gone to bed, end of story.

"Remember when you found Natalie and me up there?" James stuck his hands in his pockets, not looking at June.

"I knew you were making out." A triumphant smile crossed June's face.

"Not really, you took care of that." He mock-punched her arm then smiled. "But what happened after we left?"

"You're just wondering *now*?" June stopped on her heels. "My stupid lantern battery burned out, that's what happened. I had to pick my way down the hill in pitch dark." June adjusted her ponytail, pulling it tighter and higher on her head. "It was awful. I was dirty when I got back, so I went down to the lake, by the creek, to clean off. Some people were still at the campfire, a ways away, so I changed behind that big cottonwood down there. Was that bad?" June thrust her right hip out and placed her small fist on it. Her new pose.

"Changed into what?" James resisted reacting to her pose. It was difficult. She looked like a dwarf with attitude.

"Down to my underpants."

Her underpants? "Holy Christ, June."

"Well, I don't wear a bra yet. That's where all the girls change." June looked away, feigning impatience.

"Did you see anybody? Anybody at all?"

"I got a little scared when I thought maybe I saw someone running behind a cabin, but I wasn't sure." June slouched as she continued up the muddy trail.

"Probably one of the campers, you think?" James tensed. *Please let it be one of the campers.*

"I don't know. I could only see a shadow. Strange, huh?" June turned away from James and continued hiking up the incline.

What the hell? "Has this shadow ever approached you?" James touched her elbow.

"Oh, heck no. I don't even know if anyone was actually there." June trudged on.

"I shouldn't have left you alone that night." James put his arm around June's shoulder. "I'm sorry for not being around more this summer. I'll do better, I promise." He tousled June's soft blond hair.

She threw her arms around his waist. "I know you will."

They had reached the mouth of the hideout, hidden under the massive boughs. Climbers could reach this treed ledge only through one narrow entry between boulders. James held up a thickly tasseled branch. June went first, then he followed her into a space so black that James felt as though he had fallen down a rabbit hole. The waterfall's roar had subsided when they stepped inside.

James turned on his flashlight just to get a sense, shining it around 360 degrees. Empty, cool, dark. He sat down, soft needles and moss crushing beneath him. They sat cross-legged, wordless in this special place. He set the flashlight on end, illuminating the network of branches overhead like webs.

June fidgeted with her hair, twisting and untwisting the ponytail like twine. She forced an impish smile at her brother, as if trying to hide some embarrassing new thought, then her eyes twinkled. She stepped over to the wall of boulders and reached into a crack between them. Her hand emerged with the headless Barbie, still jaunty in her black-and-white striped swimsuit. June brought the doll back to her seat next to James.

"Could you fix her?" Her voice was small, a child's voice, her eyes downcast.

"Uh. We'd need to find her head to do that." James smiled, almost chuckled at his cleverness. She was not amused. He put out his hand to take the doll. June gave it to him solemnly.

"How did it happen?" James found himself swinging Barbie's hard-plastic arms back and forth.

"I just found her like that." June grazed her hand over the soft humus floor.

"Where?"

"There." She pointed to the ground a few feet from them.

James shined the flashlight on the spot. "Maybe the head is around here somewhere. You want to look with me?" James handed the doll back to June and started to feel around on the dark ground.

June moved Barbie's arms back and forth scissor-like, over and over, as James had done. There wasn't much you could move. The doll had a marcher's arms and legs. June did not answer him. She tried repeatedly to make Barbie stand on her tiny black pumps, but the top-heavy doll fell on her face every time. James tried to explain the physics to her. It just wasn't going to work without Barbie's metal stand. After a few more stubborn tries, she stopped. Her small shoulders started to shake, a little at first then they were heaving. June sobbed, her head hung down.

"What's wrong?" James wasn't sure what to do. He didn't want to presume, but he went ahead and put his arm around her shoulder. She took a minute before she wiped her face with the back of her hand and gazed intently at her brother. He pulled back.

"If I tell you a secret will you promise on our mother's grave not to tell a soul?"

That was extreme, but okay, he could do it. "Sure." His eyes followed June, the image of his mother's corpse tacked onto his mental billboard. June returned to the stonewall, to one of many cracks between gray rocks. She reached in and brought out Barbie's head.

James gasped. The doll's yellow ponytail had been cut to a stub as if with scissors. June stuck the head on her baby finger and wiggled it at him. "I did it."

"What the heck, June?"

June sat back down next to him and met his eyes. "I did it — I pulled off her head."

James's mouth was bone dry. His head throbbed with the weirdness of it all.

"After I cut her ponytail."

That was too much. Somehow his response just flipped from shock to laughter. What the hell?

June had stopped crying and held the two parts, one in each hand, thrusting them at James, her eyelashes wet, catching light.

"Can you fix her? Please."

James stopped grinning. June's unease endeared her to him. His little sister was more complicated than he had thought. Her attachment to and anger towards her doll matched James's own broken toys and bonds of childhood. He wouldn't laugh anymore.

"Sure. I'll try." James took the parts and set about trying to push the hard plastic lip encircling the neck into the much smaller, tighter opening between the shoulders. June sat watching, her hands folded in her lap. He could see she was grateful that he hadn't scolded her.

James tried to push the head into the body again and again, with heightened frustration each time. Mattel had surely designed Barbies this way so you'd have to buy a whole new doll if a head or limb came off. Smart for the company, sure, but lousy for the kids.

"Sorry, June. I can't do it." The weight of failing her sat heavy on him.

"It's okay." June took the parts and returned them to their respective cubbies in the rock wall.

"Hey, why put it back?" James said irritably. "It's broken." Seemed pointless. "I'll get you a new Barbie."

"Really?" June turned to him, blue eyes wide like a younger child. "Would you really? Oh, James." Another hug. "Thank you." He promised her he would buy it when he went to Longview. He'd even go to Portland if he had to. Without a car, he'd have to hitch a ride into town, but he'd do it. He took off his smudgy glasses and lay on his back, gazing sleepily at the shadows towering above them. Each tree limb extended at intervals like bicycle spokes. Over the distant drone of the falls, orioles shrieked their bottle-rocket songs and two noisy squirrels barked over an acorn.

James had nearly fallen to sleep when a branch snapped brightly overhead where the mountain rose up. He sat up quietly, putting his finger to his lips when June opened her mouth to speak. James put on his glasses and stepped to the mouth of the hideout to peek under the bough. Cast in deep shade, this emerald world remained dim. So impenetrable was nature's cathedral of conifers that not even a memory of sunlight could reach the ground. Panning with his flashlight, James squinted into the forest and thought he saw some movement behind the trees, a shimmer, something, but he couldn't be sure.

"Did you catch that?" June asked.

"I saw something move, I think." He didn't want to scare her. "Sis, maybe we're getting a little nervous in the woods. It's probably a deer." Even as the words left his lips, James knew they were lame. Something, someone, had been there.

27

She awakes from a vivid dream of a merry go-round with real horses she cannot control. Her palomino tries to bound off the platform, but she holds him back with the strength of Wonder Woman. She has to keep the spooked horse in the same pose throughout The Yellow Brick Road song. She doesn't know if she can hold on till the end. Because because because because because.

She feels clearer each time she awakes like maybe she's swimming in shallower water where sunlight brightens the indigo depths of Spirit Lake. She cannot believe Elias would hurt her. He told her he loved her. Why would he lie?

Because of the wonderful things he does! At last she remembered the line!

The ribbons around her wrist have loosened enough to wiggle her hands out, one hand then the other. She pushes off the blindfold to see utter darkness. She quickly places it back over her eyes and slips her hands into the ribbon. It is loose now. What will he do when he sees? Is Max the wizard?

28

June bolted ahead down the trail, skipping that funny yellow-brick-road skip, singing, "We're off to see the wizard…" and laughing between the verses. Little sisters were okay if you had the time, which James did since Natalie broke it off. He could see more of June and Tess, take more hikes with Ben. Still he thought of Natalie. They hadn't talked since that night when she stood him up while he waited on the dock.

But, of course, when June and James walked into the kitchen, there was Natalie standing by the sink. As she focused on him, her eyes went dead as buttons, even though she flashed a phony grin. Horrified, James realized he was doing the same thing and instantly frowned to compensate. It was tough being near Natalie. Gloria separated them, sending James to the dining hall to fold silverware into napkins. He was now an expert.

He absently stared at Loowit. Funny. Since Ben told him the Indian legends, James used her native name. Particularly when she smoked or shook — which she did regularly — he called her Loowit.

Ben and Hank returned from Longview to South Shore Landing midafternoon, same time as Aunt Marie, Tess and Kay, the better to help lift supplies and share the boat ride back. Like every Monday, gallons of milk, hampers of eggs, sides of pork and more than a dozen chickens started moving off the boat.

Kay took James aside as he was helping. "How did June do while we were gone?"

"Fine."

"Fine?"

"What was she supposed to do, Mom? Who was watching her? You just left her here with … who? Gloria? She was busy working. I didn't know I was supposed to babysit."

"Listen to you, big brother, who's been too busy all summer to spend one minute with your little sister." Arms akimbo, Kay was on the offense.

"That's right, Mom. Twist it around. Well, now she's on your watch."

"I have to help with dinner. She can sit in her room for the time being."

James stormed into the living room, away from the argument. *Dammit!* There was June sitting on the staircase hidden behind a post rail, where she'd been the whole time. She had heard every spiteful word he'd said. James's eyes met hers. Scrunching her face to push back tears, she ran upstairs.

At that moment, Tess tapped James's shoulder. "Let's go with Ben to take a look at Sweden Mine. He thinks they've started drilling." James was relieved for a distraction and followed Tess to the dock where the runabout idled. They took off for Coe Creek, Tess's favorite swim spot. But as they approached the cove, they saw the clear water had been sullied. The creek bottom undulated with ridges of yellowish crud.

29

TESS

She saw the muck in her dream. Copper mud spreading down the creek, spilling into the clear sweet water of Spirit Lake. In the dream it was killing every creature it touched. She saw the beautiful trout flopping, gasping for life. It got worse. She saw June trying to swim in the ochre mud, she too gasping for life. Who was watching June? Where was Aunt Kay? There was no one to save June from the rising brown mud. June was in a cave, in the way that dreams just shift and make no sense. Tess heard the seeping of wet rock, the scurry of salamanders, the rush of black bats.

The scene shifted from June, wriggling like the fish, to St. Helens, towering over them all, growing larger, larger, swelling huge, spitting boulders into the lake, sizzling, boiling, killing every creature, every living thing that she loved. Tess screamed and yelled, "Help! Help! Dear God, help!"

30

A deep frown cut into Ben's face. "Damned copper." He threw out the anchor, hopped out into knee-deep water, and was already splashing up the creek with the authority of someone born to protect the wilderness.

"No!" Tess screamed suddenly and pointed. There on the stippled creek bank were scattered dozens of rainbow trout, all dead. Tess's back began to shake as she covered her eyes, sobbing. After a moment, she stooped to pick up a freshly killed fish. Its scales, once vibrant with many colors, were a dull iron. So were the eyes. She placed the trout on a bed of ferns then looked at James and Ben, weeping.

"But what if a bear or fox eats it? They too will be poisoned! And the whole of Spirit Lake." Tess shook. Gathering all the dead fish into a towel, she set them in the boat. She stood and rubbed her hands on her jeans then wiped her eyes with the back of her hand. No words.

The long climb up the north ridge to the mine grew muddier the farther up they hiked. Fresh brown spoils had leaked from the mine. James's gut clenched with every step, anticipating the worst. They all stopped abruptly at the settling pond. Ochre-colored ooze dripped down the creek, staining rocks and ferns, settling on the bottom. Tess took a sample of the sediment in a tin she carried in her field pack. Drilling machinery and a generator stood next to the mine.

The mine's mouth was off kilter, a clear danger to anyone fool enough to enter. Ben stepped under the log-lined entrance first, followed by Tess and James. It seemed deserted, dusty. Farther inside, the air was cooler. Empty cans of baked beans and candy wrappers littered the ground. James lifted his chin. A waft of human perspiration rode atop dank layers of history. He nodded to Ben who had clearly reached the same conclusion. Someone had left quickly.

James knew who was responsible for the poisoned trout, the poisoned lake, and for the stomach-churning unease everyone at Harmony Falls felt whenever he came around.

31
MAX

Whoosh! Bats exploded out of the mine at the sound of two men's voices. One of them swatted at the bats yelling, "Git, Git! The damn mine's a bust! Nothing but sludge."

"I told you there was nothin'," Max said. "But I did the drillin' so you owe me. Ain't my fault it's no good."

"How about that Lost Spaniard's Treasure? Under the waterfalls? Did you search all the falls around here?"

"No, you ignoramus." Max stamped his foot. "I went to Harmony. But there was no dagblasted treasure, not there or in any waterfall. It's a tale, that's all. Another dumb tall tale out of yer stupid tourist book."

"We need a Plan B."

"We had a Plan B. Got no plan now. Just pay me my wage and I'll leave."

"You damn troglodyte. Why should I pay you for nothing?"

32

"It was only a matter of time," Ben said. He and Hank stood in the front hall of the lodge. "They'll dig up the mine then abandon it when there's no gold and leave a toxic lake behind them."

"Dad, dozens of trout lay dead in the mouth of the creek," Tess wailed.

"I'm sorry, Tess. I know how you feel for them. But we've got a bigger problem. Craft is gone. Harry Newman said he left yesterday."

James wondered if Craft had already checked out when he came to Harmony Falls the day before. Had he stopped to see June on his way out? James should tell them. Then Gloria, Hank, Tess, and Kay all talked at once. Where's Craft? How do we stop the spillover? What about the people who bought shares?

But the six o'clock dinner had begun, and Marie hushed the kitchen crew before she started seating diners. All she needed was a stampede of angry people who'd bought into the scheme. But when Natalie heard Craft was gone, she forgot and hissed, "Where did he go?" and louder, "Where's the gold?"

The couple seated nearest the kitchen heard "gold" and started murmuring, first to each other, then to their neighbors. By the time the tables were full, the news had rippled through them all. Natalie and Tess bore the brunt of the men's fury as they served their meals, refilled their ice tea. Some had left their families to stand with other men, their voices crashing into each other.

"Let's go to the mine and see for ourselves," one yelled.

"Sure, you can do that, but I'm going to find Elias Craft, that no-good con."

"I heard he's staying at Harry's. Let's go there."

"Yeah! Let's get our money back and then some."

Uncle Hank had told James that out west, they were all gamblers. All the homesteaders, the timber barons and loggers, the mountaineers and miners, they'd all taken impossible risks, and some had cashed in big.

At once, the floor trembled under James. Christ, what was happening? The walls of the lodge shook. White cups and dishes rattled, fell and broke, and glasses shattered on the floor. Everybody reacted at once. The diners quickly gathered their shrieking children and ran for their cabins. James was tamping down his own hysteria, but some of the adults seemed a little thrilled the volcano might blow.

The crew had jumped to catch falling objects, but in the end James stood in an empty dining hall on a carpet of white shards. Frozen to the spot, he felt his mother's nudge as she handed him a broom. He swept the sharp debris, the entire time lashing himself for hurting June's feelings and spoiling their afternoon.

Later, after the tremors came the smoke. At Harmony Falls, most of the crew and campers sat on the dock, shoulder to shoulder, watching. By then the uproar over Elias Craft had been replaced by the breath-stopping spectacle of Loowit. Blood-red smoke whirled into the black night. There were no songs by the fire that night. Any human performance would have paled next to the dazzle of the Pacific Rim's youngest volcano. James couldn't pull his eyes away.

Nervous laughter skimmed over the water. As gorgeous as that pink fumarole curling up from the shimmering glacier was, it scared the hell out of James to think she could overpower them like Mount Vesuvius had done in Pompeii. James remembered how the campers had laughed at the forest ranger when he predicted that St. Helens would erupt before the end of the twentieth century. "How exciting," they'd said. "Boy, I'd love to see that." Stupid people.

All around Spirit Lake that night, at the YMCA camps and the girls' camp and at St. Helens Lodge, too, campfires glowed and folks talked and yelled. At least a dozen boats floated on the burgundy lake.

33

BEN

He had been sitting a distance away on the shore, facing Loowit. Straight-backed and alone, he drummed continuously with his sticks on a hollow log. An ever-changing cadence, the drumming was almost indistinguishable from the low roar of the waterfall.

These were not the first tremors Ben had experienced, nor the last, he was certain. He felt the vibrations before anyone else, before the ground began shaking, before the dishes began to fall and break, before the children started to scream. He felt the heat deep in his blood, an unsettling of his pulse, an irregular breath.

While others at Harmony Falls grabbed canoes and shore boats to get out on the lake and see the swirls of pink smoke more closely, Ben hung back in his solitude. He focused on the beast, as he had come to call her. He calmed his breath, his heart, the beat of his sticks on the log. In so doing, he tried to calm Loowit.

He was only one man, who knew more than he could ever tell.

34

From the dock, James could hear the beats. They eased his fears as his fingers tapped unconsciously in time with Ben.

By ten that evening, a tenuous calm had returned. Maroon-gray smoke circled the timberline, dissipating slowly. James was in no rush to meet his hard bunk so he waited for Ben to return.

The two of them sat silently at the firepit, keeping the flame long after campers had retired. James couldn't stop thinking about Loowit.

Living at the whim of a volcano was madness. Could she be boiling miles down at that very moment? All that fire hidden beneath an icy glacier? It was impossible to imagine. No one seemed to care. Live here long enough, and you forget about the danger. Instead, you focus on her dazzling beauty.

Finally, James said goodnight. Still upset over June hearing his mean words, he took a moment upstairs to look in on her. His mom snored in the lower bunk as June slept quietly on the top. Seeing her familiar round shape tucked in, James sighed. He marveled that she had slept through all the excitement. Their earlier walk must have tired her out. James tiptoed across the dark hall to his own room and eased down on his hard, yet welcoming bed.

35

DAY ONE

At six-fifteen the next morning as Ben and James were heading out the kitchen door to work, they stopped short. Thump, thump, thump, coming down the stairs, and Kay broke into the room, raving.

"Junie's gone! She's gone! I went to wake her just now, but her bunk was full of clothes." Kay whirled around imploringly to each of them.

James set down his cup of coffee with a shaking hand. "What?" Why were they all staring at him?

He had checked June's bunk last night. She was sleeping. Wasn't she?

"For God's sake, where is she?" James's mother snapped at James, who hadn't moved. "Anybody?"

"When could she have left?" James asked, but no one knew. Gloria, always up by four, said she hadn't seen June or heard any floorboards creaking.

"I'm sure June was there when I fell asleep." Kay kept shaking her head. "I could hear her breathing...." She sank into the closest chair. "I think."

James's mind raced. She might have snuck out to the woods. She loved to hide. James knew because he was always the one sent to find her. Thing is, it was fairly easy to see her. He'd catch her peeking at him through a leafy bush or from up in a tree, hardly hidden at all. Suddenly James was sure he knew where she was and, saying so, he dashed out the back door.

On the path up the hill, the same path she'd skipped down yesterday, the loose pebbles and potholes threw him off balance. James called June's name over and over all the way there, but the hideout was empty. Even the cubbies where June stashed Barbie's two body parts were empty. No head, no body, no ponytail. No June. Where else would she go?

She must be at the lake. That was it. Some days June woke up early to row along the shore to catch minnows.

Alone on the dock, James yelled her name hoarsely, over and over. Harsh winds kicked up waves that surged straight at him from the south. This couldn't be happening.

As he approached the back kitchen door, Gloria's face loomed in the window, wavy and warped from the old mullion glass. By the time he reached the kitchen door, a half dozen other faces crammed against the window to witness for themselves his failure to find June, not least among them, his mother.

Uncle Hank had already taken the boat to South Shore Landing, to the only phone booth for miles, and report June's disappearance to the Longview police. Despite Kay's protests that June was likely lost somewhere in the forest, Hank said he wouldn't let anything sway him from reporting what he felt sure was a crime.

"I've seen too many posters in Portland advertising missing kids!"

36

Kay's cheek pressed against the linoleum-topped kitchen table, with her eyes closed. Marie stroked her sister's back. The coffee percolator bubbled on the counter in that reassuring way, but mostly just drew attention to the silence of the lodge.

"I think she's hiding somewhere," Tess spoke quietly. "Maybe in a cave. We'll find her."

Aunt Marie nodded to Tess, saying to Kay, "That's right, honey."

James stood behind his mother. It was impossible to sit. His limbs twitched, but he felt useless standing there. Still, he was in no way prepared for what happened next.

The instant Uncle Hank walked in, Tess rushed to him. "What did they say?"

Kay raised her head listlessly and slowly pulled herself upright. Hank found a seat next to her. Collapsing into it, he took a deep breath before beginning.

"I'll cut to the chase, Kay. Elias Craft is not Elias Craft." He held on to one of her arms to brace her.

"What do you mean?" Kay's back stiffened.

"I got nowhere with the Longview Police. They said I'd have to wait twenty-four hours to report June missing. That wouldn't do. So I dialed Bill Haley in Portland."

"Bill's the only detective I know. When I called, oddly enough, he was about to come out here to warn us. This morning he saw the monthly list of recently released inmates. Standard procedure. He was surprised to see Elias' face. But when he looked up his name, he said he almost fell off his chair. He's on his way.

"Kay, listen. The real Elias Craft died in prison last year," Hank said, his face grave. "He's the guy who originally owned the rights to the Sweden Mine." He paused. "The man posing as Craft was his cellmate. His name is Vince Lavetti. He's a convicted felon. And probably Mr. Craft's murderer."

37

GLORIA

Gloria suddenly dropped the iron skillet of spaghetti sauce she held. It just slipped from her grip to the floor with a thud, splattering bright red on the linoleum, painting the white cupboards, burning the legs of those around her. Gloria tried to kneel down, but her legs gave way under her. She slipped on the thick sauce and slumped on the floor, shaking.

No, No, godammit! It couldn't be him! She left him and that nightmare back in Portland. He was put away in jail for what he did to her and all the others. How could he be here on Spirit Lake, somehow penetrating her shelter? Had he come for her? For the one who survived to testify against him?

No, he'd come for June. Oh my God. Where's June now? Gloria shuddered.

She had to get up, to pull herself together. She tried to stand but slipped again on the sauce. Jesus, red splotches were all over her like a nightmare returned.

James stooped to help her, but they were both trembling, swearing to themselves. Marie rushed to them with a pile of rag towels, Hank helped Gloria stand, and Tess led her to her cottage to clean up.

Tess poured clear water from the pitcher into the bowl on the stand. She soaked a fresh small towel in the bowl and squeezed out the excess water.

Gloria sat on the wood chair in her room, staring at nothing, pale and motionless. She let Tess take her hand and wipe it clean, then her arm. Tess rinsed the towel in water, tinting it red, as if cleaning a wound. She repeated with the other hand and arm. Then she tossed the pink water out the front door and refilled the bowl with fresh water. She wiped Gloria's face and throat and replaced Gloria's shirt with a clean one from her drawer. Next she removed her dirty shoes and cleaned her feet and ankles. When she began to clean the sauce off her legs, Gloria stopped her, whispering.

"I can do that."

"I don't mind, really."

"No, I prefer. I've got another skirt in the closet, if you don't mind."

Tess brought her a brightly printed long skirt, one similar to those she always wore. "Here." She kissed Gloria on the top of her head. "I'll go back to hear the rest."

Gloria didn't need to hear the rest. She already knew too well.

38

Hank cleared his gravelly throat and coughed. "In the Forties, Lavetti led a prostitution ring that moved girls over state borders. Some were moved out of the country, most of them minors."

"NO!" James yelled and punched the icebox like it was Lavetti's face. On impact he felt a strange release, a pleasurable tingling at the metal biting into his knuckles. He pulled back, clutched his hand in his lap, and swore at delayed pain. Aunt Marie brought him a dish towel with ice.

Hank's brows knit with worry as he looked at Kay. "We have reason to suspect he abducted June."

James struggled to take a breath, but kept swallowing. Next to him, his mother's thin hands shook like leaves around her head. "What do we do? *What do we do?*"

Hank grabbed both her hands firmly in his. "We get her back." Squeezing them, he made Kay look at him. "Okay?" She nodded. James handed her a tissue from a box on the table. Marie had been mopping up the spilled tomato sauce with towels, but it was a pink mess.

"Ben, you organize search groups to go out right away," Hank said. "I'll stay here. Detective Haley is on his way." He waved Tess and

Marie away. "I'll clean up this gore. Tess, go around to all the camps, tell them to search their grounds." He pushed back his chair and stood. "And tell them to keep their campers close."

"I know she's in a cave, Dad. I just know it." Tess was biting her lower lip raw.

39

TESS

What could have happened to Gloria? She was always such a strong presence, yet she just came unraveled. A private woman, she let nobody know much about her. They only knew what they saw: how well she ran her kitchen, how she assigned duties and kept everybody in line. They knew nothing of her past.

But Tess was more worried for June, of course. She'd had so many bad dreams. Creepy dreams. Like being tied up in a cave somewhere. But no one ever listened to her so what was the sense of talking about her dreams? Tess was beginning to accept that she was losing her mind. That wouldn't help anyone.

But her thoughts drifted back to the dream she'd had last night. It wasn't creepy. She felt things so vividly, as if she herself was in a cave, smelling the mold, hearing the weeping of the walls and the cries of animals. Last night she'd heard a wolf howl in the dream, yet she knew there were no more wolves. They'd all been killed, even the pups, long before Tess was even born. She was sad that she missed the chance to see one.

But in the way that pieces of dreams come back to you when you start to pull the thread, she might have felt a wolf in her dream, but it was hazy. She recalled the soft fur between her fingers, like her old dog Jake's ruff around his neck. It made her smile.

Everything about the dream seemed hazy, all the senses blurred. But not scary like the carousel dream had been. This dream was even beautiful.

40

"Now is not the time to talk about your dreams, Tessie," said Hank. The words rang out sharp and angry, so unlike him, as if losing June was already changing the family. "James, you take your mother across the lake to call Dan when she's ready, and on your way you can shout for June. Just keep calling her on the lake." Hank said the words, but no one put any stock in June answering, particularly with bad weather blowing in.

James had a purpose now. Gusts whipped at his hair as he jumped down into the icy waves to pull out a shore boat. Screeching against pumice, it came free. Kay ran down to the boat crying, "Wait! I've got to call Dan!"

James took her hand to help her into the boat. He yanked the engine to life with a sputter of smelly gas. Like a flash, they were out in the chop with a three horse-power shore boat. June couldn't possibly hear them scream over the howl of the wind, but scream they did, over and over. With each syllable, though, higher waves pounded home the impossibility of finding her.

The storm front was moving in fast. Gales rocked them, and the small motor squealed as they plunged and reared over the water. When James reached South Shore Landing, he tied up. The general store hadn't opened yet, but the phone booth was never locked. Kay squeezed in. She inserted a dime, spoke with an operator, and then waited. And waited. No answer. It was three hours later in Boston. Dan should have been at work.

Outside, James had been leaning against the glass booth, rain pelting him, trying to hear his mother's voice through the glass, to read her lips. She hung up the phone and pushed her forehead against the cold glass. Rain-spatter threw paisley lace on her skin, smearing as she slid to the floor. Kay grabbed the tethered phone book, anything to hold onto, as James pushed open the irksome louvered door. He pulled her out, hands under her armpits, while her nails raked her scalp. The second he got her out, the glass door snapped rudely back into place.

"Is he coming? Mom, isn't he coming?" They stood under the eaves of the store. James clutched her shoulders. She was fragile enough to slip to the ground.

"He was out to lunch." Her words were barely audible. "I left an emergency message at his firm."

James yelled, "Let's get back. The wind's picking up." Kay got in and he pushed off. Heaving due north, James gripped the lever, trying to steer over the peaks, only to slap down the other side. Each time it jolted his jaw, but he kept barking hoarsely "June! June!" Huddling small on the metal seat, Kay scrunched inside a drafty yellow slicker, so big she looked tiny. She yelled June's name over and over, but they heard only Spirit Lake's incessant wailing.

The sheriff's inboard eased up to the dock as James and his mother set foot on the shore. James ran over to catch their line and tie it up. A big man, Sheriff Blanchard from Longview stepped out, accompanied by one Officer Tulo. They looked grim.

Kay ran toward the dock yelling. "Just the two of you? Only two police officers to find my daughter?" Her eyes shifted between the two men, her hysteria building visibly.

"Excuse me, Ma'am. Where is June's father?" Sheriff Blanchard stared at Kay.

"He's back East working." Kay pulled herself up to her 5'10" model height, never cowing to a stranger, particularly not a rude one.

"He's back East and his family is here?" Blanchard asked.

"Who are you to judge?" She stepped into his face. "I am June Baptiste's mother. I'm the one you want to talk to."

"Ma'am, all I'm saying is …." Blanchard's retort was cut short by the arrival of another runabout, this one carrying Detective Bill Haley. Hank walked down from the lodge to meet him.

Even before the boat had stopped rocking on the waves, Haley threw the rope to James on the dock. He leaped out and strode toward the group while James tied it up.

Hank reached out to shake his hand. "Thanks for coming out, Detective. You remember meeting Lavetti here?"

Haley shook his hand and nodded. "Oh, I sure do." Then he turned to address the sheriff. "Thanks for coming out, Sheriff Blanchard. Name's Haley. Trafficking is my beat, that's why I'm here from Portland. And we'll need all the manpower we can get. For now, I'm taking over this investigation, and you'll be my second in command." Haley announced this with the natural force of authority.

"Well, I thought since …."

"Whatever you thought has now changed. Let's get out of the rain and start focusing on finding a kidnapped little girl." As Haley spoke, he glanced at Kay who had winced at his words. He moved to her side, shaking her hand in both of his. They'd met earlier, in July when he'd visited, and had spoken briefly.

"Kay, I'm sorry this is happening. We'll find her." He took her elbow and guided her up the path to the lodge. "Can you tell me where June's father is?"

"He should be at work in Boston. I called him but he wasn't at his office or home." Kay fretted, walking and wringing her hands, unwilling to look Haley in the eye.

"I have connections in my old Boston precinct. Let me get some preliminaries out of the way here, and I'll go back to the South Shore Landing and call them, see if they can help track him down."

41

KAY

She already suspected where Dan was, but was too ashamed to tell the detective. It wasn't anyone's business but her own sorry life.

When she first met Dan in New York, James was only six. She'd married him primarily to give her son a father that could send him to good schools, give him opportunities, make the right kinds of friends. What mother wouldn't want that?

They settled in Boston's Back Bay when Dan got a better job with a decent law firm. It wasn't long before Kay realized that Dan married her for reasons not unlike her own: opportunities and appearances. She quit her modeling career and bought into the country club life, the charity balls, the right friends. But Dan wasn't a generous man, not with love or money. Just a good enough provider, as he was quick to remind her. She only got whatever made them look successful and classy. And how classy was infidelity?

She and James were never enough for Dan. She knew she was losing him. Even after June was born, Kay was just arm-candy with kid baggage.

But love? Maybe Kay never had love. Marie had married for love and still had Hank to keep her warm at night. Kay? She had bridge groups, floor plans and the kids.

42

James's head felt full of bees, buzzing with guilt. Yes, he had seen something yesterday that he should have told his Mom and Uncle Hank about: June flirting with Elias, or Vince, and him teasing her back, flattering her. Even then James suspected a boundary was being crossed. Now he realized that June would have followed Vince willingly, innocently. Had James tried hard enough to stop it? The answer would always be no, but a louder no, a no that would rip him open if she was really gone.

How could he possibly tell them now? The idea made him weak. They would ask him why he had held back. He'd thought of that, of little else. The answer was that he'd been the one responsible for June, though no one had told him so. He'd failed miserably, quite possibly fatally, to protect her.

He heard Haley speaking to his mother and moved closer to listen.

"But for now let's get this investigation underway. First, I need a picture of June." He pulled a notebook out of his shirt pocket and looked at Kay.

Haley was all business, probably furious with himself for missing a child-trafficker in his midst. He had been face to face with a man he thought was Elias Craft, laughing along with him and his goddam nuggets. How could Haley not have seen what a con man he was? Or been such a poor judge of character? James hoped that his little sister wouldn't pay the price for Haley's lapse. Or for his own.

In a daze, Kay walked to get her wallet. She dug out a picture of the family at a Broadway show, *Funny Girl,* and placed it on the table. James glanced at the photograph, instantly remembering how ridiculous he had felt that day. Because it was in New York City, where Kay had been a high fashion model, she'd made them all dress up like it was Easter Sunday, suits, ties, the whole bit. June had looked miserable in a frilly pinafore.

"Thanks, Kay." He placed the picture in his notebook. "We'll crop her and make copies and paper Longview and Portland with notices. This is a crime scene now, Hank. Close Harmony Falls immediately. Nobody leaves without being questioned."

"There's no telephones here," Hank said. "You should set up at a place with phone service." James silently agreed. Harmony Falls was so isolated from the rest of the world that it had seemed to move out of time, their actions without consequences beyond Spirit Lake. Clearly delusional.

"Good point, Hank. We'll work from Newman's lodge. Sheriff Blanchard, how about you and your officer visit the cabins and begin the interviewing. That okay? Great." The Longview contingent got to work obligingly.

Haley joined Hank in the dining hall, and the two shouldered over a table. Haley pulled a map from his breast pocket, unfolded and spread it out. He traced his finger around it, talking, while James listened from the kitchen.

"We'll block off the South Shore Campground as well as St. Helens Lodge. If Vince's car is there, we'll get him. Either way, I've got guys searching Longview and Portland, putting up roadblocks on all the highways. Vince may have already gotten to the Willamette. And you know that's the quickest escape route to the coast, to the pipeline." Haley turned to James, who had moved closer to hear. "Those're the smuggling routes. Once the girls are in the pipeline, they usually vanish forever."

James nodded, numb.

"Where did June like to play?" Haley asked James to bring him around.

A simple question yet one freighted with so much guilt that James squirmed. "The hideout," and he pointed. "Up past the cabin called Shangri La."

"June played *there*?" Aunt Marie jumped into the conversation, strolling in from the hall. "That's where all the teens go to make out, didn't you know?"

Of course James knew. And June did, too. She had interrupted James and Natalie there. His face reddened. He said nothing.

"Has anyone seen Natalie?" Marie said. "She didn't show up for breakfast this morning." Shrugging her shoulders, she muttered, "Not that it would be the first time…."

Haley apparently didn't hear Marie. "June may have gone up there last night and then left from there," Haley said. "Why don't you show me this hideout. We'll rope off the area for evidence, especially the ground leading to the hiking trails, so you'll need to watch where you step."

Watch where he stepped? Right. In fact, as soon as they began the steep trek up, James slipped on pebbles and even fell to his knees once. Despite trying his best to help, he felt useless and undone.

Haley offered an arm to steady him. "It's alright, son."

Inside the dark bower, Haley stooped under some low boughs. Something shiny had caught his eye. With a gloved hand, he picked up a foil ball of a crushed Hershey's Kisses wrapper. Looking at James questioningly, Haley placed the wrapper in a plastic evidence bag.

"Yeah. June loves chocolate," mumbled James, as if the foil wrappers proved she'd been there. He tasted bile thinking of how he had teased June for gorging on chocolate, calling her 'June Balloon' and worse. She hated that, anybody referring to her weight.

Haley had already changed his focus to pine needles. Beside the place where he spotted the Kiss wrappers was a small area, maybe two by four feet, where needle duff was depressed, smoothed like maybe a child had lain there. "She might have slept here, James."

James couldn't imagine his little sister sleeping in the forest alone. He shivered. *Try to stay focused.* Stepping to the rock wall, he checked between the two protruding rocks. Nothing.

"That's one item that's not here, well two. June's Barbie doll. That's another story, her Barbie."

"Tell me about it." Haley reached down to pick a cigarette butt off the ground. "Hmm. Camels." He spotted a few more, putting each butt in a separate plastic bag.

James smiled, recalling. "You'd think Barbie was her best friend. She has a special voice for Barbie and a lower pitched voice for herself. Kind of strange... but maybe not. You can imagine how she reacted when, a few days ago, she looked into this cubby here," James showed him the space, "and saw that her Barbie had been decapitated."

"Wait, I'm taking notes."

"Anyway, she said she'd decided to just leave the headless doll up here since she couldn't really play with it. Then yesterday, when we were here together, she found Barbie still in the cubby in two parts. But someone had chopped off the doll's long blond ponytail.

"What?" Haley stopped writing and eyed James with a raised eyebrow.

"Here's the weird thing." James said. "She did it herself." Eyes wide, he nodded. "She confessed yesterday while we were here. She asked me to fix the Barbie, but the head wouldn't go back on. It's still in two parts."

"What? Why?" Haley muttered as he wrote.

"I didn't ask." James's shoe toed the duff. "I figured if she wanted to tell me she would. But if I had to guess, I'd say she's been lonely and bored out of her mind."

The two eased out of the hideout, stepping to the side of the little path to look for clues. "There's something else." James faltered. "Something I haven't told anyone." He didn't want to say it out loud, but he did, looking at his shoe.

"June was hula-hooping for Craft yesterday in the living room, kind of suggestively. He was egging her on and clapping." A deep crease tightened between James's eyebrows. "I stopped it, but he came back…."

Haley scribbled in his notebook, then looked up at James. "Not Craft. His name is Vince Lavetti."

"Jesus." James simply could not grasp Haley's words. "That was exactly twenty-four hours ago. I knew something was wrong even then." James kicked at a rock and cursed at himself.

"Don't be hard on yourself. You couldn't have known who Vince was. Nobody else did either." Haley paused, probably remembering how even he had failed to question Lavetti's intentions when he met him. They stood off the path under the dark trees. "Tell me more about Lavetti."

"Remember how he hung around here with his gold nuggets? Well, when he first came to Harmony Falls, he had his eye on Natalie." James paused, putting it together, and continued. "Then he turned his gaze to June." James's breath caught in his throat. He looked up at the trees to keep the tears from rolling down his face.

"Something pointed Lavetti to June," said Haley.

James said what he hated to admit. "It could have been June herself, trying to get attention." He wiped his face with his shirt sleeve when Haley wasn't looking. Haley nodded and silently considered the connection. James followed his thought.

"June watches older girls and copies them. She did it with Natalie." James's mind drifted to awful places. "Dancing and hooping must make her feel pretty, and grown-up."

"Yes," Haley said, then turned away, pursing his lips together.

As they started back down the path, James caught sight of the bright pink tube. Hidden behind brush, the hula-hoop had been cast aside, perhaps when June wasn't looking or didn't care anymore. James climbed down to retrieve it and brought up the bent thing to show Haley. Big raindrops suddenly plunked on them, chopping up the trail, washing away the evidence.

In the lodge, Haley left James to speak with Uncle Hank. "Seal off June's room," he said, "even from her mother." Then he went to see Kay for a piece of June's favorite clothing or a toy. She brought out one of June's shirts — a white one with wide red stripes. But now, Kay held the soft cotton to her cheek, inhaling its fragrance as she squeezed her eyes shut.

Everyone was milling around the dining hall, whispering. James wanted desperately to be alone, to try to think. If only he could get to the lake. Submersion was his only solace, but the weather was still stormy. James went to his room. Once there, he overheard Haley speaking to his mother at the top of the steps. James cracked his door.

"I need to see her room," Haley said. Kay nodded and walked him to the closed door. "Thanks, we'll take it from here." He opened the door, went in and eased it almost closed behind him, enough that James had a sliver of a view.

Sitting on the bottom bunk, Haley looked through June's possessions. Nearly two dozen comics tumbled out of her over-night case, along with barrettes and crayons, a sketchbook and her wallet, her Daily Diary and her lucky rabbit foot, the soft fur worn to bone from June's faithful, if misguided, rubbing. The noise of June's stuff falling on the floor brought James to the door. Haley was pulling out her undershirts and panties. June was shamefully exposed though she wasn't even there.

"I can't open the diary," barked Haley. "Is there a key?"

James pushed open the door.

"Here, take it." Haley tossed the little pink book at him.

James caught it and picked at the flimsy clasp. "I don't know where the key is."

"Well, break it open."

James didn't want to, as if it might add to June's violations, but he opened up his pocketknife and broke the lock. Inside, she'd written pages during the school year, right up to when they'd left Attleboro mid-June to drive out to Harmony Falls.

After that, there was only one entry. A recent one. Yesterday. It was written in her loopy cursive handwriting. James read out loud, "My first date." Pink shiny star stickers adorned the page.

Haley's mouth opened, stayed that way for a second before he made it produce words. "What else did she say?"

James skimmed through the remaining pages. All blank. "Nothing more."

The pile of tumbled clothes on the floor drew James over. Something was missing. "Where's her yellow sundress?" As it dawned on him, James slapped his forehead "Christ. Her first date … she wore her favorite dress."

Haley locked eyes with James, both of them realizing. June had gone willingly.

"I'm done here," he said to James. "Come on out." James followed him and watched while Haley slid a lock on the door.

James returned to his room. Just thinking about what he should have done squeezed his gut. I should have interfered faster. I should have made her go to her room. I should have made him leave sooner.

So many should haves.

43

DAY TWO

"Natalie isn't in her cabin," Aunt Marie said to Haley. "No one's seen her since supper last night. Can you call to see if she's at her folks' in Longview?" James's aunt, being short, seemed to stand on her tiptoes when she was trying to be heard. She touched Haley's elbow. "I'm concerned."

James hadn't noticed Natalie's absence. Had she taken off with Vince? He wouldn't have been surprised. Was she with June? No. Too much to hold in his head, too many pictures. James just wanted to find June. That would be enough to hope for.

"I'll look into it," Haley said, then turned to Kay and spoke quietly. "My guys will find your husband," he said. "Boston is, used to be, my home. I'll let you know." He nodded at her and to James who, seated next to her, seemed to be included in the promise. Was Dan missing, too? His mother had given him no clue.

Speaking to all gathered in the living room, the detective cautioned, "Keep your walkie talkies on and stay inside."

"Can I volunteer?" Gloria called out from the back, waving her hand in the air.

"Sorry, but the search is limited to law enforcement only. Standard procedure," Haley said, glancing quizzically at the big bohemian-looking woman before he turned to leave. "There's still a small chance June could wander back here." Everyone was quiet.

Haley cleared his throat. "Okay, Blanchard reported in. All of the cabins are emptying. He'll be ferrying the last of the campers across the lake. Gloria, you move into the lodge. Keep the doors locked. We'll be back in the morning."

"What about Natalie?" Gloria said. "Where will she go?"

"Home. When we find her." Haley shut the lodge's thick wooden door behind him. He would set up temporary headquarters over at Newman's St. Helens Lodge then drive to Longview.

Though it was barely dusk, a tangible darkness had blown in and chilled James to the bone as Detective Haley closed the door. Harmony Falls had been left to the ghosts of Spirit Lake. And to Vince. Within minutes, Ben walked in, looking as if he were about to say something, then stopped, seeing the few people who remained at Harmony Falls.

"Where is everyone?" He was followed by Joe Delaney, who owned a camp on the lake and was a logger for Weyerhauser, the latter a fact that everyone tried to forget because they liked him. Ben and Joe had spent the day searching for June in the lava tubes. Wet, muddy, tired, and hungry, yet they were both prepared to keep searching. Joe's young mutt, Jonah, part bloodhound, panted behind Ben, tired from searching with the men.

"They're all gone," Kay muttered the obvious.

"Haley wants us to stay put," Hank said. "Standard procedure." James knew exactly what Ben's response would be.

Ben's one eye opened frightfully wide then his chest expanded. "Sit and wait? Do nothing? I can't do that. I know these woods. We're going back out."

"You're supposed to sign in with the cops over at Newman's," Hank said.

Ben's legs spread the slightest bit. "Like hell."

"I'm coming, too," James blurted out. He stood abruptly as if answering roll call.

"Me too," Tess chimed in.

"If you guys go out, we can't call the cops if you get into trouble." Hank looked intently at each one. "Okay. You better hustle, it'll be dark in an hour."

It was a good team: Ben was an experienced tracker, Joe knew these woods better than anyone, and Jonah, his hound, would sniff her out. All of them able and willing — they only needed a plan. Since they'd searched the lava tubes, Ben suggested Sweden Mine.

"Ape Cave would have been a great hiding place, except it's too far for them to hike," Tess said, slumping in her chair. "There are so many hiding places in the Cascades, too many even for hundreds of searchers."

Hearing her resignation reminded James how tired they all were. More than that, his cousin had sunk into a black mood. It had been raining for days, and now all the campers were gone. He had an idea.

"Are you still having dreams?" He knew she was. He could hear Tess moan and cry. He moved to a chair closer to her. "Yesterday when June and I hiked up to the hideout, she sang 'Follow the Yellow Brick Road.' Like in your dream of the carousel."

"Oh, everybody sings that song since the movie came out," Tess said. "It doesn't mean anything."

He sighed. "Why do you doubt yourself? What if your dreams could lead us to June?" James felt desperate. They had few options. He needed her.

"But I have nightmares almost every darn night. I don't know what they mean." She bit her lower lip.

"How about when you dreamed about the copper mine leaking? Or the volcano sputtering? Or when you heard the girls crying in the carousel? Maybe they really are crying somewhere, and you have to discover where." James looked at her, his head leaning in.

Tess grew thoughtful. "What's strange is, in the cave I can't see anything. Just hear. And feel. I feel salamanders on my legs. I hear wolves howling. And doves. I can hear doves."

44

What? James recoiled. "Salamanders?" No one else believed Tess. Why should he? Because without Tess's implausible dreams they had no hope at all. Miles and miles of dense Pacific Northwest forests. There were folks out searching their damnedest. But really. What were the odds?

"Let's go!" Ben hollered at them. Tess and James jumped up and met the others on the dock. Kay waved June's shirt in front of Jonah before they left and, once he got outside, he followed her scent right up the path to the hideout. From there they took Trail 211, around Spirit Lake.

Jonah trotted on ahead, not particularly focused.

"This isn't right!" Tess protested. "I saw a cave in my dream!" She stubbornly walked in the other direction. James hesitated for a moment, trying to decide which direction to take. He chose Jonah's nose over Tess's untested clairvoyance.

Jonah started bellowing deeply, urgently, splitting the night around them.

"Tess, let's just see where Jonah's leading us." Ben touched her arm. "Those caves will get searched all day tomorrow by other volunteers. Come on."

As Jonah trotted north of the Portland YMCA camp, towards the Swedish Mine, everyone fell in line behind him, hurrying to keep up. Tess aimed her eyes at the ground. "She's not there," she said to no one, the pain of their doubting her vision so clear on her face.

When night took hold, their flashlights illuminated a ghostly landscape. Beyond the dimming beams was utter darkness. As fear gripped him, James tried to walk quietly, not to disturb the forest's creatures, but his footsteps spooked a ptarmigan out of the bushes near the trail, and a weasel ran for cover. Owls took flight and bats flapped bony wings against the intrusion.

Jonah bellowed again and sped farther ahead of them. *What the hell?* Now clearly on a scent, the dog was not concerned with anything else around him. Joe sprinted forward to keep up with his dog. Seemingly out of nowhere, a mountain lion dropped from thick branches above the dog. As if frozen in mid-air, it was caught in Joe's excruciatingly bright light. Then it landed hard on poor Jonah's back, who splayed flat under the force. The dog screamed and then emitted a pitiful baying that pierced the night. James heard a sickening crunch as the cat bit deep into Jonah's neck and sank its claws into his side.

Joe sprang at the cat instantly. He jumped behind it and, reaching around with his Bowie, cut deep into the wild cat's throat. A bowlful of blood arced from the beast onto Jonah's convulsing body.

Oh God. Oh God! James choked, sickened for poor Jonah. He sat down on a rock and waited to stop shaking. He'd never seen an animal die violently.

Joe tossed the lion's carcass off Jonah as if it were a house cat. Falling to his knees, he used his bandana to wipe the blood from Jonah.

But it was no good. Jonah's artery had been cut and pumped profusely as the dog shook with shock.

"No, goddam it! He's bleeding out!" Joe stuttered, "No! No!"

Ben leaned down to help Joe gather Jonah into his arms. Joe held his dying hound like a baby. "I've got to get him home." In his master's arms Jonah stopped shaking. He exhaled his last breath.

"Dear God." Joe cried and pulled Jonah to his chest. He held on a long minute with his eyes squeezed shut.

"He's a good dog, dammit. I shouldn't have brought him out tonight." He patted Jonah's head. "He was too tired." Joe laid the dog down and squatted beside him, petting him with long strokes.

Ben offered to say a valor prayer for Jonah. Joe nodded and Ben kneeled next to Joe, commending the loyal hound to the care of the Ghost Wolves, who would watch over his spirit. James and Tess formed a circle around them. Tears flowed. James squeezed his eyes and wiped them with the back of his hand.

Joe carried his hound on his shoulders all the way back. The group followed sadly behind, giving him a wide berth back to Harmony Falls. James put one foot in front of the other. Couldn't any goddam thing go right? His bones were leaden. By the time they'd stumbled back to the lodge, it was almost eleven, a night with no moon and black as tar. James felt as drained as if the lion's claws had bled him, too. The forest crawled with dangerous creatures. Their chances of finding June alive were plummeting. This was the second night, and they'd made no headway.

James stopped at his mother's room, but the door was closed. He hoped she'd fallen asleep. Maybe Aunt Marie gave her a pill. It would have been hard to fall asleep without June in the top bunk, her absence bearing down on her.

Sleep was a long time coming. James turned over and over, tangling the sheet. There was grace in surviving, he remembered somebody saying, probably a blind preacher. But nobody wanted to be left behind. God, June. Don't leave me. Don't do that. Don't do that. It was a prayer that James must have whispered a hundred times before he finally slept.

45

DAY THREE

When James heard the six a.m. knock on his door, he awoke from a dream. His first thought thrilled him: they found June! And she was fine! And where was she now? That was the point when the dream unraveled, like a part of his body spooling out into thin air. With each waking second, his anxiety grew. He suddenly pulled his knees to his chest, collapsing in a sob. June was gone.

Ben knocked again. "James? Come on."

"Be right down." But it was twenty minutes before James could get it together to join the others in the kitchen. Ben, Aunt Marie, and Gloria were equally stricken. By the time Hank walked through, James was pacing. Haley had said how critical the first twenty-four hours were, and they were now past that.

"Where's my mom?" James poured a mug of coffee and sat at the table.

"Still sleeping," Aunt Marie said. "I gave her a pill."

"Seems like she should be here with us," James said.

"Let her sleep. She'll need it," Uncle Hank added.

"I want to find that bastard!" Gloria lifted a rolling pin like a torch. She pulled up her apron to show that she wore her hiking pants. "I'll bring the sandwiches."

Waiting on the dock, Joe stood beside a big, frisky bloodhound named Rosie that he'd borrowed from a friend. Rosie wagged her tail when Tess held out June's shirt for her to smell. Joe didn't smile. His mouth was a flat line. Overnight, gray circles had formed under eyes that had gone dead. Jonah's death was haunting him.

James squinted back tears on the ride across the lake. Poor Jonah. Thick mist levitated as a solid mass above steel water. Shorebirds shrieked, trout splashed, but behind this foreground of particulars was a great silence. Not an absence but a silent presence that James breathed in with fog.

Rosie sat next to him for the boat ride, letting him obsessively stroke her long silky ears. She licked his hand thoroughly.

Ben guided the boat onto the beach at Coe Creek with a shrill scratch so they could step easily into shallow water. He handed Rosie over to Joe, and as soon as her paws touched the ground, her pure-bred nose began to sweep the dirt for June's scent.

Forty minutes later, after climbing a steep half-mile, they slowed. Gloria had fallen behind, out of sight, but the others had kept going. When they got to Sweden Mine, the place looked deserted, the creek still brown from spills. Dust balls and bits of trash blew on currents outside. The machinery stood abandoned.

"Do you think June could be in there?" James asked, his voice pinched and high as he fixed on Ben.

"Give me a minute." Ben was examining something. He pointed to a partially swept footprint in the humus. "Someone has been here."

Rosie began barking and tugging at her leash. They followed her into a damp tunnel deep in the mine. It smelled of dirt walls weeping moisture. Ben found a little pallet, not much bigger than a box, around which Rosie bayed. Joe walked in deeper and, poking around rocks, found an empty can of condensed Carnation milk, a few Blue Ribbon bottles and a cluster of Camel butts.

James dropped his pack with a thud, his entire body feeling beat. *Goddamit*. They'd missed her.

Tess stepped up to be heard. "It's crazy to go any deeper into this mine, guys. We're wasting time. I know June's not here. She's in a cave." Tess shook her head, refusing to go further. James wanted to scream.

"Come on, Tess, they were here, right? Maybe they still are," James pleaded.

Joe frowned at Tess. "Let us do our job, okay?"

"I'm trying to help. I have . . . special gifts." Tess's voice began confident but tapered off to a whisper when she got to 'gifts'. Everyone was quiet. James was about to stand up for her but before he could speak, Rosie trotted back to the mouth of the mine. They all followed.

Ben waited for Gloria outside, who only now stumbled up the hill. He met her and offered his arm, which she took. Ben filled her in. They had come to a dead end. Joe looked at Gloria curiously. She caught his glance. "Look, just because I'm a slow hiker doesn't mean I'm not determined to nail that bastard. Hell, I'll kill him myself."

"You better leave that to the law," Joe said. "In fact, you might be more helpful back at the lodge."

Gloria shook her head slowly. "Not on your life."

"You won't be killing anyone today. Let's make that clear right now."

"Sure, Joe," she snarled.

James avoided looking at Gloria; the bitter bite in her words was so unlike her.

"What's this about?" Joe took a step toward her. "Why are you even here?"

"Leave her alone," Ben said to Joe.

46

GLORIA

She had dreaded this moment for sixteen years, when she promised herself to keep the secret forever. Too much pain, even more shame, it was a nightmare that could never heal. She carried the weight in every cell of her body, not just in the scars down the backs of her legs. His cruelty scarred her heart, her womb, her brain, her life.

No one would know.

But the monster had come back. He had taken June to do the same unspeakable injuries to her. Even if the child survived, her life would be worse than death. No one here knew how he would cut June apart and steal her soul. He would pimp this innocent girl to the very worst of men. She would be unrecognizable, even to herself. Only Gloria understood.

How could Gloria let this happen? She was boiling with rage, no matter the cost to herself. She felt fury rising, transforming into an act of revenge she never dreamed herself capable of. She felt power surging through her, resurrecting her, healing her shame at last.

She would kill him in the worst way.

47

James thought Gloria was storming off. But she stopped abruptly with her back to them. She took in a deep breath and lifted her loose pedal pushers up to her thighs.

"Jesus Christ," James said as the others gasped. Dozens of horizontal one-inch scars notched the backs of her legs. From the middle of Gloria's calves, extending upwards to an invisible end point under her hiked-up pants, the ugly welts looked like a lunatic had sliced deeply into her skin with great precision. The cuts were all parallel and equally spaced.

As Gloria dropped the hems of her pants, she turned back to face them. Her eyes glistened an angry red; her mouth, a hateful grimace. A full minute passed.

"Vince did this to me." Gloria glared at Joe then took in each one of them. Catching herself, she must have remembered this wasn't about her. "We've got to get him. He'll do the same to June."

Gloria spilled her secret. "Vince captured me and pimped me out when I was barely fifteen. Every time, he notched me." She stood tall, taller than before. "I was kidnapped a virgin. Two weeks later I was rescued and pregnant. That was sixteen years ago." She looked hard at Ben. He held her gaze gently with no judgment. No shame. He walked to her and took her in his big arms and held her while she wept.

When Tess saw Gloria's gashes, she had blanched and whispered to James, "I've seen those cuts. I've seen the trapped girls, too."

Tess's dreams. James's breath caught, sweat beaded his lip. *What the hell?*

Then Rosie caught a scent and nosed north.

A light drizzle fell as James trod behind Ben and Joe. After him came Tess and Gloria. They stopped at a clearing to have lunch. Gloria passed around tuna salad sandwiches and chips, and presented a tin-foil package of kosher pickles. It was only a brief rest.

James, and probably all the others, took Gloria's offering with thanks, with a new respect for her suffering and courage.

Hours passed. They were way off-path, swatting through deep forest. Jutting branches and tangled vines scratched their arms as they climbed over fallen logs. James felt lost. He'd even lost faith in Rosie's nose. She had, too, apparently for she came to a small clearing and just stopped.

Rosie lay on the ground, panting. James glanced around and realized what Ben already knew. Here was where the mountain lion got Jonah. Rosie had delivered them to the same crossroads. The big cat's carcass lay ahead, singing with black flies. James wanted to cover the lion, but when he lowered fir boughs onto it, a solid fan of flies buzzed up into his face. He spit them from his tongue and removed his glasses to wipe his eyes. Joe helped him secure the boughs with rocks. Saddened,

Ben kneeled over the mountain lion and said a valor prayer for her. And for her kits. The lion's teats had been full. The kits, wherever they were, would soon die too.

Tess watched, tears streaming down her cheeks.

It was almost eight. Gloria limped behind Ben on a sprained ankle. Even the dog was bone tired, but when Joe suggested they head back, James shrieked.

"We can't give up now! June will be out here another long night." James folded his arms across his chest. "I'm not going back. I'll stay and look for her. We know she was around here somewhere. Come *on*, guys." His voice broke into a shudder of sobbing, and he covered his face with his hands.

Be a man, he kept telling himself, be a goddamn man. But he was no man. He was a kid who left his little sister alone in the woods. Ben put his arm around James's shoulders and pulled the boy to him. He was the only one there who could have. When Ben pulled back from James, he held both his shoulders.

"We're going to find her." Ben nodded. "But I can't let you stay out here alone. Then both of you would be missing. We stay together."

Ben rotated James toward home and followed close behind him. James's thoughts kept heaving with bad memories of teasing June, calling her "chatty chubby" and "booger." Why was that even funny? James needed sleep bad and agreed with Ben to return there early tomorrow morning and start the search at their landmark: the mountain lion's grave.

48

It was nearly ten as Ben grabbed the smooth branch handle of Harmony Falls' front door and opened it for James and the crew. Inside, Kay, Marie and Hank sat close together on the sofa, Kay in the middle. They looked wild-eyed at the searchers walking in. James rushed to his mother and squeezed beside her on the couch just as Hank kindly got up. James took her hand with both of his as she leaned into his shoulder and cried. He hadn't seen her the night before nor this morning and had missed talking to her. She needed him, he knew.

Joe came in and found a seat on the great river-stone hearth, looking pretty beat. "I know Haley and the officers believe Vince has left the woods with June, that he would want to get her up river as fast as he could. But that doesn't sit right with Ben and me. We think he's still here."

"Really? There's still a chance to find her?" Kay perked up instantly.

Ben jumped in. "It looks like she was taken up the lake in a boat, to Sweden Mine. We found the place where he had her. Maybe she's still somewhere near the mine."

James hugged his mother as he sat beside her. He felt terrified knowing that June's life still hung on chance.

Hank nodded at Ben. "Get word to Haley at St. Helens Lodge. We'll try again in the morning. You guys, grab some venizen stew in the kitchen."

Turning to Joe, Ben stood to get food and gestured for Joe to join him. "But then I'll take you back to your truck and pick you up around eight."

Joe thanked Marie and gathered a tired Rosie in his arms to ride back to South Shore Landing. The only thing left for James to do after eating was to go to bed. While he read MAD by lamplight, his mother cracked open his door. "Can we talk?" she asked. It was the first time she'd ever asked permission to talk to him.

"Sure, Mom. Come on in." He sat up.

Kay sat on the edge of his bed. "What was it like seeing where he took her?" Tears brimmed in her eyes. "How could Ben tell?"

James told her about finding the small pallet, but just thinking of June frightened on the cold ground started them both crying. "I'm so sorry, Mom. I'm so sorry."

"It's not your fault, James, certainly no more than mine. I left you both. That was wrong." His mother sighed, a long exhalation escaping her mouth. "There's something you need to know. Haley stopped in after you all left this morning. His partner in Boston found Dan after putting some pressure on his firm."

"Why did he need a policeman to make Dan come out here? You left a message, an emergency message, right?"

"Let me finish, James. His coworkers suggested he check at Frances Veray's house. That's Dan's secretary and his old girlfriend. No surprise, Dan was there. Practically living with her. He told the cop that he had to wrap up a few things at work, that he'd be on the next plane. Tomorrow." Kay was looking down at her lap, her voice wavering.

"What an ass." James's anger at his mother shifted to Dan. He was a bit thrilled that Dan had been caught screwing around, more for his mom's sake. Dan was a jerk. James moved closer to Kay on the bunk. "Mom. I'm sorry."

"Don't be." His mother forced a quick smile. "I knew it was coming. I've been a wreck all summer. I'm sorry. For everything." Sitting up taller she swept her hair into a twist and secured it with a clip from her pocket. She left with a hug. "Love you. 'Night."

———◆———

No one else could sleep. Ben kept the fire hot, pulling in embers from the edge. Steadily crackling and sparking, its rhythm lulled James. They all gathered at the pit. Gloria, Tess and Aunt Marie sat listless on damp benches, yellowed by the flame's half-light. Standing with Uncle Hank, James watched Ben whittle a branch of silver fir with his Bowie. The spotted owl hooted softly nearby, a call James knew well. Time stopped long enough for Gloria and Marie to yawn repeatedly, opening at last to sleep.

After they and Hank left for bed, James remained. Being alone with Ben was the medicine he craved. The man asked so little of those around him, yet James trusted him with his life, something he couldn't say of anyone else on earth. When they finally sat on the opposing benches, James told him Dan's story. Ben listened, whittling, watching James at those times when the words stopped. After a long thoughtful silence, Ben chucked a birch branch on the fire sending tiny sparks flying. "We'll find June tomorrow."

"How can you assume that after today?" James stood, looking bewildered. He kicked the dirt near the fire.

"I think she's still here. I suspect she's somewhere near Sweden Mine, maybe in a cave, like Tess said."

Could it be possible? James envisioned June's face, her dimpled smile and wide, wondrous eyes. For an instant, she lit up as if coming home from a long journey. Old June Bug. Of course she is still here. But as soon as James embraced one positive thought, another prickly one took hold. "But what'll we do when we find her? What about Vince? Do we shoot him?"

"Of course not. We can't have a shoot-out. We want June alive. And we'll have Tess and Gloria along. No, that'd be crazy. And if Vince takes June hostage, we'll lose her."

We *can't* lose her. "What if Joe just starts shooting?"

"He won't. I have it planned. I'll go in there before sunrise to find the cave and observe them." Ben must have read a scrap of hope in James's face. "No, you cannot come so don't get any ideas. This is no time to test your manhood."

James heard Ben's words as a hollow pinging of a submarine too distant to matter. Didn't Ben know? This was no trial run.

49

TESS

She had seen the bald eagle pair deliver morsels to their tiny chicks in a big nest high up on the old snag. She liked to watch the mated pair take turns flying to the nest, but it took binoculars to see the eaglets leaning over the branched nest with little beaks wide open, waiting for their meal. Tess had mixed feelings about the predator birds, about the sweet birds and furred mammals they delivered bloody to their brood. She accepted it as the circle of life, but she put out seed for the songbirds and chipmunks every day, only to imagine them yanked away by the huge claws to a grizzly death.

That night, after the fruitless search for June, Tess dreamed of the nest, of the eagle family together. Did they sleep? She didn't know. But she knew they protected their young. She dreamed of their nest high up on the dead tree. She'd circled it many times and noticed how much life was supported by the old snag. There were holes of woodpeckers and bigger ones at the base for some kind of mammal. Though long dead, the tree was full of life. She loved that about the forest.

As she walked around the snag in her dream, she heard all of nature's cries, owls and wolves, nightjars and bats. Yes bats. Somehow she knew they were nearby in a cave that she'd never before seen. She wanted to walk into the cave, but it was night and there might be bears sleeping inside. She noted where the eagle's nest was and resolved to return to the cave. She thought she could hear June singing in there, something about because, because because....

🌲

50

DAY FOUR

James awoke from a dream. June had come home. Why didn't everyone look happy? Instantly, hope vanished and nausea gripped him anew. He went downstairs by seven, but as he approached the kitchen, he overheard Ben talking. James stopped to listen.

"I went out, but where I thought it was, east of the mine, there was nothing but deep woods." Ben spoke softly.

"What now?" Hank said,

James felt panic rise in his chest as he walked into the kitchen, grateful for the full cup Gloria handed him. If Ben couldn't find the cave, no one could.

"I'm going to get Joe. He's waiting at the parking lot." Ben breezed by James, saying "Mornin'" and was gone before James could answer.

When Joe and Ben returned to the lodge, Joe said Rosie's owner kept her home to rest, which lifted James's spirits: Rosie would live another day. Tess was already outside, geared up to search.

Gloria was ready, too. Her baggy pants were dusted with as much flour as her apron. Showing off her sprained ankle, she grinned. "It doesn't even hurt this morning. Soaked it in mineral salts last night and rubbed it with witch hazel. I'm going."

By ten they all stood at Lion's Fall, as they now called it, and looked north to a place on the hills Ben pointed to. "That's where I thought it was." He shielded his eyes and squinted, continuing to look.

"I could have told you it wasn't over there." Tess put her nose in the air and turned about ninety degrees east. "It's up there." She nodded. "I saw it in my dream." Out of all options, they leaned in to hear Tess's hunch. Ben nodded slightly at her.

Then Joe shuffled his feet and said, "Yeah."

"Just show me the way," Gloria said. All eyes went to James.

"Let's go." He tried to sound enthusiastic, but the lunacy of following a dream tore at him.

"We should spread out," Joe suggested, now on board with Tess's lead. He pulled out his compass. "Due northeast. If you see something or get lost, make this call," and he made a crow *caw*.

Resolute, they headed northeast, scrabbling around boulders, brush, and creeks, staying mostly parallel. Joe took front and center, with Ben, back maybe ten yards. That way, when Joe held up, the movement rippled back to the rest of them. A good plan, theoretically. Looking up, Tess staked out the south end, James, then Gloria.

After rain, the air felt fresh, cedar-fresh. Their boot heels cracked enough branches to alert anyone, but the woods felt empty. Dusty motes of dim sunlight sliced through darkness, illuminating the forest in an instant of beauty. Deep woods sheltered all life, James realized. Even a monster like Vince could be safe in the forest's lawless embrace. James stomped through the woody debris, feeling more anxious with every step. He stopped short when he heard Tess muttering loudly to herself about "going the wrong damn way again."

"Tess, Tess! Wait up," James said. Gloria hurried behind him.

Tess looked back at him, her face corkscrewed from fighting tears. James slowed his step slightly. She whispered, "What?"

He took a deep breath. "Do you think we should split off from the others?"

"Yes, I do." Tess looked ahead. "I know it's not this way." She had stopped and turned 360 degrees like radar, her forehead lined. There it was. The eagle's nest.

By then, Gloria had caught up. "What're we doing?"

"Follow me." Tess smiled. "I know now." Tess hiked in the direction of true north, James close behind her, and Gloria trailing him. The forest floor was almost impassable. Boulders bigger than Gloria, toppled trees and snags, prickly bushes, and small brooks grown wider from summer's thaw, all of it slowed them. Tess soon reached a hiking trail and ran for about a hundred yards. She veered back into the bushes. James watched her closely, letting Gloria catch up. In a few moments Tess returned to them.

"Stay low, guys. Hide inside thick bushes. See if you can spot anyone. Stay out of sight. Seriously."

James grabbed a few yards of vine maple to wrap around himself. It didn't take much. Each leaf was wide enough to cover his torso. Then he waited and crouched down as still as a heron. Gloria's girth needed more yards of vine, but she pulled them on her at last and sat on the ground, muttering, "Snakes be damned."

Tess walked a bit farther on the path but suddenly jumped into a clutch of bushes. James couldn't see what spooked her. His legs ached, but when he stretched them slightly to get a better view, Gloria hissed, "Stop moving."

Now he could see where Tess was looking.

"It's Max," said Tess. She turned to James wide-eyed. "Could he be in on this?

The old man had emerged from a small cave and was stoking a cook fire. James recognized the prospector from his first day. The man rigged a tin pot on a couple Y branches and poured something in it. Then, he leaned on a low cottonwood limb and gazed out at the woods. He looked at James. Right at him.

Holding his breath, James couldn't tell if Max actually saw him. He was looking for someone, maybe Vince, that was certain. But his eyes rested on James as if thinking of something far away. Just then his tin pot set to boiling, and he quickly poured steaming milk into a cup and blew on it.

That *had* to be for June—she loved warm milk, unlikely to be his beverage of choice. Did Max take June? She was inside the cave, James was sure. He shivered to be so close.

The old man turned around and took the pot inside.

James eased out his breath, though he stayed still. Tess held up a pointed finger, did he see him? James nodded, forgetting how moving made the big vines shake. Hell, he was shaking as it was. Gloria and Tess both had knives, but they were no match if Vince had a gun. Max probably had a sawed-off shotgun. Regardless, James would get inside first chance he had.

While Max was still in the cave, Tess squeezed out of her brush cover and ran to James. "I'm going back to get Ben and Joe."

"Wait!" James's breath turned shallow and fast. What would he do if Vince showed up? "Shouldn't we be sure June's in there?"

Tess shook her head. "Lord, no. Vince could already be in there. Joe has a gun that we might need. I have an idea where they are. It's not far. Just stay low, James. Here, take this." She handed James her beloved Buck in the leather sheath. "But don't use it."

James took it, but as far as not using it, well, the minute he had a chance, he would get into that cave and to hell with the others. As Tess ran off, Gloria held her position, watching intently and mouthing to James, "Is that Max?"

A crow screeched as James nodded back at her. He thought it might be Joe's *caw*, but no. It was a real crow that flew off a high branch of a dead tree. James pulled the knife from the sheath. The Buck had done its share of skinnings, still razor sharp, the edge jagged from use. It had been a gift from her dad when she turned fourteen. James turned it over and over in his palm.

Shit, he couldn't use this damn thing. He didn't even know how to hold it. Wait. He remembered how Joe held the Bowie to slash the neck of the mountain lion. James bounced the bone handle of the Buck in his hand, getting familiar with its heft, holding it lightly, not gripping. He did the slasher hold then the stab hold, repeating each over and over, thinking of how he'd slit Vince's throat. God. He might have to kill a man.

Meanwhile, he was crouching in a mess of vine maple, but not enough of it. He felt like he was lit up with an arrow pointing at his head. Without bigger trees for cover, he had to get in the cave.

"Hey, when Max comes out again, think you could distract him?" he whispered to Gloria. "Throw a rock?"

She put up her thumb.

When Max emerged, again he scanned the woods. Rail thin, he swam in his raggedy clothes and dashed from one side of his camp to the other, looking out in all directions. As his head swiveled, white matted hair stuck out from under a dusty Stetson. He picked up his cooking gear and hurried back in the cave.

51

James didn't like it that Max had been in there so long. What was his part in this anyway? It had been twenty minutes. Okay, now he limped out, again staring in James's direction then gasped.

Vince had suddenly crept up behind him quiet as a cat. Just as the prospector squinted at James, finally seeing his face, he doubled over. Vince had put an arm lock on him.

"Max. You imbecile. Thought you'd skate off with her, did you? Her buyer's waiting, and you don't fuck with these people." Vince yanked up Max's arm another two inches. Max cried out. His Stetson fell from his head revealing a bunch of white knots like the fur of an old animal.

James tried to sort it out. Had Max taken June from Vince?

"I should kill you for this. I'm hours behind now. Where is she?" But Max just shook his head. Vince punched the back of his neck and dropped him right there. He kicked him out of the way and ran into the cave. Max didn't move. James wanted to help him, but he wanted to help June more.

Outside the cave Gloria edged closer to James. "Let's get him now." Her big leaves swished as she rallied.

"We can't just barrel in there. Vince is there. Maybe with June." Truth was, James was scared shitless. He reached over and grabbed Gloria's arm to stop her.

"Don't touch me!" She jerked her arm away from him.

"Hey, come on, Gloria. June's the priority here, right?" But not for Gloria. Where were Ben and Joe? Where was Tess? This was it. There was no one else but James and Gloria. They had to find a way to save June.

"Let's go, dammit!" Gloria threw off her vines with a disgusted flick of her arm and ran to the cave leaving James following behind her, leaves trailing. At the opening, they crouched down to peer in. Curly moss dropped tiny beads of moisture on their faces as they stood and entered sideways. It was silent, but for the constant dripping, weeping sound. The cave was dimly lighted by an oil lamp and smelled of earthy mold. As his eyes adjusted, James saw they were in a cavern that tunneled deeper into green rock. James's heartbeat quickened and he elbowed Gloria, whispering, "This is it." She nervously rotated her knife in her palm and, for a moment, the blade reflected a star of light from deep inside.

"They're in there," James said. Gloria thrust her chin at him as if to say, *well, go on in.* James edged in, his back against the wall of rock. In a far corner, a wood ladder led up about six feet to a rocky ledge. James felt his way in, Gloria pressed tight against him, shuffling quietly on the dirt.

52

She shrank from the men arguing beneath her, even as she awoke from a vivid dream about circus elephants.

The trainer was coming, an angry voice getting louder. She must be still. His boots scraped the rungs of the ladder. He was coming to hurt the baby elephant with a bull hook.

"Well here you are, after all that. You were playing hide and seek on Vince, were you?" He reached for her feet where she lay, nudging her awake. He climbed up to the ledge and said, "C'mon, Sugar, rouse yourself and be sweet for me."

"Git away from her, man!" Max yelled, heaving up the ladder. He tried to pull Vince off of her.

"Why should I?" Vince snarled. "She's my girl, ain't you, Sugar? Ain't you Vince's girl?" He rubbed her legs, moving his fingers up the inside of her thigh.

"NOOO! I wanna go home." She cried for the elephant. He was hurt.

"Let her go, man!" She saw Vince kick Max in his head and heard Max scream. He fell backwards. She heard "kerthump" on the ground below.

"Where are those goddam opi-chocolates, man?" But Max wasn't answering. Vince looked around and there, by the girl's bare feet, was the greasy paper bag of chocolate-dipped opium balls.

"Here sugar, something sweet." He gave her two chocolates. She hungrily ate them.

53

"C'mon, sugar, rouse yourself and be sweet for me." Vince was on the ledge.

Holy Jesus, no!

James couldn't comprehend that Vince was calling June his sugar, telling her to be sweet. James gulped back the fresh bile urging him to scream, to run to June, to keep Vince from touching her. Instead, he pushed his back tighter against the wet rock, deeper into shadow. Gloria had heard Vince too and grabbed James's shoulder. Wait, she mouthed and looked toward the cave entrance.

Max lurched by James and Gloria, not seeing them, nor much of anything as he aimed haltingly towards the ladder. He'd been left for dead outside the cave when Vince had knocked him out, but he'd resurrected, limping, yelping.

"Git away from her, man!" Max scrabbled up the ladder like a cricket with a broken leg. He stood on the highest rung.

"Why should I?" Vince snarled from the top. "She's my girl, ain't you, sugar? Ain't you Vince's girl?" James inched closer to see June jerk away from him.

"Noooo. I want to go home." *Oh God. June.*

"Let her go, man!" Max tried to pull Vince away from June, but Vince's foot back-kicked his chin with a crack and snapped the old man's head back. James heard Max scream while his arms pin-wheeled backwards. With a loud crunch Max landed on the rocky ground. A split-second later the ladder fell on his chest.

James stood, frozen, his eyes glued on Max's crumpled form.

"Where are those opi-chocolates, man?" Vince muttered to no one. Still on the ledge, he looked around and found the paper bag. "Here, Sugar." He must have given her one. "Something sweet."

Vince turned around and caught the glint of Gloria's knife. He peered into the shadow. James tried like hell to disappear.

"Well, well. What are you two losers doing here?" Vince laughed like a gun popping off. Jumping down from the ledge, he moved fast and agile. He ran at her, but Gloria held her big Buck so he'd go right into it. Instead, he knocked it easily from her hand and punched her hard in the gut. Gloria twisted around and, screaming as she fell to the ground, one of her pant legs flew up and exposed the back of her thigh. She was still. A smirk passed Vince's lips, and he growled at her. "You're one of mine."

James had positioned himself to jump Vince from behind. He sprang up and grabbed his neck, but Vince immediately rammed him against the wall, the impact sending James's knife flying. James's back cracked with pain, but he refused to fall. He rallied every muscle to fight and stood shakily. Where was the goddamn Buck?

Gloria had rolled into a ball after the kidney strike but was now trying to stand. She was halfway up when Vince landed a kick to her chin. As she fell backwards, her eyes rolled back in her head before she hit the ground.

James ran at Vince with the retrieved knife, but Vince blocked James's strike with his forearm. Vince's fist planted deep in James's left rib cage. Then a right hook to his cheekbone dropped him to his knees and spun his head around, sending his eyeglasses flying.

Dazed, James remained kneeling, wavering, watching a blurred Vince fit the ladder back in place. There was blurry June in her yellow dress, standing shakily. Was she looking at him?

Vince climbed up to the ledge, watching James watch her, grinning his Burt Lancaster grin. He hefted June up over his shoulder as she murmured dim protests.

"Forget about her, kid," Vince said to James as he climbed down the ladder. "She's already gone." Vince had swung June around and paraded her by James. Hanging upside down, June was dead weight that Vince carried like a dozen shot rabbits. Near the mouth of the cave, he sat her down against the wall, facing James. Her chin dropped to her chest.

"Say goodbye to your big brother, Junie. He won't be saving you today."

Vince ambled back to James carrying multiple sections of rope. Then he kicked him hard in the side of his head. James keeled over.

54

Dripping. Seeping. What the hell?

Muted voices jolted James from a daze. Suddenly, a blurry Tess walked in, followed by a blurry Ben and Joe. Where were his glasses?

"Oh my God! Look at you two!" Her touch on James's forehead warmed a chill that had spread into his bones. "Here, let's get these back on." Yes. He could see her now.

"Help him," James whispered.

Tess shifted her eyes from James to Max and ran to him. "Oh dear, a faint pulse," she said as she pressed his neck. When Max whispered to Tess, she lowered her ear to the old man's mouth.

Ben had gone right to Gloria, also hogtied, and shook her shoulders. "Wake up, you." She raised her head to see Ben then fell back again. Joe cut James and Gloria free from their ropes. Instant relief spread through James's shoulders and arms as he stretched them out, but a vise squeezed his head. He discovered, tenderly, a lump the size of a lime protruding from the side of his head. James stood carefully, still spinning, and stepped over to see Max. Yes, he had been an accomplice, but he wasn't the bad guy there.

"Max kept June safe!" James blurted out, eager to set the record straight. "He hid her from Vince, but Vince found them and beat up Max pretty bad. We saw it. Then somehow Max came in the cave to stop Vince from messing with June. At the top of the ladder, Vince kicked him in the face and pushed him over. I saw it, Ben," James pleaded. "We all got a beating."

"Max doesn't have much chance of leaving this cave alive." Ben shook his head as he assessed the damage. "His back's probably broke, his ribs definitely. The way he's breathing, probably a punctured lung, so there's not much time. Joe, get to higher ground and radio Hank for a rescue."

"Sure." When Joe returned to his team, he said, "Got news on Natalie. She's still missing. Haley thinks she left with Vince at the same time as June. That's all I know."

Gloria had slowly moved to a sitting position, rubbing her chin, feeling her side.

Ben went to her to help her stand. She held on to him, her eyes focusing.

If Natalie's missing, too, was she kidnapped? Is she with June somewhere? What's the connection? James was asking himself the same questions they were all likely thinking. They just had to keep going. James didn't want Natalie to distract anyone from finding June.

"Okay. Let's synchronize," Joe said into the silence. "7:30, already dusk."

"Listen, we've got to move fast," Tess said. "Max just told me Vince took June down to the YMCA camp. He's already got some time on us."

Joe leaned in close to Max and placed his Stetson next to him. "Hang on, mate. And thanks, for June's sake."

James retrieved the Buck and handed it to Tess. "No. You keep it." She remained on her knees as the others got up. "Guys, I'm staying with Max 'til Rescue shows up. Somebody's got to stay. I can help him breathe."

James remembered Ben talking about the WWII soldiers he stayed with at the end. "If it was me," Ben had said, "I wouldn't want to be left alone."

There were two kinds of people in the world.

55

TESS

The bats returned to the cave all at once when the others left. They whooshed in like black smoke and found their places high up on the cave walls, rustling into each other. Max watched them, his eyes still bright, and smiled. "My friends," he whispered.

Tess grinned back. "Mine, too."

Max lay on the dirt where he fell. His Stetson lay in the dust a few feet from him, upside down like an offering. Tess dared not move him, but she placed a weightless hand on the arm closest to her. His arm under the ragged shirt was skin and bones. His breathing was raspy, his voice dry as paper.

"I'll watch over you. They're coming." She knew he wouldn't last. How she wished he could.

Dusk had fallen and the cave's mouth disappeared in shadow. The constant seeping sound and dank-earth smell unnerved Tess. She turned on her flashlight, but kept it down, shining away from Max, away from the bats. After a moment, Max's lips moved but emitted no sound. Tess moved her ear closer to catch the halting whisper, as quiet as a spring breeze.

"Thanks… you found us… how?" He looked up at her with nearly colorless eyes that reminded Tess of small clouds in a vast sky.

"I saw the cave in a dream. Under the eagle's nest. And June called to me." Tess braced herself for the ridicule that so often came when she mentioned her dreams. But Max only smiled, his thin lips pulling over yellowed teeth, his eyes widening frightfully.

"You… have a gift. Use it to find the other children." He gasped for air.

Tess felt dazed by his words and the implied responsibility. She dug deep into herself, trying to map the boundaries of compassion. But what did it matter now? He was dying.

He choked. Tess held his hand and shook her head as tears rushed down her cheeks. Max's white tangled garden of hair poked out with new white shoots and grayed branches. He was losing ground. He swallowed.

"Vince got away… with June, right? I tried to save her… watched out for her in the woods… almost did save her. Oh, God… she looks like my little girl… couldn't let him take June… or touch her. He will sell her tonight … if your guys don't kill him.

"Don't worry, Max. They'll get her tonight. You did save her."

Gasping for air, Max coughed, a raggedy drawn-out cough that ended by coloring his lips red. He tried to reach something in his breast pocket, but his hand shook and fell back on the ground. He asked Tess with his eyes, and she reached into his pocket and pulled out a folded paper, felted soft and browned with time. She opened the folds: it was a sort of map. Looked like the Columbia River snaking through the center.

Max whispered. "Gold. Find it… find my girl Suzy… Abbot, last seen in Idaho. Give her some. You keep some."

His eyes widened as if seeing Tess for the first time. "You have the Sight. Yes, find the missing kids… You can…." He inhaled as if to finish the sentence, but he never exhaled. A small red bubble formed on Max's lips. He was gone.

Tess let the tears come, let them fall on the old man's still face. There would be no others shed for Max.

56

The only blessing James could count was that Vince was pressed for time and, evidently, he liked money more than he liked little girls. Woozy, James stood with difficulty and rubbed his head. Vince had gotten him in his ribs, too. As consciousness returned to James so too came the exact location of each blow. He took a few steps and just kept going.

Heavy fog rendered their flashlights useless as they headed toward the Y Camp. Ben was energized. He and Joe made a good pair. Joe had a gun and Ben, his Bowie. Gloria and James followed quite a few yards behind them, losing distance with each step.

After an indeterminate amount of time, a tree root tripped James and, while he didn't fall, it jarred him. Soon, as James's feet dragged, Ben returned to prod him.

"Come on, guys. We've got to find Vince and June before they leave Spirit Lake. Before it's too late." Ben launched into a trot and surged ahead. James rallied, weaving through the trees and underbrush. Gloria tried to keep up.

Ben spoke quietly into his walkie talkie. James could hear him say to Hank, "Better evacuate the Y. You don't want a hostage situation."

A deafening roar, and the tree in front of James splintered, shooting bark into his face that stung like a nest of hornets. He jumped back, taking cover behind an elderberry bush. He thought he'd been shot. Immediately two more booms shook the ground. Ben, then Joe, dropped to the ground. James almost hollered but slapped his hand on his mouth in case Vince was still shooting. Like Gloria, he waited a few seconds to look around before running to help them.

Ben clawed at his pants trying to get at the wound, where blood poured from his shin. He ripped his bandanna off his neck and gave it to James. "Make a tourniquet and tie it. Quick."

"Oh no, Joe's down." Kneeling beside him, Gloria felt the artery on his neck. "Wait a minute, he's got a pulse." She examined the wound. "Thank God. Just a shallow scrape from the bullet." She tore off her scarf to wipe blood from the side of Joe's head.

When Gloria pulled Joe up to a seated position, James saw a goose egg on the back of Joe's skull. "Hey. Feel the bump," James said. "Is it bleeding?"

Sitting down, Gloria found it. "No blood."

"Goddammit, the bone is shattered!" yelled Ben. James had cut open the leg of his pants to reveal a broken shin bone. "I can't walk." He gripped his bloody leg, his hands corded and white.

"Did I cinch it too tight?"

His face mottled with agony, Ben slowly lowered his back to the ground. "No. Listen. Vince isn't headed to the Y Camp. He must have split off a ways back." His eyes squeezed shut. Weakening, Ben growled. "You go there, James. He's going to Bear Cove. It's a few miles west of here, but you can do it. Pull Joe over to me. And Gloria, I'll keep the walkie talkie and call Hank. The police can meet you there. Grab Joe's revolver."

"Already got it."

James dragged Joe over to Ben. Leaning down, Gloria wrapped her arm around Ben.

"Go!" He ordered hoarsely.

Gloria and James tore off to Bear Cove. Vince had ambushed them, had lied to Max that he was headed down Coe Creek to the Y Camp. He waited for them and backtracked around to the cove. It made sense. His boat was moored there, no doubt, far from the YMCA water traffic, giving easy access to the South Shore parking lot and the state road.

Then it hit James. Saving June was up to Gloria and him. They had to reach Vince before he launched. They had no boat waiting on Spirit Lake, so this was it. This was their last chance to rescue June and the last chance to personally take out a monster who had left a trail of victims, many of them children, for at least twenty years. They couldn't kill Vince enough times.

Gloria's energy surged. James could tell she was eaten up with revenge. It was 9:26. Once on smoother ground, Gloria amped up her speed. James soon saw silver columns of Spirit Lake between tall trees, glimmering with moonlight. He slowed.

"This is it," James whispered. "He could be anywhere. Be quiet and take cover." He moved into the spread of a salmonberry bush. Suddenly James heard *whoosh*, and a net of bats flew into their faces. He remained still, having learned that was best with bats.

There, about a hundred feet ahead, a moonbeam shone on Vince's head, his hair glassy with oil. That instant, Vince turned around with June hanging under an arm. He'd likely heard the small branch snap under James's shoe. Gloria and James soundlessly ducked deeper into the bush. Vince turned back around.

"Just take the shot, Gloria," James hissed. "It'll slow him down at least." James figured she'd aim for a foot or a knee.

57

GLORIA

Take the shot? Of course she would take the shot. She'd waited and trained for this moment ever since Vince was sent to prison. She would have been a fool not to know how to protect herself. As soon as she was old enough to get a firearms license, she bought a Smith & Wesson 38 Special. Every Saturday she trained at the local firing range in San Francisco, one of the few women to compete as a sharp shooter.

She wasn't afraid to take the shot; she just didn't want to shoot June. Her thoughts drifted to the consequences of this act. He could shoot back, maybe kill her or June or James. She might go to prison. Or she might possibly get a great deal of satisfaction in killing him. He got life the last time he was convicted, but here he was, just fifteen years later. Somebody in the Seattle mob got him out, she was sure of it. They'd get him out again, too, if she didn't end his wretched life today. She had to do it. James was useless with a weapon. Guess they didn't teach that skill at his prep school. No, it was up to her.

Maybe doing it would finally wipe the shame from her life, and she could stand tall enough to find her son. She'd like that. She'd like to know what kind of person he'd become. More than anything, she'd like him to be proud of his mother. This act – as bloody as it would be -- could put her on a righteous path.

One thing for sure. Better shoot him where he can't shoot back.

58

"James. I can do this." Gloria steadied her elbows on a boulder and slowed her breathing, exhaling fully. She waited a few moments, watching to see what Vince would do next. Inexplicably, Vince set June down against a tree trunk. She had her chance. Standing up straight, he stretched his back and scanned the woods.

Gloria took the shot.

The gun popped out of Vince's hand and launched into the air before a loud boom blew through James's eardrums. What was left of Vince's hand was a useless bloody stump. He cussed a demon's rant and squatted behind June, holding her in front of him with his good hand. James had to get behind him while Gloria held the gun on him. He had to surprise him, maybe grab a small log and crush his skull? Yeah. Plenty of wood around. Or use the Buck. But did he have the nerve to use the Buck? The man scared the hell out of him.

Gloria was stalking Vince, edging ever closer, squeezing him, as James silently padded around behind him, the knife handle now slick in his palm. James wiped his hands on his jeans and the handle on his shirt. He was close enough to see June's face. Her mouth hung open as Vince tried to hold her up by the straps of her sundress. Some shield. Drugged, she fell to the ground from his weakened grip. James hesitated.

Instantly, Vince was knocked backwards with the force: A blast from Gloria's revolver had sent another bullet into him. He bellowed like a horse in a slaughterhouse, clutching his groin with his good hand.

"God, Gloria," James whispered. "You shot him in the balls." He stood riveted by all the blood.

"Hey!" Gloria screamed, "Tie his arms behind him with your belt."

Vince spat curses at James. The belt caught in James's loops while he frantically tugged at it. Finally freeing it, he tried to hold Vince's slippery arms.

"You little shit!" Vince said, and easily slid his bloody arms out of James's hold. Gloria kicked Vince in his mouth, silencing him. She tried to secure his arms herself. Even as they both fought him, Vince's good hand flew out and grabbed at the gun on the ground. Like a flash, Gloria stomped on Vince's wrist, applying her formidable weight until the gun dropped from his hand. She stood over him, a strange calm smile on her face.

Vince struggled to free his slippery hand, and might have, but Gloria fired close range into his chest. His body jumped, shuddered and fell still.

"That's for the all the kids who weren't as lucky as me." She turned away.

Vince Lavetti lay dead, grimacing in a widening pool of blood.

"James? James! Is June okay?" But James was staring at Vince with his mouth open. Shaking, he roused himself. Blood had splattered onto June's face. He picked her up to wipe the scattershot with his shirttail. When he shook her shoulders to wake her up, her eyes rolled back. How much opium had she had? How much opium could a young girl take? Holding her in his arms, James pulled her close, warming her chilled body. Just then, she reached for his neck. Feeling June take hold, choosing life, gave James the strength to face what they had just done.

59

There had to be a getaway plan. Vince must have a boat at Bear Cove with a buddy who'd be waiting for him. Surely that guy heard the shots. Hell, he could have a gun on them that very moment. Gloria inched ahead first, holding the revolver with both hands, eyes darting right and left. James stepped carefully behind her, carrying June but flinching at every step. He half expected a shot to come from behind the trees. Where was Vince's man?

James checked the compass. Still heading southwest. Good. James's arms and shoulders throbbed from carrying June. Seventy-five pounds, he remembered. Each step weighed two forty. As minutes passed, James arms were weakening. Regardless, he held June tight to his chest.

"Look!" Gloria whispered. Spirit Lake glowed through the trees. James stumbled to the clearing. On the dim moonlit shore were small figures milling around a man. It looked like Haley's lawmen had anchored Hank's old lifeboat in the cove. One was cuffing Vince's buddy. James breathed easier.

He and Gloria trudged toward the beach with June. Uncle Hank saw them and jumped off the boat, smiling and laughing. He splashed up to them and said, "Oh man. We heard the shots." Starting to choke up,

Hank pulled James into a hug that put June in the middle. "Thank God you're alright."

Haley got to them next, "Where's Vince? How'd you get her away from him? When did you—" He stopped his questions when Gloria pointed up in the direction of Vince's body.

"Dead. Here, take this." She handed Haley the revolver, handle first.

The detective looked from Gloria to James, who said nothing. Puzzled, Haley must have been trying to grasp how the two of them could have killed Vince, a trafficker who had eluded so many others, including Haley. Then he looked at June, a bit of a miracle resting in James's arms, and he seemed to soften.

"Vince's man just told us the buyers are waiting on their rig in Stella to take her up the Willamette to the coast," the detective said. "And some other kids, too. How the heck did you do it?" Haley squinted, as if to see Gloria more clearly. He likely made it easier for Gloria to tell him the truth.

"I shot him, sir. I shot him three times 'cause he was going to kill us."

"Okay." Haley radioed his men at St. Helens Lodge for backup at Bear Cove, for ballistics and recovery. He turned back to Gloria. "Are you certain this was self-defense?"

"Yes, sir. I'm certain." Gloria nodded and looked at James. He nodded too.

"Hey, what about Ben?" James couldn't wait. "And Joe? Are they okay?"

"Ben and Joe are on their way to Longview. St. John's Hospital. They'll be alright." Haley must have noticed James's skepticism, who had, after all, seen their injuries.

Holding June close, James slogged through the shallows to reach Uncle Hank's boat. It was midnight, he was told, as he sat down on a boat bench. A calm spread through him as he exhaled. June had fallen asleep in his arms. Sharp angles now defined her face. How could she have thinned so in just four days? James brushed bits of moss and dirt from her hair that had pressed against her head when she had lain on the ground.

The lifeboat eased away from Bear Cove. The night was speckled with stars millions of light years away. James took in the vast sky while June held on to him, her cheek pressed against his shirt. He kissed her head without thinking.

At that instant, James looked up. He was dazzled by at least a dozen bonfires encircling Spirit Lake. Huge fires blazed around the lake's perimeter. Chills raised the skin on the back of James's neck. "What's going on?"

At the wheel, Hank turned back to them and smiled broadly. "As word spread that you found June, everyone around the lake — every boys' camp and girls' camp and every cabin — they all built fires for her. At first we weren't sure if June was alive." Hank smiled wide, "You can imagine the bonfires got a good deal bigger with that news."

James nudged June. "Hey, wake up, sleepyhead. Look at the fires they made for your homecoming." June lifted her head but promptly let it fall back against James's chest.

With a glance, James shared the moment with Gloria. She put her arm around James's shoulder. Together they took in the fires blazing for them, for what they had done.

Spirit Lake glowed brilliantly. As the boat glided over the water, James felt buoyed by those ancient forces of the depths, the forces of legend. The spirits of the lake.

Then the drums. James could hear them. It was as Ben had said: the deep bass beats rode on the wind, across the water, around all the campfires.

James heard a something else. *Impossible*! But there it was. For the first time ever, James heard the howls of wild wolves. They were answering each other around the lake. There had been no passage of time. The air felt electric with the ancestral spirits of ghost wolves. They had returned, James believed, to trumpet the way home.

60

His mother would be waiting on the dock, her eyes lifted southward. Through a scrim of night mist, their pale bow lights would emerge as if from nothing. At last James made out dark shapes and familiar voices.

"They're coming," his mother screamed.

"Come *on,*" Aunt Marie cried. Neighbors had joined in, and when the lifeboat eased up to the dock, their cheering and clapping out-roared the waterfall.

James stood in the lifeboat, holding June, who was limp. But safe.

This is what it felt like to be golden. He who had previously done nothing remarkable in his life suddenly had. James drank in the praise. On impulse, he held June up for just a second, alive and safe, like a trophy. But it was his mother's loving smile that filled James with what he'd long craved. She offered her hand to him as he climbed onto the dock and into her strong embrace.

"Oh my God, my babies." She drew back to look at them better and caressed June's cheek. Even as groggy as June was, she whimpered when she saw her, whispering "Mommy," then snuggled closer into James's embrace.

"Mom." James could find no words.

"Thank you, son.

Then James caught sight of Dan.

What the hell? James's stepdad was the last person in the world he wanted to see. Dan approached the tight circle on the dock, relief flashing across his face as he closed the gap between June and himself.

"Hey, James. You okay?" Dan shook his hand with an elbow grab, and then moved to June. She had his blue-green eyes and turned-up nose: she was his progeny. Suddenly James's arms felt dead. A part of him desperately wanted to set June down so he could rest them, if only for a moment, but June clung to his neck.

Flashing perfect white teeth in a practiced smile, Dan repeated his phrase for every successful occasion: "Well done."

Same shit. "Yeah. Thanks."

Dan clasped him too hard on the shoulder. "I never doubted you'd bring her back to us, James. You're amazing!"

James turned away. Even when Dan smiled, the corners of his mouth turned down. A tiny thing, but you could see it if you looked close.

Then James's mother reached for June, who adjusted unconsciously to her mother's hold. Kay, too, had to adjust to carrying her daughter's weight. But she did, and straight-backed, stepping past Dan and on up to the lodge. James and Gloria followed. Off to the left, a bonfire cast its pink-orange glow on the neighbors gathered there toasting June's future.

When James sat next to his mother on the living room couch, June moved toward him. She tightened her hold on him when Dan, who had followed them in, took a seat nearby in a straight wood chair.

Aunt Marie asked him, "Coffee or hot cocoa?" But she glared at his expression, stiffened and backed away.

"Marie, I'm disappointed. How did this happen? Spirit Lake is packed with kids' camps. How could you let them roam around these woods without any supervision?" The left side of his mouth tugged downward. "Who was watching my little girl?"

Silence. They all seemed to know that any answer would surely become fodder for a custody case.

James couldn't give June up to Dan. After all, June was Spirit Lake's victory. They'd all fought hard for her. Max had died for her, as had Jonah, and Ben and Joe were both in the hospital. None of them had slept well for days, and everybody on the lake had rallied to help.

But Dan had given no help. Hell, he couldn't even be located. He couldn't claim any part in her rescue. Yet he had an irrefutable claim on June.

"Come on, Junie, come to Daddy." He held out his arms for her to climb into, but she remained in James's embrace. Dan's voice elevated a notch. "I flew all the way across the country just to see you. Come on."

James stood and raised both his hands in the air to show Dan that June was holding on by herself, her legs now wrapped around his waist. As she clutched him tightly, James felt his rage build. "Can't you see she's frightened? Leave her alone." James's arms wrapped firmly around her and she relaxed into them.

Dan raised his voice, suddenly shifting into his inner courtroom. "James and Kay, I'll tell you what she's frightened of. People who can't keep her out of harm's way, family members who abandon her. What the hell was she doing alone in the woods, anyway?"

When Dan tried to transition from courtroom talk to Daddy talk, though, he seemed self-conscious and ill-equipped. "Come on, Junie," he pleaded. "I won't let any bad men near you." Dan murmured to her, as he edged closer. June's face still lay hidden against James's shirt. It was obvious she didn't want to be seen or touched by anyone, particularly by Dan. She began to whimper.

Dan stood, his arms pinned to his sides like a spoiled child. June must have heard something in her father's voice. James felt a shiver charge through her body.

Kay stepped up closer to Dan, blocking him from June. "My daughter needs some warm clothes, she needs bed rest, maybe medical attention." She reached for June.

"I know what she needs. I'm her father."

Gloria stepped in to block the two from each other with her girth and faced Dan. "So, if you know she needs rest, wouldn't you want to give her that?"

"Who the hell are you, some beatnik? And you're telling me what my daughter needs? Mind your own business and go back to San Francisco." As he turned away from Gloria, James smiled. It would take a lot more than Daniel Hart III to shut up Gloria. She knew all about shame. She knew it was bullshit. June dozed in James's lap while he watched her.

Gloria didn't blink. "Being her father, you should care what a ten-year-old girl needs to survive an abduction."

"Somebody shut this witch up, fast, before I do."

"Hart!" Detective Haley yelled. "Cut the talk. Gloria just saved June's life. And you can't just take her. She needs medical attention immediately. There's due process here." Kay stepped closer to take Gloria's arm in a show of solidarity.

"You're going to preach due process to me, sir? I'm a criminal lawyer."

Haley took another step closer. "Mister, if you think you can obstruct this investigation by removing your daughter, I'm here to tell you different. I have no problem bringing you in on charges. You'll spend a night in jail, and I don't care if you are a lawyer."

Dan's lips tightened. He shut up, but the sneer on his mouth said he was far from beaten.

61

Kay reached for June, who moved into her arms. "Can you stand up, honey?" June nodded and stood, wobbly. "Walk with me?" Kay took June's hand and together they went into the front hall where a doctor, called there by Hank and Marie, waited to meet her.

"Hello, June." Dr. Blair held out his hand to shake though she was too groggy to respond. He gestured for her to go before him upstairs. She bravely climbed slowly to her bedroom, mumbling something about finally getting the bottom bunk. Kay followed closely and James, after her. When James reached the top, he stopped to listen and stepped down a few steps.

Haley had stepped near the stairwell when his walkie talkie buzzed. He listened and put it down. With a pallor as sad as fog, he turned to the group in the living room.

"It's Natalie." Haley looked at Hank. "We found her."

"Thank God," said Hank and some cheers followed.

Haley shook his head. "She's in bad shape. Longview cops found her deep in the mine. They're calling her folks to come." He looked up at Marie's face. "But she's alive."

"What's this? Another kidnapping victim?" Dan looked back and forth from Marie to Hank. "Another case of negligence? I'll check into that."

Detective Haley stepped to where Dan sat and he stood, staring him down. "My men were the ones out there doing the 'checking,' risking their lives to bring June back, and Vince was taken down in the process. What have *you* done?"

Dan's smile twitched, pulling left.

Marie stared sadly out the front windows. She suddenly screamed, "She's here!" and ran out the front door, followed by everyone in the lodge, including James, who dashed ahead to the dock to help. After catching the rope, Marie tied the boat up as James helped lift out the stretcher. Natalie was covered by burgundy blankets that failed to cover flecks of blood around her eyes and matted in her brown hair. Her face was purplish, her eyes closed. She was evidently unconscious.

"Excuse me," said Natalie's father, moving to her. He and his teary wife stayed with their daughter as James and an officer carried the stretcher up to his room, a private place where the doctor could see her.

A few minutes later, Tess dragged into the lodge. She had stayed with Max until his body had been airlifted to the morgue. Rivulets of tears had made clean stripes through the dirt on her cheeks. Hank went to her and pulled her into his arms. James watched from the dining room, glad to see his uncle's rare affection shown her.

"I'm so sorry, Tessie," he said, stroking her hair. Hank kept his arm around Tess's shoulder, pulling back to say, "Here's the good news. June is back. That's what counts. And you found her, Tess. Imagine that." His pride showed in his smile.

Kay walked down the stairs to the living room, looking at everyone but Dan. "Dr. Blair says June is okay, relatively speaking."

"Which means what?" Dan said.

"Meaning her injuries are not physical." Gloria added her translation just to rile him.

"Daniel, do not spoil this moment!" Kay pleaded. "June is alive. We should be celebrating." She turned to go into the kitchen. Dan followed, talking.

"Excuse me if I'm not popping the bubbly, Kay, but I still want to know how she got kidnapped in the first place." He reached for her arm to get her to turn to him. She swiveled so fast it knocked his hand off her. They were alone in the dining room.

"Kay, I'm suing you for divorce and custody. You best get yourself a lawyer. After your negligence, you'll be lucky to get visitation." He stood as if he had made his case and hissed, "I can't *wait* to leave this godforsaken place. At least, June'll be safe with me."

"Why on earth are you doing this now?" Kay had gotten her strength back the instant he said 'custody.' "You can't rip a child from her mother, Daniel, especially right after a trauma. You know how much she needs me." Kay turned to walk upstairs and spat her last words at him. "And you don't even care."

Hank approached Dan. "We'd prefer that you leave now. It's nearly one in the morning and everyone is too tired to make decisions. The police will keep you informed over at Harry's. You are staying at St. Helens Lodge, aren't you?" Hank tried to guide Dan towards the door with his hand touching Dan's shoulder, but Dan bristled and knocked Hank's hand off. He planted his feet.

"I'm not leaving here until I know that my daughter is alright."

"She's alright now, Daniel, I can assure you." Hank's blue eyes bored into him like icicles.

"No. I need to know what they did to her." Dan sat down on the nearest chair.

Tess jumped in, to her father's chagrin. "It wasn't 'they.' It was 'he.' It was Vince. Max did nothing to June. He swore it with his dying breath and I believe him. In fact, Max was why June wasn't already in the pipeline." Tess had everyone's attention now.

Hank's voice quieted. "Let's allow Detective Haley to explain these details to Mr. Hart, Tess. It's a legal issue."

Tess shook her head. "Max told me how Vince brought June and Natalie up to the mine, how he drugged them with opium. When Vince went off with Natalie, Max grabbed June and carried her to a secret cave. He kept her sleepy so she wouldn't worry or make noise."

"Then why didn't he just bring her back to Harmony Falls?" Dan asked.

"Max was afraid that Vince would kill him and take June. He already had a buyer.

"Screw Max. I want to know what was done to June." It was obvious, even to James, that Dan cared primarily if June had been violated. Why? Would Dan treat her differently if she had?

62

Wood stairs creaked. All eyes shifted to Natalie's parents leading their daughter carefully down the steps. Natalie's father looked hard at Dan. He must have heard him. Turning to help her, he said, "Come on, baby."

After a few minutes she got down the stairs. Wrapped in a robe, Natalie took tiny steps like her shoes belonged to a doll. Her hair was wet from her mother cleaning out the blood. She had cinched it in a ponytail. Natalie seemed almost normal until she lifted her face from under her bangs. Her right eye and the left side of her mouth swelled badly in angry bruises. There was a bandage high on her right cheek.

Her parents led her to one of the overstuffed chairs. At first she held her head down but soon pushed herself up straight. When she spoke, only one side of her mouth moved and that, with some difficulty. "I didn't know. Elias said we could go up to the hideout then out on the lake at midnight. He said to bring June. That it would be fun."

"On the lake at midnight?" Dan naturally assumed his inquisitor stance, clasping his hands behind his back.

"Sit down, Hart. I'll ask the questions." Haley turned to Natalie. "How did you get June up to the hideout?"

She gulped, looked at her parents, and began. "I said we'd have fun." She looked around at the dumbfounded faces staring back at her, and she began to cry into her hands.

"What? It was *you* that took June? You kidnapped June?" Dan demanded.

"That's enough, Hart!" Haley boomed, surprising those who thought they knew him. "You're obstructing the investigation. You're out." He hailed Hank. "Take him across now!" He thought a few seconds. "Gloria, you, James and Tess, you all need to leave, too."

The three left the living room, but they remained hushed in the hall. James watched Dan leave with his uncle, glad he didn't have to say another word to him.

Natalie settled carefully into the chair. "June wanted to come. She thought it was a party."

Haley asked, "Natalie, why would she think that?" He sat across from her, on the coffee table.

She paused a moment then whispered, "Because I told her it was."

Wait a damn minute. James tried to stop the runaway train charging through his head. Natalie admitted taking June from the lodge? Gloria's and Tess's faces mirrored his shock back at him. They had to be quiet.

"Maybe you'd better explain what you did when you left Harmony Falls." Haley continued. Her parents took a seat on the sofa as Hank and Marie shifted to make room so they could sit next to Natalie. She began.

"That night, St. Helens kept everybody outside late, watching. I asked June to meet me after dinner in the kitchen. From there we walked up to the hideout. Elias was waiting. After a while, when everybody at the lodge had gone to bed, he took us in a boat to the mine where we thought the party was. We were already loaded."

"Loaded?" Haley pressed.

"Chocolate balls. With opium centers."

James struggled with the idea. It didn't make sense to him.

"Elias had a bag of them. June and I ate one before we left the hideout. They were bitter, but kind of sweet. June liked them, too."

"Holy shit!" Gloria whispered loudly from the hall. "Opium *candy*?"

Could Vince have given opium to a ten-year-old? It seemed impossible. Yet June willingly ate it. *She'd do anything on a dare.*

"What way did you go?" Haley got Natalie back on track.

"Elias had a shore boat anchored at Harmony Creek. We took it across the lake to the Portland Y camp where he tied it, and we hiked up to the mine from there. It was a really long walk. I was starting to wonder where we were going, but he kept laughing and telling jokes. I was high so I just kept walking. June complained of being sleepy. When we got to the mine, she laid down on Max's jacket. Then Elias took me deeper into the mine to mess around. He was kind of rough." She glanced at her father who quickly looked away. She picked at her fingernails where the hot-pink polish had flaked, wincing as she shifted in the chair.

"Later, when Elias hollered for Max, there was no answer. Max must have taken June somewhere to hide her. Elias went berserk and beat me up. He thought I was part of it, that I knew where they went, but I didn't."

"Then what happened?"

"You can see what happened. I thought he was going to kill me. That's all I know." Natalie looked at her father who stood up and said, "She's had enough, Detective Haley. Our next conversation will have a lawyer present."

"Yeah, good idea," said Haley. "Marie, you got room?"

"Sure. Natalie, you and your parents can sleep upstairs in James's room, if you like. We'll move in a cot. James can take the couch."

Within moments, the doctor stepped down the stairs to report on June. "She says she wasn't molested, which seems accurate as far as I can tell. She has no marks, no bruises anywhere." He recommended that June remain upstairs to rest for the next day or two. "Her spirits are good." Saying goodnight, he accepted a boat ride back to the landing.

Later, after they'd settled around the warm fireplace, Tess whispered to James, "I have a secret about Max."

"What? Okay. In the morning."

"We all need some shut-eye," Haley announced. "Let's reconvene at nine." He left for Harry Newman's lodge.

Upstairs, James cracked June's door for a glimpse of her sleeping soundly on the bottom bunk. His mom lay on the bunk above her.

"James?" Kay's head appeared over the edge of the bed.

"Hi, Mom." James pushed the door open and stepped into the dark room. "Can't sleep?"

"I will now, thanks to you. What you did was so brave."

He kissed her cheek. "I love you, Mom. 'Night." He slipped downstairs to the couch. But sleep wouldn't come until James had retraced every detail of the most incredible day of his life.

63

"They're arresting Natalie!"

What the hell? It wasn't even seven yet.

"Come on, guys!" Gloria yelled. "They're arresting Natalie!"

James roused himself on the couch and, still in yesterday's shirt and Levis, he threw off the blanket angrily. No doubt Dan had a hand in this. James and Tess met at the front door then followed the somber procession to the boat. Natalie stepped slowly, her parents walking behind her. Her mother sniffled and her father demanded the charges from the two officers who escorted Natalie to the inboard.

Aunt Marie, Hank and Ben watched Natalie go. Hank said she was being charged as a juvenile offender with conspiracy and accessory to a kidnapping, as well as drugging a minor.

It was all Gloria could do to hold her tongue as Natalie passed. James was acutely aware of that because he, too, wanted to pound Natalie for being so stupid, for putting June and the rest of them through this nightmare. Yeah, he was pissed. On the other hand, he didn't want Natalie to do time. These were federal charges. They could change her life.

Regardless, Natalie was no one that James knew. Sure, maybe at first he'd had a crush on her, but now he couldn't honestly remember why.

Haley tapped him on the shoulder. "How about you and Gloria and I get some coffee?" Once in the privacy of an empty kitchen, Haley poured them cups. Gloria placed a plate of fresh berry muffins where they gathered at the table.

"I've got some news," Haley said. "Vincent Mario Lavetti's death at 11:05 last night was from one gunshot wound to his heart. The other shots—one in the right hand, and the other in his lower pelvis —were not fatal though they caused considerable blood loss before the killing shot.

"Our findings concur with your story, Gloria. They were your bullets, your prints on the gun. Now, tell me why it was self-defense. My guys are up at the site looking for his bullet marks."

By the third cup of coffee, James was busting to leave. They'd gone over and over it. He stood and stretched then ambled into the living room. When he heard Haley raise his voice, he stepped nearer to the dining room to listen.

"Why'd you shoot Vince in the heart after he let June go?" the detective demanded.

"He reached for his gun on the ground, sir. He had already shot at us!"

"That's true!" James poked his head into the kitchen. "He would have shot us at close range, I'm sure of it."

"Hey, if you don't mind, I'm talking to her right now. Give us a moment."

"Sure." James returned to the river-stone fireplace, where two fir logs burned slowly to dry the damp lodge more than to warm it. He settled into the overstuffed chair closest to the hearth. Up until this moment he had been certain Vince would have shot one or both of them if he had been able. After all, he had murdered Max and tried his best to kill Ben and Joe. No question, the guy deserved to be killed. James had been ready to cut his throat. But now, afterwards, James realized he'd never actually questioned that assumption of self-defense. A quiet, shrill voice inside him asked how Vince could have shot anyone with Gloria standing on, and crushing, his one good arm? No, James remembered. He was a killer and a trafficker.

Sparks flew out at James abruptly from the fireplace when one of the logs rolled over the other and settled. A low hissing emitted from the throbbing embers, reminding James that Vince had the chance to shoot them in the cave. Why didn't he take it?

James's hands were as bloody as Gloria's. Well, almost. As soon as Haley allowed, James headed upstairs to check on his sister whose safety was the single justification for this godawful mess. Surely she'd wake soon. They were all far behind the clock that morning. It was nearly eleven.

Kay sat on June's bunk speaking softly to her. James listened from the hall.

Just waking, June's first words were "I don't want to go, Mommy." She looked younger than her years, sleepy, and bundled into warm blankets.

"I know, honey. I don't want you to, either." Kay patted her over the covers.

"Neither do I." James interrupted, standing in the doorway.

Startled, June and Kay turned to him, and June smiled broadly.

"What's going on?" Where the hell was June going?

"Hi, James!" June raised herself on an elbow, her eyes brightening. Seeing June's sunny face filled James with peace. He stepped to her and held her hand.

"Dan left early this morning to arrange June's temporary release into his custody," Kay said and looked away.

"What?"

"No!" June yelled. She pulled her hand away.

"No, Mom!" James felt his rage build. "He can't do that."

"He can do that, James, if the judge agrees. But we can fight it. Hank's taking me to an attorney in Longview today." Kay stood and stepped over to the yellowed mirror and frowned.

"That's not fair!" June pulled up her covers to her shoulders and shook her head. "You're saying I have to go with him?" She jumped out of bed and ran over to Kay and started hitting her, not hard, but hard enough.

"Hey June, come on!" James said. "Mom's going to do everything she can to get you back. Right, Mom?" James looked at Kay, expecting an instant affirmation. For a split second, a shadow passed across his mother's face. The next second, though, she opened up with that razzle-dazzle smile.

"That's right. It'll be fine, June. We'll get you back," she said, straightening June's bangs to perfection.

"Promise?" June searched her mother's face and then put her hands together as if praying.

"I promise we'll get you back." Kay had covered June's prayer hands with her own as she had done so many times before. She kissed June's brow.

Kay's assurance rang thin. James doubted his mother's resolve when he remembered how remote she'd been with them all summer. He decided then that if he had to light a bonfire under his mother to get some fight into her, he would.

"Hey June, *I* promise, okay?" He reached over and they shook on it, her face relaxing with a trust she hadn't shown with her mother.

Outside, mist drifted like slow music over the morning lake. A great blue heron took flight. At first, its huge wings flapped erratically. Then a deep, strong cadence took hold and lifted the great bird upward on an eight-foot wingspan, up into the sky. Alone on the dock, James's spirit soared with it. His promise to June had meant everything.

The balsam-chilled air cleared his foggy brain and he inhaled as much as he could. James breathed deeply and raised his face to Loowit, her peak still in the clouds. Before her, he felt humbled. She was surely omniscient, seeing all, seeing even the tiniest spider, and cleaving the whole wilderness to her as if it all might fly off into space without the motherlode to hold it down.

James doubted he would ever climb her now. No way could Ben go with a busted leg. And school would start soon. He involuntarily pushed Loowit to the back of his mind. All that mattered now was June.

64

At noon the following day, Gloria strode out the front door, down to the dock where James waited. "Let's go."

They jumped in the outboard and raced full throttle to South Shore Landing. There stood Gloria's Chevy pickup, parked for the season. It choked to life with a puff of gray smoke. They drove off, away from Spirit Lake.

They had planned it the previous night, to drive to see Ben at St. John's Hospital. James rolled the window down all the way and stuck his face out to smell the sweet scent of noble firs shouldering Highway 504, a thin ribbon of road sunk between evergreens so tall they blocked the sky. Getting out of the fishbowl drama of Harmony Falls liberated him, but the thought of losing June again dragged him down. He couldn't afford to lose her again, not after all that had happened. He thought of how he would feel in her absence, and it ate at him. Gloria, on the other hand, was singing Brenda Lee out the car window, oblivious to the turmoil he was going through.

When she parked at St. John's, James took his chance. "How do you feel about what we did … to Vince?" The last two words were barely audible.

"After sixteen years, I got something back, you know? Something that belonged to me. Now I want to put him behind me." Gloria looked straight ahead.

"Yeah. Me too," said James. But could he?

Turning the corner into Room 323, neither of them was prepared for the elaborate metal traction that suspended Ben's bent knee high above him. His leg, from his toes to mid-thigh, hung rigid in a splint. Seeing them walk in the open door, Ben grinned like a joker on a worn deck of cards, no doubt loopy from painkillers. Shock stretched James's smile into a grimace. He could feel it, but he couldn't help it. Seeing rubber tubes going into his friend's arms and under his sheet to God knows where turned James's stomach. He stood near the door for a quick exit.

Having no such reserve, Gloria beamed at Ben. "Hey there, hon."

Ben's eyes stayed on her as he opened his arms for her. "Come on over here."

"I've been worried about you," she said with a hug.

"Good," Ben pronounced and laughed deeply. The second bed in Room 323 was mercifully empty. Ben was loud enough for two.

"I thought you might want this." Gloria handed him his knapsack, AKA survival pack, clearly pleased that she had anticipated his needs.

He took it from her. "Thanks. I do. Just not this moment." Ben dropped it to the floor.

"Ben, what's this contraption for?" James couldn't hold back. The ropes and pulleys unnerved him. Obligingly, Ben began the story of his shattered tibia and the surgery.

"Doc said I might not walk again." Ben shrugged. "You bet I'll walk again. I'm a tough old cowboy." He must have seen the fear on James's face.

"I know you're tough enough to do anything, Ben, no matter what the docs say." Behind his confident words, though, James had to wonder what life on crutches, or worse, would do to a proud man like Ben. He took the chair closest to him while Gloria fluffed the patient's pillows and refilled the ice in his water glass. When she could think of nothing else to do, she sat on the edge of Ben's bed.

⸪

A half-hour later, after chatting and laughing, Gloria said, "I'll let you guys have your fun." Pointing at James, she chided, "but remember, Ben needs some rest, and so do you." Gloria's voice sang with cheer.

She leaned over Ben and pecked his cheek. "See you later this afternoon." Gloria swept out the door, a flash of loud colors, trailing scents of cinnamon and clove.

James perched on the vacant hospital bed, trying to smooth the already smooth blanket. His rough skin snagged on the woolen threads. Once soft from holding nothing heavier than books, his hands now bore callouses from cutting firewood and shaving shingles.

Ben remained quiet. He just stared at James, watching him. James felt Ben was waiting for something from him. He watched as Ben tried to shift in his traction, flinching, probably from the pain. He had been reserved since Gloria left, holding something back. James could wait no longer.

"My stepdad's got a mistress and he's going to marry her and he's taking custody of June and Mom wants to leave." James blurted it out all at once, each word tumbling over the last. He shut his eyes, blinking back a tear, and then he looked up to Ben. "Everything has changed. Especially me. I don't belong back East now."

Ben sucked water up through the flex-straw in a glass from the bed table. He breathed deeply and nodded. "You have changed." His steady gaze held James for a minute before he looked away. "I killed a man once."

James blinked at the turn of conversation. Did Ben think James had shot Vince? "I didn't kill Vince, Ben. Gloria shot him. Three times." James shuddered. Red splotches circled his brain.

"I understand," Ben said. "In a way, though, you are also responsible for his death. True, you didn't shoot him, but you didn't stop Gloria, either."

James was taking none of that. "Ben, it was self-defense. He was reaching for his gun." Why was Ben making him feel guilty?

"I'm not saying you shouldn't have done it, James. I am proud of you." A long minute passed.

"I just want you to know, taking a life takes something in return, something you may not know you've lost until later – maybe much later."

"Even if it was self-defense?"

"Let's consider that. We both know Gloria wanted Vince dead from the moment she recognized him as her kidnapper. Remember, she told Joe she wanted to kill him. Maybe you wanted that too. So how is that self-defense? Can you see this in a different light? The way a jury might see it?"

"But Ben, everyone said we were heroes, that what we did was brave." James didn't like hearing the edge in Ben's voice.

Ben reached for the water glass. He drew a slow sip and swallowed. He didn't look at James when he spoke. "Do you feel brave?"

James hadn't stopped to consider it. "Not really."

"So, turn away from their praise for a moment and look inside yourself. What do you see? How are you different?"

James wasn't sure what Ben meant.

"In some cultures, after a deadly victory, a true hero must make peace with himself, with the killer he has become. Sometimes he catches a fleeting image in the mirror, but the face isn't his. It is the face of the man he killed."

Ben reached for James's hand and then tapped it lightly. "To act bravely doesn't make you a hero. You did what you had to do to save your sister. But courage is different. It is not one action. It is a quality of mind and spirit, something you live by."

"In some tribes when a man kills another," Ben continued, "he is expected to take responsibility for the dead man's wife, for his children, and for his livestock, too. After all, he left them with no provider. To willingly take on that responsibility, to do it well, now that takes courage." Ben paused a full minute. "There'd sure be a lower murder rate, wouldn't there?"

Ben shifted in his traction, grimaced, closed his eyes, and sighed.

"Soon you will leave Spirit Lake, James. You will take his ghost with you."

"It *had* to be me, Ben." James continued to plead his case. "We had the opportunity. Gloria and I were June's last best chance for freedom. It *had* to be us."

Ben was silent. James was missing the point. After a moment he said, "If the praise of men leaves you empty, if you seek something beyond flattery…." Ben's voice trailed off.

James squinted at him. Ben looked old as if tired from the effort of explaining it all. He shifted slightly and grew quiet.

"Then what?" James asked.

"Way I see it, you've got nothing to lose now and everything to gain. You have no home. No father. And now June is leaving. All the arrows point up that mountain." Ben nodded toward the window, which framed Loowit. From Longview, it was a small, distant peak.

"Ben, I can't go without you," James mumbled, slightly embarrassed.

Without warning, Ben's head swiveled back toward the window. Soaring overhead, a red-tailed hawk circled, its wings wide and still, riding the current. "Red Boy is back." Ben watched it disappear over the tops of pines. "An excellent sign. Perseverance furthers."

"I've got a plan. But before we go over that, let's start at the beginning." Ben patted a space on the foot of his bed for James to sit.

"Hank and I have a place on Loowit, a solo campsite," Ben said. "It's a small ledge on the east side. We go there to camp alone for a night, maybe more. Below the timberline is an indented spot. I'm sure others have stayed there. We climb to the summit and then hike down, but only one of us stays on the volcano. The other returns at a designated time.

James watched Ben with full concentration. He craved this, to be alone in the wild, to become a man. He would have to keep the fire burning all night and stay watchful. Alone. He sputtered, "I can't do this, Ben." He had read about initiation rites in Greek myths, mostly *Classic Comics*, which he admittedly read like crazy, enough to know he was no hero.

"Hank will take you up…."

"What? Uncle Hank?"

"Yes. You didn't know your uncle is an accomplished alpine climber? He knows the mountain better than I do. I'll make arrangements. This evening I'll tell you everything you need to know to survive in the wilderness without me. I've made notes. Look, I've got maps."

Ben reached into his weathered pack and pulled out a mess of creased maps of hiking trails and creeks on and around Loowit. "Let's go through them, okay?"

James pulled a chair close to Ben's bed to better spread them out. He liked the way Ben simplified the important things in life. He helped James see a way out of the quicksand he was sinking in.

James would depart with his uncle in the very early morning of the following night. His uncle would guide him to the summit and then lead him down to Ben's one-man camp below the timberline. Hank would return the next afternoon, climbing back up to walk James down.

It was late afternoon before Gloria arrived to take him back. In the few moments, before she came, Ben gave final instructions. "Here. Take my pack. It's got everything you need. Hank has the climbing gear." James grabbed the strap and pulled it over his shoulder.

Gloria burst in the door with a bag of warm huckleberry muffins. She placed them on Ben's bed and hugged him. "How're you doin'?" She passed them both a muffin and sat on the bed. "Can't stay long."

Ben put his hand on James's shoulder. "You're going to do fine." But Ben's smile seemed wistful.

James didn't want to leave. Gloria took a playful slap at his back. "Let's go. You got the pack?"

"Yeah." James turned and nodded at Ben, who gave him a thumbs-up.

In the truck, Gloria handed James a paper bag. "I stopped at Woolworth's for you."

James looked inside and smiled wide. "A Barbie doll. June'll love it."

65

It was 7:30 p.m. when James waltzed through the lodge's front door wielding the Barbie like a blue-ribbon prize. In his excitement, he had overlooked the somber mood in the kitchen. Kay sat at the table, sniffling and wiping her eyes, while Marie and Tess hovered, consoling her, "Come on, honey. You can fight it," Marie said.

"What the hell is going on now?" James's annoyance surprised everyone.

"June is gone," Kay said through her tears. "Dan got temporary custody of her this afternoon. He packed her bags and left about a half-hour ago."

"What?" James swung around to see who else was responsible for letting June go. He sank to a chair and swallowed hard, then said more to himself than anyone else, "But she didn't want to go. How did he make her?"

"She swore she wouldn't go," Kay said, nodding. She turned to look at him with bloodshot eyes. "They waited about ten minutes for you. Then Dan put his foot down and showed June the signed custody release. 'This says you're coming with me,' he said. 'And that's all there is to it.' June tried to run back to me, calling me, but he caught her." Kay started sobbing again.

"She looked terrified," Tess added, beginning to cry too.

Damn that Barbie doll anyway. He threw the boxed Barbie to the kitchen table and it clattered to the floor. "To hell with this!"

"June wanted to say goodbye to you," Kay said. "They did wait," choking back sobs, "but Dan thought it was better this way." Her voice cracked.

''Oh, I'm sure,'' James muttered. ''Better for him.'' He and Gloria must have passed them on Route 504.

''I'm sorry, James.'' Gloria put her arm around his back. "I didn't know."

"I blocked the door," Kay said to him, "but Dan waved his signed release in my face." Kay's arms wrapped around her stomach like she might be sick. She rocked back and forth.

Bolting from the kitchen, James left his mother and Tess sitting there. He hefted open the front door and flew down the cedar slab steps without stopping, down to the end of the dock. He sat on the weathered wood and hung his feet over the dock. Head in his hands, he rubbed his forehead, hard.

Dammit. James twisted around to his left and with his right hand punched the old planks as hard as he could, again and again, hard enough to feel the wood splinter deep into his knuckles.

June was gone. Again. Wiping tears from his eyes he smeared blood on his cheeks. He looked at his red fist and wiped the rest on his jeans.

The image of June being ripped from Harmony Falls, crying, confused and scared, kept pummeling James. If Dan got permanent custody, James might never see her again. Suddenly, he thought of her, of how she must feel going back East, motherless and brotherless, and his heart burned for her.

But James could do nothing. Not about June, nor Dan, nor his mother. And he sure couldn't bring his father back to life. James stood, unzipped, and pulled off his jeans down to his boxers in one motion. Then his shirt, overhead. And he dove in. His knuckles stung but he found his stroke and headed to the Boys Scout camp.

His darkest thought kept scrolling in his head, somehow matching his stroke like a German march. Saving June had been the single justification for killing Vince, but with her gone, was there any reason for Vince's death? Had James been right to be a part of it... or was he damned? With each stroke, a dozen questions echoed in his lonely chamber. Upon his return, he took a deep breath and took his questions to the bottom of the lake. He wondered if he should stay there.

66

The next morning after resuming his daily swim, James trudged to his room, dripping, and changed into dry trunks. He grabbed a bar of Lux, a washcloth, and a towel and walked dully back down the stairs to the deck. Seeing the diving tower brought back memories of sweet times when he and Natalie had lain there gazing at the stars. Now the place was a ghost tower, not a soul in sight, not Natalie nor Tess nor June swimming below. James dropped his towel and soap onto the dock and put his glasses on top. He climbed up the ladder, but with the creaky thing listing, even the tower seemed adrift.

James jumped off the stiff diving board, gaining what little height he could, and tucked tight into his practiced cannonball, always terrific to splash everyone within ten feet. But today there was no one to splash.

As he hit the water twelve feet below, a sudden *whoosh* of bubbles exploded around him, tickling, as he straightened out and exhaled, descending feet-first into icy, sapphire depths. In a single thrust, he expelled his breath and all the pea-sized bubbles shot up while he sank, emptying air. For James, the coolest part of submersion was the silence. Underwater, all the noise of life just vanished.

When he opened his eyes, James saw golden swords of sunlight piercing each undulating swell of water. The effect was blurry and impressionistic. His lungs screamed for air though he refused to surface. He could hold his breath longer than five minutes, he knew. He'd been practicing.

He could have stayed underwater much longer if the hum of an approaching motor hadn't disturbed his meditation. James launched himself to the surface for a furious suck of air. Coughing, he swam over to the police boat, cursing it with every stroke for interrupting his ritual. He would have to start over when they left. Soon, his toes scratched on the pumice bottom and he raised his body slowly. He climbed to the dock.

Retrieving his glasses, James quickly toweled off his face and put out his hand. "Hello, Sir." Haley shook his hand and drew James in for a brief hug, even with his wet, shivering body.

"Congratulations again on getting our man," Haley said, then told James about an F.B.I. raid on the tanker up-river in Stella, the one that would have transported June. They strolled up to the lodge and took seats on the sunny deck while James shivered under his damp towel.

"Last night when the Feds busted them, they broke wide open an international trafficking ring. Got four of them last night, each one guilty enough to give us more names. This is big, James. It's a breakthrough in this ugly business. Did you know they had three more girls on the ship, younger than June? Poor kids clung to each other in the hold, drugged up, lying on a mound of smelly hay. But they're safe now. They're home, thank God. Oh, and something else. Because of nailing Vince and his connections in trafficking, the F.B.I might find some of the kids who were already sold. Can you imagine? Like bringing someone back from the dead."

"That's great, Detective Haley." James didn't want to hear any more about poor kids caught in this 'ugly business'. Thinking of them trapped on the tanker sat heavily on James.

A bright indigo bunting sang from a perch nearby: a bit of beauty in a bitter world.

Haley pulled out a folded page of *The Oregonian.* "Take a look at this." Smiling broadly, he opened it to a front-page story.

RELEASED CONVICT KILLED

A released convict from the Oregon State Penitentiary was killed Friday night. Vincent Lavetti, 45, died of gunshot wounds while fleeing with a minor whom he drugged and held captive with intent to cross state lines. Lavetti had been released two months prior. He assumed an alias and papers of a deceased prisoner, Elias Craft. Lavetti was a long-time player in Portland prostitution rings. In a 1945 federal round-up, he was arrested for prostituting minors. Released in 1953, Lavetti was incarcerated again in '56 for the attempted murder of a minor. Released on June 9, he used the name Elias Craft and was at large until Friday, August 25. Vincent Lavetti is survived by two brothers, Anthony, 38, and Mario, 41, from Seattle, both serving five-year sentences since their 1956 convictions for racketeering and prostitution.

James nodded, glad no mention was made of Lavetti's killer. James hadn't known about his brothers. But there was something odd about Haley's visit. James knew the busy detective hadn't come across the lake just to show him a news clip. Though James could ask such things more easily now, he feared he already knew the answer.

"So, why are you here?" James ran his palm over the smooth railing of the deck.

Haley averted his eyes. "To escort Gloria to the sheriff's department to answer some questions." The detective then stood up as if recognizing the lines of hospitality had been crossed.

James's mouth dropped open as he stood, too.

"I'm sure they just need to verify the self-defense." Haley turned toward the front door. "She should be back later tonight."

"*Should* be?"

"Sure, if everything lines up." He opened the front door and held it.

James didn't want to hear "if" in that sentence. He liked Haley, but whose side was he on? Chances were, not Gloria's. She had a record, a small thing, but once she had said to James, laughing, that if she got arrested again, "they'd get out the stake and kindling." Gloria was more than a cook and baker; she was an herbalist who practiced homeopathy quite privately, mindful that, less than a century before, women were burned for less.

"Detective Haley," James said, "I was a witness, the only one. I should go with Gloria." James followed Haley into the hall.

"It's not going to come to that. As far as I'm concerned, Gloria is a hero." Haley smiled. "So are you, James."

James remembered Ben's words about praise. Was Haley flattering him?

"James, take it easy. I'll do whatever I can for her, okay?" With that, he went to find Gloria in the kitchen. Sitting on her stool spread-legged in a long cerulean-blue skirt, she leaned over the trash and snapped beans for dinner. Her pot roast infused the lodge with aromas of sweet onion and rosemary.

"Hello, Detective Haley. Looking for me?" Gloria stood and slowly dried her hands on a dishtowel, took off her apron, and hung it on a hook. "I'm ready." She nodded at him and followed him out.

James had paced the hallway, shaking his head. Another good friend was ripped from him. He stepped outside. Gloria soon strolled out the front door, holding her head high. As Haley chatted with Uncle Hank, she turned to James and hugged him. For a long moment, they held on. James thought of Gloria's long-lost son, who should have been the one there to hug her. One day, James would tell him what a cool mom he had.

"Be safe, little brother. See you soon." Swishing her skirt, she walked to the dock and waved to James with a clatter of bangles. Haley took her hand to help her into the boat. James's eyes stung as she left. A thought jolted him. If the self-defense plea didn't hold, could James be charged as an accessory to murder? Was that what Ben meant about consequences?

James had felt foolish when Haley told him he was a hero. Maybe he had been a hero saving June. For about five minutes. Now that she had gone, that little bit of righteousness went with her. There was no one to save but himself.

----------◆----------

Kay stood at the open door like a sentinel. James blurted out, "What's happening to Harmony Falls? Everyone's leaving."

"I don't know." She shook her head but paused as if she had more to say.

James didn't want to ask, but he had to know. "Did you see the lawyer?"

"Yesterday afternoon. He referred me to someone in Boston, someone good. We'll see." She looked around briefly and started back in, then turned to James. "I'm thinking we should leave, too, James, head back and get June's custody settled. Tomorrow or the next day. If I delay, Dan might use it against me. What do you think?" Her forehead was furrowed.

James froze as soon as he heard the words 'leave too'. She couldn't mean that. "Mom, no!" His heart thundered. "We can't leave till I'm back from my climb up Loowit."

As he spoke, she backed through the front door, edged to a hall chair, and sank into it. "What are you *talking* about, James? Climbing the summit?"

"I told you about it, Mom. Remember?" But she hadn't remembered. He could see it on her face. "Ben and I were going to climb up and camp at the timberline?"

"Ben clearly can't go now. And you're not going up there alone, not up a glacier-covered volcano. You need a guide! The weather is unpredictable. Winds can be fifty miles an hour."

"That's why Uncle Hank is taking me up," James said. "It's all been arranged." He needed her to understand. This was no crazy scheme. "Ben went over everything. He gave me maps. He told me what to watch for."

"I don't care. Maybe young men out west do this sort of thing, but you weren't raised in the wild. Hardly. You hated Cub Scouts, remember? You can't defend yourself against bullies at school never mind against wolves or bears. No. You are *not* going."

"Mom, I have to go. I have stuff to sort out. I need to do it alone."

Uncle Hank must have heard their conversation. He walked in the front door, his eyes pinned on his sister-in-law. "Come on, Kay. Let me take my nephew up Mount St. Helens. It's an experience of a lifetime. He needs this. We'll leave early in the morning, alright?"

"No Hank, it's too dangerous up there and he's not a climber."

"Kay, he's sixteen. He's been hiking the backcountry for weeks. And he's learned a lot about the wilderness in the last week. Kay. He needs to go." Hank held her stare. "Trust me."

"I do, Hank. But *I* need James with me. I've lost half a family, you know." She looked at James. "I can't lose you, too." She started to tear up. With some hesitation, James placed his hand on her shoulder. Kay crushed in against him, hugging, sniffling.

"You won't lose me, Mom. It's only one night." He said the words, but what he was feeling couldn't have found words. Warm honey filled his being. His mother cared.

Kay looked from James to Hank and gave a brave smile. "I'm holding you responsible, Hank, if anything goes wrong." She turned to James and hugged him close.

"You better come back to me," she managed, tearfully. "Then we'll get June."

67

That night, the wind carried a lonesome song from the campfire to James's bedroom window, ruffling on the breeze, in and out of earshot. Even though he had to leave in a few hours, he wasn't tired. The music, the wind, or maybe just the company pulled him outside, where a blood moon hung low in the western sky.

How could he leave this place?

An ebbing campfire burned, illuminating the faces of Uncle Hank and Aunt Marie, while she sang a sorrowful Irish ballad called "Jimmy Whalen" in a deep, practiced voice. Tess managed Ben's job of keeping the fire, adding in harmonies with her mother. The little spotted owl perched on a cottonwood branch, a regular in the evenings.

"Could I take over the fire, Tess?" James offered.

"Sure." She picked up her guitar and sat on a log. Strumming lightly, she began a tune that James easily recognized, "The Tennessee Waltz." Aunt Marie sang alto harmony to Tess's melody. It soothed James. He closed his eyes and listened, thinking of June, probably at home by now. What was she doing?

After Tess's song, before James could steal away to bed, she nudged his arm. "Stay. I want to tell you about Max," she whispered, and then sat beside James. "He spoke about his daughter, but also gold mining the Northwest." Tess unfolded a paper map as soft as flannel with marks barely visible. "Look. This shows where he buried his gold."

"Buried gold? And you *believed* him?" The marks looked like they'd been made by a wolverine.

"Sure I believed him. He said, 'Go get it, Tess. Share it with my daughter, when you find her'. Look at this old map. It's in Oregon somewhere. We'll go when you come back."

Though she seemed to assume he would return, James wasn't sure of anything anymore.

He was awake before the alarm buzzed. He'd given up on sleeping. Nothing was going to make him feel better. He dressed in layers of clothes he had washed in the lake and dried the day before, to keep his scent down. Sitting on the edge of the bunk, he riffled through Ben's survival pack. Neatly arranged in interior pockets were:

1) Fish hooks, lures, and plenty of lines

2) Ben's Buck, in a leather sheath

3) small hatchet

4) packets of salmon jerky

5) toothbrush and paste

6) small towel

7) First Aid pack with snake bite med

8) aluminum cup and cook kit

9) kitchen matches

10) compass

11) rolled-up piece of canvas

12) thin sleeping bag

13) flashlight and batteries

In a side pocket of the pack was a small doe-skin bag with fringe and a bear beaded brightly in blue and black on the front. James would wait to see the contents when he made camp that evening.

His Timex read three a.m. when he walked into Harmony Falls' dark kitchen. There was no sign that Gloria had returned last night. By four, the kitchen would typically be ablaze with light and chatter, Gloria dispensing her 'crumbs of wisdom', as she called it. But today, still early, there was only the coffee percolator, bubbling with that reassuring gurgle, on a small fire on the woodstove. In walked Uncle Hank, bright-eyed and chatty.

"There, I found you a good staff. An alpenstock. One of my extras." He gave James a staff of noble fir, taller than him by six inches. It was fit for a real mountaineer. The fir had grown in this wilderness and had been carved and polished by his uncle's hands.

"You may keep it. It'll come in handy." Hank's smile stretched wide and warm.

"Thank you. It's cool." James was moved by the gift and ran his palm over the staff. It suited him. "Hey, did Gloria get back?"

"No. I looked in her room. She wasn't there." Uncle Hank ran his hand over the smooth cane, too. "Maybe with Ben," he said, an afterthought.

His pack drew James's attention. "What you got in there?"

"My bag's always packed to climb St. Helens. I take campers up, often, and I go up sometimes for no reason at all. Rest easy, James. You've got a good guide." He pulled open the bag and showed James coiled ropes and harnesses, crampons, extra socks and gloves, sweaters, and long underwear. Hank grabbed a couple of banana muffins, tossed one to James and they walked outside.

Thick mist blurred the lacy edges of night. They sipped their steaming coffee on the deck before starting. Hank had kindly tied a boat to the dock, saving them from wading in the icy lake. Pushing off into the night, they slid silently over the inky water to the South Shore Landing, where they would begin. Not another soul was on the lake. Fog hung like a shroud.

After pulling the boat onto the beach, they headed up Trail 100 to the timberline viewpoint. At three thousand two hundred feet, the viewpoint took only a few hours to hike but was the gateway for every climber. Then they followed Ben's map southeast to his campsite, though James's uncle already knew the way. There was no path, he said. The site was marked by a totem snag.

An easy trail, 100 bore the press of a thousand wandering boot heels. With each step, James crushed a fresh layer of pine needles, and the soft earth sighed, yielding. He felt dazed and sleepy. It was too early to talk. Bats whizzed by, disturbed by their lights.

When they took an off-trail pit stop, something screeching flew near James's face scaring the bejesus out of him. He shooed it, jumping backward a foot or more. It flew up to a nearby branch. There, in the spot of his flashlight was a screech owl; it couldn't have been more than seven inches high, staring at him with angry yellow eyes, warning James away with a quavering whistle. She must have had a nest nearby. Owls can be plain mean, particularly the mothers, but today James wanted to see the goodness in every living thing. Ben had said there was always a reason when a creature crossed a quester's path if for none other than to remind us that we too are animals. James picked up a two-inch gray feather shed by the owl and saved it in his shirt pocket. Maybe the reason would come to him.

Now wide awake, he began to hear the Great North Woods awaken too. By six, they passed the timberline viewpoint in a cloudy haze. Creatures shuffled and skittered beyond James's sight. As dawn broke, birds of varied colors, blue, yellow, and orange, seemed to mill about the two of them, twittering and cooing. Was he still dreaming?

They had set out at three in the morning to a black and gray world, a maze of shadows. Now in the half-light, the mist had cleared to a brooding landscape. While they walked, Uncle Hank spoke of the ancient Indian legends that portrayed Loowit as a lovely maiden, so fair that gods fell in love with her and fought over her, causing bloodshed and destruction. Indians told early settlers that Loowit shot out hot rocks. They tried to warn them.

"They must have thought white men were just plain mental for continuing to die on her summit, where they repeatedly skied into crevasses or succumbed to avalanche. At one time," Hank said, "Mount St. Helens was called 'Death Mountain.'"

James's toes curled in his boots.

68

To come upon a wind-worn totem in the wilderness, tucked into the side of a volcano, seemed a great mystery. Yet it was there to mark the north corner of a flat rectangular clearing, approximately six feet by eight feet on a ledge, facing east and overlooking the world. This was a sacred place, Hank said. Despite the mist that still clouded their view, the sheer height, nearly five thousand feet, hitched James's heart.

Ben had carved the totem from the snag of noble fir, years ago. It loomed maybe eight feet high and three feet wide. Colored dully with mineral dyes, the five animal heads were massive and stacked one on top of the other: coyote, eagle, wolf, owl, and bear. James wondered what each one meant and would ask Ben when he saw him.

Leaving his treasures and his big pack at the site, James followed Uncle Hank on a search for sagebrush, which was good kindling. James cut an armful of scratchy branches, releasing the fresh-cut Thanksgiving smell of herbs. They took it back, and then they set out for firewood: bright red alder. Not as plentiful as sagebrush, alder sent them afar in two separate directions. Using their hatchets to sever big branches, they dragged them back for James to cut later.

At last, they tightened their packs. They were ready. It was already eight a.m. Time to hike up to Dog's Head. The timberline fell away behind them. James caught Hank watching his face, which must have lit up, must have opened wide to the heavens above.

"The beauty," his uncle said, panting. "I know. It's easy to forget the danger." Hank talked while he climbed. "The snowpacks are pretty, but they've been known to shift when Loowit trembles and the heavy snow yields to avalanches. Even these talus rocks called 'scree' can give way underfoot, so step carefully. Use your staff like this." His uncle demonstrated. James was a quick study given the circumstances. Then Hank picked up a rock and threw it at James.

"Hey, what're you doing?" James's hand popped up to block it, but the pumiceous rock bounced off his hand as lightly as a chalk eraser. "Okay. Very funny."

It had been an easy climb on the lower slopes, but as they hoofed up the rocky back of Dog's Head, wind gusts began to blow erratically. Hank stopped on top of Dog's Head where he pulled from his pack the necessary harnesses, gloves, and crampons for the upper glacial climb. As his uncle showed him the proper way to wear the gear, a little snake of vertigo shot up James's spine sending nausea to his throat. The volcano was 9,500 feet high. Now the fog was beneath them, and the blinding mass of ice called Nelson Glacier radiated with morning's pink light. Sheer ice. Holy crap.

Gusts increased drastically the higher they climbed. James had hiked plenty during the last few weeks and his legs were strong. But the altitude. He breathed, no, he panted, thin, dizzying air. Above the ground fog, he could see everything as if from an airplane. The snowy tip of Mount Adams floated above the clouds in the dreamy distance. Blue sky splashed purple shadows on bright white ice. Dazzled dumb without realizing it, James had stopped walking.

"James. Come on. Stay alert." Hank had attached their ropes, and James's attention returned as his crampons cut deep into the white crust. He had wanted to climb Loowit from his first day at Spirit Lake, even before he could see her peak. Here was his reward at last.

The route traversing upper Nelson steepened and, as they crested Forsythe Glacier, nearing the top, wind whipped at their pants and jackets, snapping them loudly like loose sails. The wind became James's wickedest enemy, one that toyed cruelly with him.

Uncle Hank urged him: "Just the last twenty-six hundred feet." James focused on Hank's broad back. One boot in front of the other.

He wanted this.

Soon the route leveled. James silently thanked God. Bending over, hands on his knees, he sucked in thin gulps of air. He couldn't have taken another step.

"This isn't the top, James." His uncle stretched and turned to him, smiling.

"What?" James panted. Was he joking?

"It's a false summit."

"Where's the real one?"

"Just another hundred feet. You're so close. You can do it." Hank patted him on his back. In fact, from there, getting to the summit was easy. Eager to pay homage to Loowit, James marched past Hank, right up to the crater rim. "Ah, at last...."

"Hey, come back here!" James heard the edge in his uncle's voice before Hank dove towards him and grabbed his arm to pull him back. A bit annoyed, James hoped his uncle hadn't thought he was stupid enough to fall in.

"The rim has been known to crumble right under a climber," Hank said. "Don't put your weight on it." His uncle had regained some composure.

"Ten feet back?" James wasn't sarcastic. Hank had spooked him.

"No, right here." Hank stood about seven feet from the edge. Trembling, James gazed down into the crater to see… snow. A great deal of snow. What did he expect, boiling lava? Maybe something?

"You're looking at an adolescent volcano, James, an active volcano. She's bustin' at the seams. Kind of like you." His uncle winked at him.

James would have to think about that.

"See that bulge down there? That's the dome. It's growing all the time, being pushed up by the volatile gases deep inside. That's what makes her cone so pretty, so symmetrical. It's also what makes Loowit so dangerous."

When James first looked in the crater, he had been blinded by white. Now he could make out the dome, the youngest part, and grasp the extent of Uncle Hank's comparison. He nodded his head, deep in thought. Uncle Hank kept talking, as was his inclination.

"Loowit has erupted, on average, every hundred years, over thousands of years, say the scientists. That's high frequency in geologic terms." Reading the question on James's face, Hank said, "Yeah. We're due for one this century, they say."

News flash: Loowit didn't give a damn whether James paid homage or not. She was going to blow when she had to. James was looking into the heart of the wildest beast of all. He was speechless.

James didn't stare for long. Like most climbers on Loowit, his descent was quicker than his ascent by a third. He formed a theory about that on his way down. After peering into the top of an active volcano, climbers probably turned away with such a heightened conviction to seize life that they wasted no more time. They flew down the mountain.

James and Hank shook hands goodbye at the campsite. His uncle, already on his way back to earth, yelled, "See you tomorrow around three and not before."

69

James scraped a kitchen match on dry rock and lit the scraggly mound of sagebrush, setting off tiny crackling fireworks. He was alone now, and he had work to do. Burning sage readied the campsite, Ben had explained. James lit a compressed sage bundle, releasing a fragrant smoke that James inhaled deeply.

He took out a packet of Gloria's herbs called Death Camas. Not edible like the Blue Camas, an Indian staple, Death Camas was believed by natives to form a magical barrier when its dried flowers were crushed and sprinkled around the perimeter of a campsite, protecting it from harm. James took small handfuls and spread them, doubly protecting his site.

Ben found this spot years ago, he'd said, for his spiritual journey. It satisfied the requirements: the ledge was remote and rugged and perilously exposed to the elements. It was nature at her most dramatic, most inspirational. Sacred places, Ben had said, often call the creation to mind.

Inside Ben's knapsack were packets of food Gloria had included, dried blueberries and salmon jerky, M&M's, and almonds. James poured a handful of M&M's and almonds and ate them slowly for quick energy.

He filled the tin cup with spring water from his packed bottle. The cup always hung from a strap on Ben's pack and brought him to mind. "That's all you need for the best tasting water in the country," he had said. "A cup to scoop it out of any stream flowing down to Spirit Lake."

<hr>

After a while, James dug into the side of Ben's pack for something to hold the mementos of his journey. He found the small deerskin bag. A bear was beaded on the front, but inside, James found nothing. He placed the owl feather inside it for safe-keeping.

For hours James sat so still that nature lost interest in him, cross-legged, gazing out over an infinity of cirrus clouds. Sitting below the timberline on the volcano's flank was traditionally where Cowlitz Indians camped on their quests so they wouldn't offend Loowit's often-angry spirits. Squirrels rustled in some bushes making soft barking sounds and tiny chipmunks scurried far from him. James could hear individual voices at once. Were wolf ears his compensation for not being able to see well?

Sitting gave James a chance to turn inward, to scratch through the scree and see what still stung. Salt burned the edges of every thought James had of June. He had lost her just when he began to appreciate her. His jaw ached from clenching his teeth, grinding them. Stuffing his anger was all he could do. He would be going back East in a few days and when James got home, June would not be there. She will be with Dan at his apartment in Cambridge, rented until they work out the terms of their divorce.

How could Dan steal June from his mother and him after that nightmare? She would have so many emotions to sort out. Not to mention dealing with the divorce. What did Dan know about Vince? Nothing. Or about June's lonely summer? He would just sweep June's feelings under one of his antique Orientals.

James inhaled, but his breath caught. He remembered their last afternoon together, as they left the waterfall, how June double-skipped down the trail like she was Dorothy singing "Follow The Yellow Brick Road." June was a free spirit then. She was alive. Will she be free again?

A cold wind gusted close by, sending a fast shudder through James. Suddenly, James heard drumming. Sitting high in the clouds, staring at the small flame somehow transported him to another time. James felt a deep kinship with others who had sat there before him, on the side of a powerful young volcano. What would be the way of his life? James lifted his face to the sky, opening to answers.

He lay back on the ledge, counting clouds. As he breathed the pine-scented air, he exhaled fully. How could he leave Spirit Lake? His body was rooted like the great forests and streams. His heart beat with the wild. It was unthinkable to go back to the bullies at school and the posh cubicle his mother called home. James had found his place and himself right here.

70

Off to his right, a sudden moan pierced his sensory high. It was a low-pitched animal groan coming from somewhere nearby. James stood up and listened from a place of inner stillness. His ear slowly tracked 180 degrees as he turned around. Hearing it better, James thought it sounded more like heavy breath, a loud wheeze, maybe. James left his site, drawn to ease the animal's suffering, not knowing what he might find, what danger he might walk into. The moans grew louder and more urgent as James approached the noise, about two hundred feet from his camp. There in loamy soil, a wild dog lay on its side, weak, its back leg impaled in a bloody steel trap. James moved toward the dog warily. When he got a few feet from it, it opened its eyes but didn't start or raise its head at the sight of him. Just a yearling, a female. She was dying. She had been bleeding out for some time. *I have to help her.*

He had never opened a steel trap, particularly one already embedded in a dog's leg. She was too weak to bite James, barely looking at him as he worked to pull the trap apart. His fingers fumbled between the jaws, so tightly sprung and slippery with blood. James took hold and pulled with all his might, shaking as he opened it just long enough to allow the mangled leg to fall out. The godawful trap slammed shut, the teeth almost crushing James's fingers. Who in hell would trap on Loowit?

The dog glanced back at James showing relief on her face. Then her head fell on the grass as if she could finally rest. He wrapped his bandana around her short snout and raised her over his shoulder. She wasn't scraggly looking like a coyote, somewhat larger. More like a pale-furred young wolf. James carried her back to camp to clean her wound.

While he walked, he tried to decipher what meaning there could be for him finding this dog. There was no question he would care for her, even though she may die. If she did, he'd feel like crap and blame himself. But if she lived she would require care, care he couldn't give when he left to go back East. Stuck. As always, good intentions were useless without the right action. Yet walking away and leaving her there was not an option.

Back at the site, James dug into Ben's first aid kit for hydrogen peroxide, antibacterial cream, and gauze. He poured on some peroxide like Tess had shown him many times and cleaned her wounds with his bandanna. Her leg showed three deep punctures and a mess of crushed bones. James wrapped an excess of gauze around it. She lay quiet then.

Nighthawks swooped above James, hunting for flying insects and calling *peent, peent*. Taking out his small bottle of water, he wet a wad of cloth from Ben's pack and held it against the dog's mouth, squeezing out some water. She licked it and wanted more. Finally, James grabbed his tin cup and poured himself a drink too.

He sat down next to the dog and cut strips of alder. Soon, a little fire crackled and warmed them. He would go out for more wood at first light, but they'd get by until then. The dog slept while James waited out the long night, listening for wildlife, staying alert.

Wolves started howling after midnight, not too far away. Ben had said there were no more wolves. Was James dreaming? No. The howling was real.

There would be no sleep tonight.

———— ╎ ————

Nor would there be stars. Clouds had consumed the constellations.

The dog startled abruptly, pulling herself partly up.

"It's okay, girl, you're going to be fine." James tried to croon softly, but the dog knew better. She had heard something. James shone his flashlight where the dog looked. There, beyond a stand of cedars, three sets of yellow eyes glowed. James shuddered then froze. His dog issued a low growl, one probably ringing with fear that the wolves could already smell. They stood their ground. Behind James, the dog whined and tried to raise herself onto her legs but fell back. Oh, they were quite the team.

Nothing happened for an unbearable hour or so, but then, after one a.m., one of the beasts began to approach. Dog, as James had begun to call her, had been keeping vigil with him, growling quietly. James grabbed two half-burning logs and stood up tall, holding them high, like torches. He yelled furiously, "Git! Git!" and shook the logs at them.

All three wolves advanced. James tried like hell to put his faith in Gloria's Death Camas, a boundary of measly flowers encircling them. Yet there the wolves oddly remained. James held his fire sticks up and stared at each wolf's feet, back and forth, avoiding those six yellow eyes.

James and Dog were perched on the edge of disaster. The wolves could have just leaped on them, for crissakes, they were that close. But they didn't. Now the wolves were sitting, watching James, no longer menacing. His arms fell, heavy from hoisting logs, one of which he laid back in the fire. His breathing slowed.

James should have been petrified. But after a while, the wolves lay down and seemed to settle in. He did, too. He wasn't afraid of them. Even Dog slept.

Vast wilderness surrounded James. And wolves.

Dozens of ghostly sounds reverberated through the black night. Two or three different kinds of owls hooted. Distant coyotes cried mournfully. They sounded as lonely as James felt. He had nothing but his thoughts to keep him company once the wolves fell asleep, or he assumed they were.

Saving his dwindling stack of wood, James let the fire die down but kept the embers glowing. He eased into the thin sleeping bag and laid his head back on his rolled-up sweater. Dog snored gently beside him, emitting enough heat from her thick blond coat for both of them. James could hear the wolves breathe and, without realizing, he found himself inhaling in sync with them and with Dog. He felt a vast swelling and emptying, swelling and emptying, as if the world breathed in unison.

Exposed to the night air, James felt free. The roll of canvas he brought along was to be used only in case of rain to keep firewood and provisions dry.

His senses opened. Like jazz, forest racket filled him with music. Hearing the cicadas and nightjars, and the little Pacific tree frogs croaking high above the Bufo frogs' booming bass, he listened to each melody distinctly and heard in each creature's song a sheer joy in making noise. With Dog beside him, James felt protected. He smiled. He must have fallen asleep that way.

<hr>

James awoke abruptly to a piercing whistle, then a trill. The hermit thrush! Had he fallen asleep? In pale dawn, James turned over to greet Dog. But the place where she had been was empty. James felt the stone-cold ground. She was gone.

Impossible.

She couldn't even walk. James didn't understand. He looked closely, but there were no paw prints or fresh marks on the ground where she could have been dragged away. He sat up and walked to where the three wolves had slept. No wolves, no prints. He rubbed his gritty eyes and face, reaching for the cloth he had dampened for Dog. But there was no cloth, and his water bottle was still in his pack, half full. His bandanna was still wound around his neck. There was no blood.

James scratched his head, noting how itchy his scalp had become. A prickly stubble irritated his face. Standing on the ledge, he saw below him a sea of pink clouds flowing over the Cascade valleys. Sunrise silhouetted Mount Adams to the south and Rainier far north. It was gorgeous, but all James could think of was Dog. His bare feet pressed into the sharp pebbly ledge. He was alone.

71

He'd expected to be sore from lying on the damp ground all night. He stretched tall, and with a few clicks of his spine, he felt aligned, ready to clean up at the creek and fill his water bottle. Ben's map showed a brook in the forest a few hundred feet beneath the timberline.

James wasn't sure why, but he longed to bathe. He hadn't sweated or shoveled dirt or anything, though he felt as if he had. He just wanted fresh cold water on his face and chest. In the wilderness, said Ben, staying clean keeps your scent down, which is critical around wildlife.

The lively music of the stream lured James long before he saw the water. He followed a footpath into dark woods where a mossy bank gave easy access to a fast-moving creek. Almost other-worldly, a shady understory framed the brook like a picturesque painting from the last century. James sat down where the ferns lay pressed, figuring it was where other hikers sat to drink. His eyes moved over the lower trunks of firs and cedars where big patches of bark had been rubbed or scraped off, probably where varmints searched for insects.

As James leaned over the creek to fill his bottle, a light mist settled on his eyelashes and blurred his glasses. He took them off to clean with his shirttail, but the heavy horn-rimmed frames slipped through his wet fingers into the foaming water. Panic seized him! He couldn't see much of anything, so he tried to feel around the slick rocks. The current pulled his hand, and then his whole arm, downstream, away from where the glasses had fallen.

James freaked at the thought of losing his vision. He imagined the glasses downstream crushed against rocks. As he rolled up his Levis to the knees he held on to a sapling and toed his way into the eddying water. Knee-deep in spots, the stream sent ice rods up James's legs, bluing his skin and shrinking his vitals.

He kept searching with his feet. Then he got down on his knees to feel the bottom with his hands. Methodically, he covered the brook's width back and forth. With every second, James grew more desperate. He was chilled to the bone and shaking with alarm. How would he find his way back to the camp? Just then, his hand knocked randomly against something hard. Yes! His heart pounded. It was the glasses. His frames had wedged in an outcropping about ten feet down from where he'd dropped them. He carefully loosened them from the rocks. Putting his glasses on filled James with incredible relief. Then he realized that both lenses were badly scratched. Still, he could see better with them than without them. Chilled solid, his feet and fingers were beyond numb. He unzipped his soaking Levis and pulled them down and off each foot. He could dry them in the sun when he got back.

Man, that was close. If he'd lost his glasses, he might not have been able to find his way anywhere. And as far as defending himself? He wouldn't know a small bear from a big beaver.

James rubbed the lenses hard with his shirt, but they were deeply crosshatched with lines, the right lens worse than the left, and the frames listed sideways. He hated to be so dependent on these things, but he nearly lost them. Trembling and wet, James sat back on the bank to catch his breath. Regulating his pulse, he let go of the helpless feeling. It was a small miracle to find his glasses like that. James fingered a smooth round stone at the brook's edge and pocketed it in his jeans to remember.

72

Back at his camp ledge, the cloud cover below him was evaporating, revealing vast patches of deep green. Even through scratched glasses, James could make out hazy distances, dreamy and distorted. Suddenly, huge feathered wings swooped near his face. Squawking loudly, the large owl seemed to warn James. "Look around!" A pure-white feather floated down on James's head. He saved it and the brook stone in his beaded bear purse. He sat up and rubbed his gritty eyes, dreading what he had to do.

Getting back into the icy brook would damn near kill him, but James had to wash off his body odor. He carefully found his way back and kneeled beside the rushing stream. He floated his hands on the bubbling current. Cupping them with water, James raised his hands to drink the purest taste he'd ever known. Swallowing a cold, delicious mouthful, he looked up with a start. He stopped moving when he heard odd noises, shuffling, splashing, grunting, panting. James froze, staring.

Two golden eyes gleamed from behind large vine maple leaves. Maybe it was Dog? James's smile vanished when a hulking form emerged from behind the bush, snorting and scratching at the ground. The bear was so black against the brush that it had at first appeared small. Now it rose on its great hind legs and, for one godawful moment, he and

James looked eye to eye. James knew it was deadly to look a predator in the eye, but he couldn't help it. Warm urine ran down James's legs. He looked down. He was naked.

The bear bared his teeth and roared.

James fell to his knees and rolled away to stand just in time to see the bear lunge at him.

But the bear stopped. For a split second, there was nothing. Then the ground trembled with a thunderous gallop. James squinted to look. A blur of dust…. Wolves! At least a dozen of them in all colors flew at the bear, growling and snapping their jaws. James began shaking violently. He grabbed at a sapling but missed. A force seemed to throw him backward.

73

Days pass in a kind of fugue: a *ping, ping, ping* of machines, cold fingers on his wrist, IV poles clinking, and rustlings of stiff white skirts like so many birds. James sleeps constantly, it seems, even while he hears noises. The usual line between his conscious and unconscious mind is awash in a blur. The dreams seem real; the hospital noises, surreal. The only sensation that defines consciousness is pain, throbbing, killing pain.

When he feels no pain, he is likely dreaming. Often it is the same dream, one that gives him comfort and peace of mind. It starts as James runs through the forest, fast and weightless. To his left runs a pale wolf. Behind her and all around him runs her pack. They're taking him along tonight. Whenever they gain elevation, James sees the moon brilliantly reflecting on Spirit Lake.

How can he keep up with them? But he can. Branches whip his face as he leaps over fallen trees, the trunks thicker than he is tall. They are flying through ancient timber around the lake – two-hundred-foot noble firs and hemlocks and red cedars. Some of the firs are older than Christ.

James smells life bursting around and inside him, rotting and fresh life, both. When the wind blows a waft of new kill in their direction, they all stop running and lift their heads to the scent. And then they howl. James throws his head back and howls with them.

———— | ————

Two shapes in the doorway blot out the light. One short, one tall. Voices clash far away while he dozes. He barely hears them, yet he knows them. They pause at the open door, his door.

"Excuse me," says a nurse wearing a noisy starched skirt. James hears the clank of metal as she changes the IV.

Gloria moves to James's side. She sniffles and makes strange noises. James can feel Ben's presence. What does he see? What has happened? A knife cuts deep into his brain.

Ben returns later, wheeling himself in. He sits with James, silent, seeming to be there whenever James awakens. With Ben nearby, he can fall back to sleep.

James sees a blurry life-size Madonna extending her palms to him. She stands across the hall. James isn't sure if she is an apparition or an angel.

When James finally swims to the surface of his migraine and can speak a sentence, there is Ben.

"What'd the bear do?" James remembers the roar.

"Nothing." Ben smiles wide. "You fell and split your head open on a boulder. Good to hear your voice."

"Where's my mom?"

"Back East."

She left him again. James turns away and drifts into an uneasy sleep.

Later, his mind returned in bits. James could sip water and talk a little with Ben. "Whazzit say?"

Ben was sitting in his wheelchair as he held James's medical clipboard on his lap. "It says that you must have a powerful guardian spirit to be alive." Ben winked. "The doctor will be around this morning. You were unconscious for three days. They thought we were going to lose you."

James blinked twice. Time passed.

He awoke to Ben again.

"Jesus. I can't see a damn thing. Did Mom get me glasses?"

"And a good day to you, too. Hank's picking them up today," Ben said.

James turned his face away from Ben. He wished he would go, leave him alone. But Ben rested his hand on the blanket. James imagined him scanning the bandages wrapping his skull.

Ben shook his head. "I sent you into danger without preparing you." His voice was scratched, hoarse.

"It wasn't your fault." James thought of Dog and the wolves. He tried to hoist himself up to tell Ben, but dizzying pain stabbed into his skull. He eased back on the pillow.

"Settle down, guy." Ben smiled. "We'll have plenty of time to talk. I'm not leaving the ward anytime soon."

James was nodding off but jerked awake when a doctor marched in with a booming voice and a strange over-wide smile. "So we've decided to come back, have we?" He felt James's pulse briefly and shone a little flashlight in his eyes. "Well, let's take a look at the sutures, all hundred and two of them. Sir, if you don't mind?"

Ben wheeled himself out.

The doctor unwrapped James's bandage, chatting about how treacherous black bears were, how they were killing all the beautiful Douglas Firs by eating the bark. "Darn. No mirror. I wanted to show you the stitches. Don't worry, your bear won't be around for long. We're winning the tree fight. For the past few years, the annual bear kill in Washington alone has been five to seven thousand, each year. That's pretty good, wouldn't you say? Bet you'd like to shoot one yourself after that scuffle."

The more he talked, the more James gagged. He doubted he would have had the stomach to look in a mirror after that, even without his glasses.

"The good Lord must have stopped him," the doctor muttered as he touched the stitches with rubber gloves.

"It wasn't the Lord, doctor, it was a pack of wolves," James said, with more muster than he'd said anything in a while. After all, they deserved the credit.

"What? No, that would be impossible. We killed all of them, every last one. And if a wolf had been there, don't kid yourself, it would have finished off whatever the bear left of you. We wiped wolves out decades ago. Had to make the New World safe for our families. Oh, sorry, son. Did I upset you?"

James dry-heaved in nasty burps that sent stinging acid up his throat. All he wanted was for the doctor to shut up. "Sorry. I need sleep."

"Sure, James. I'll check in later." With a click of his heel, he turned and left.

James rolled to his side and pulled his legs close to his chest. He wrapped his arms tight around his knees and just wept outright for all those beautiful gray wolves and black bears that would be steel-trapped or shot. Would Dog be among them?

74

Uncle Hank visited the next day, slipped in, hat in hand, keeping quiet, and sat near James. He must have assumed his nephew was sleeping. James opened his eyes, trying to focus on the blurry man beside him.

"James? Oh, hey, I've got your new glasses." He tried to hand them to James before realizing he would have to help him. "Let me get that for you. There. They're not as clunky as the others, much lighter."

"I can see." James felt his head slip into alignment now that clean lines and angles had been restored. "Cool. They feel light."

"James, I waited days for you to be conscious enough to understand what I'm going to tell you. Are you still dopey? No? I figured by now you might want to hear how I found you.

"What? Sure, I'm awake."

"I returned for you on the next day at three as we agreed," Hank said, as he cranked up James's bed a bit. "I had no reason to worry. But when I found the camp empty, something was wrong. I raced straightaway down to the brook." Hank curled the brim of his hat in his fingers.

"The trampled ground around the stream bank said some big animals had tussled there, but I found no injured animal. And no you."

"Your broken eyeglasses flashed on the ground. When I stooped to pick them up, I saw wide drag marks in the dirt. I mulled over those marks and moved closer to examine the prints." He scratched his beard. "They were wolf prints, undeniably. Dozens of them flanked the smooth drag. Yet wolves haven't been in the Pacific Northwest for generations. So I followed the prints. They led to a small cave. I shone my flashlight into the closed space. There you were at my feet, lying naked on your side. As still as stone.

"I stooped into the cave to feel your artery. It pumped, though weakly. You needed a doctor, and fast, so I radioed for an airlift to St. John's. Here's the strange thing. Well, hell, there's plenty that's strange in this story. James, there was no blood inside the cave nor any blood at all on your head, despite the deep wound. Not a speck.

"I wouldn't have believed it if I hadn't seen it with my own eyes. Your gash had been cleaned of blood and dirt. How you breathed at all was a mystery. But it was no mystery how you got into the cave. The prints told the story, unbelievable though it is. Wolves had evidently stopped the bear and ran it off. They dragged you to their den.

"It was still warm when I got there." Hank shook his head. 'Tell you the truth, it smelled like they had just left." Hank sighed. "The scent was so rich, so familiar. I haven't smelled a wolf since I was a boy." He shook his head.

"You wouldn't wake up so I took off my shirt and vest and draped them over you. Then I sat with you, squeezing fresh water from my bandanna into your mouth. Your hand felt like marble, James. Cool marble. So I lay down next to you, warming you up until help came."

He'd almost died? Christ, that rattled James. Even in his druggy state of mind, he grasped the basics. Dog saved his life. The bear would've killed him. And if Uncle Hank had come any later, he'd have found a corpse. A very clean corpse.

75

Hank returned later with Tess. They slipped into James's hospital room as quietly as a whisper. Though they sat in two chairs beside him, James kept his eyes shut. His head throbbed. He felt remote even from family. They removed their jackets, settling in to stay. He was a wise one, that Uncle Hank, so James opened his eyes and blinked to focus. Couldn't focus worth crap. Then he remembered the new glasses on the table. Tess reached over and placed them on him.

"Hi, guys," James whispered. "Good to see you."

Hank's face lit up. "Good to be alive, you mean?" He hushed himself seeing James flinch.

"Thank God you're alright," said Tess. "I prayed. We all prayed." She put her hand on James's shoulder and smiled.

"Have you seen my mom? I thought I heard her."

"You did," Tess said, "but you were unconscious, or maybe not. Anyway, I'm sorry to tell you that yesterday she had to fly back East."

"Why?" *Why in hell would she leave me half dead in a strange hospital?* "To get a divorce?" James would forgive her for that.

"Yes. And to get June." Tess was excited to tell James. "June was miserable at Dan's apartment. She wouldn't eat, wouldn't talk to him, she just cried for you and Aunt Kay. He didn't know what to do with her. He has to go to work, of course. So he agreed to let her live with Kay."

Hearing this, James missed June like never before. Of course, she was sad. And lonely. What did this mean….

Hank read his mind. "Dan dropped the temporary custody judgment. They'll share custody."

"Good! She'll bring June back here?" A thrill surged through James. A new start for a new family, one without Dan.

"No." Hank took James's hand. He knew this would be tough news for him. "She wants to stay back East, wants June to go to private school, too."

James bristled at the mention of his former excuse for a life.

"Your mother is trying to get Dan to pay your tuition." Hank watched James intently.

"What if I don't want to go back?" Barely audible, James spoke in the general direction of his navel.

Silence. Hank reached for a tissue to give him. "She's going to want you back there, James," Hank said. "I'm sure June would want that, too."

James stuffed his anger. Clearly, it didn't matter what he wanted.

"So." Uncle Hank shifted. "The nurses are putting in a call to Kay now. Let's wheel you down there."

———————◆———————

"James, how are you, honey?" The tinny voice pleading from a million miles away sounded nothing like his mother. "Are you alright?"

James picked at the days-old bandage covering his head, trying to unravel the gauze. He didn't answer her. It hurt to hold the phone receiver against his ear. He leaned heavily on the white Formica counter of the nurse's station. "Why did you leave?"

"I'm so sorry, James. I hated to leave you. But I had to get June. She's doing much better now. Aren't you glad?" She waited for another answer. Then, hearing none she plunged over the cliff. "I can't come back out, though. I'm sorry. I must stay here with her."

"Of course. It's okay, Mom. I have Uncle Hank and everybody here to help me. And June does need you. Can you come back when she's better?" James was screaming inside, PLEASE?

"I am so proud of you, honey. I want you to stay with Hank and Marie only until you're well enough to travel, just a couple of weeks probably."

"*What?*" James sat straight in the chair, his broad shoulders squared. "No Mom, no." He spoke in the direction of the ceiling as tears welled up. "Listen to me. June doesn't need that fancy school and neither do I. Just come back here, please."

"No, honey, I have a life in Attleboro, whether I'm married to Dan or not. I'm looking for a job. I think my friends in my bridge group or my country club friends will help me find one. Regardless, I can't just uproot us across the country."

"Why not?" The tip of the pencil James was doodling with snapped off on the nurses' notepad. "Yes, you can!" He gripped the pencil like a knife and started stabbing into the pad. He could hear his blood pumping, working up to a massive migraine.

"Why not do this for your kids, Mom? We've got June back. Let's start over. Let's get as far from Dan as we can." The phone felt heavier and heavier in James's hand. He sagged from the effort. She was impossible. "I thought being a family mattered to you."

"James. That's not fair." She said it loudly. James pulled the receiver away too late. His head was throbbing. "Of course family matters to me," she went on. "I have to get the divorce settled and the terms of custody. I can't do that overnight."

"Mom." James's voice was quiet but deadly firm. "Please. I don't want to go back."

"You've got to. June needs you. We're Northeast people. You know that. Hamilton will guarantee a first-rate college next year. Think of your future."

"I am." Two pictures swam to the surface of his mental magic eight ball, side by side: James, the ivy league student, and James, the adventurer, heading into the wilderness. "I am."

76

Hank came back ten minutes later to wheel James to his room. Seeing him, James quickly wiped his eyes and closed them. Why couldn't his mother see that they'd be better off out here, living close to her sister and Uncle Hank? Close to Harmony Falls.

Now more than ever James loathed everything about his life back East. Even things he didn't use to mind, like after-school TV, or his so-called friends at Hamilton. They seemed lame to him now.

Though he hadn't realized to what extent, James had dreaded every day of private school. He tried to ignore those phony brats who cut him down. They ridiculed his swimming and his submersion. *What kind of sport is that?* James would never be one of them. He knew that now. They had known it instantly, of course. It was a class thing. James hated his mother's pretensions. The bridge, the charities, the country club. He hated them almost as much as Dan's Back Bay golf buddies.

But even with Dan out of the picture, James's mother still wouldn't leave Attleboro. Why had he ever imagined she could give up her phony life? She lacked the courage to pull away from the herd. Yet despite her Manhattan airs, James suspected that his mom didn't belong back East any more than he did.

"Hey." Hank interrupted James's thinking. "Whether your mother comes or not, we'd be happy to have you stay." His uncle looked James over. "You're already going to miss a month with that concussion. Think about it."

James thought about it. Hell, every minute he lay in that dreary hospital bed he thought about it. More than anything in the world, he wanted to live near Spirit Lake and Harmony Falls. Problem was, he would have to leave if his mother stayed back East. He would fly there as soon as he was healthy enough. But not because of his mother.

He'd go back because he had promised June, and his promise meant something. Wouldn't he be as selfish as his mother if he stayed out here without them? That logic might have been sound, but it didn't comfort him. How could he leave the wild, uncivilized land that had, in one summer, raised him to a man?

Ben understood, of course. They took their hospital exercises together, twice a day, at dawn and dusk at Ben's insistence. He said those were good times for discussing spiritual, or what he called 'deterministic' matters, though James hadn't a clue what the word meant. The only determinism James knew was being determined to keep up with Ben's ten laps around their floor twice daily. Hardly fair. Ben had the wheelchair.

Insisting on turning the wheels on his chair, Ben pushed while James walked stiffly alongside, fighting dizziness. Ben had to do time with crutches, too, which just about killed him. But he was indeed a tough old cowboy. The way James figured, during those early days, just being ambulatory was good enough for them.

It was on their first tour of action that James told Ben in detail about Dog and the other wolves. Ben asked a dozen questions and James answered each one. Dog's color? Blond. The others? Gray or black. How close did they come to James? Dog permitted James's touch, even welcomed it. The rest came within two feet of him. What was the tone of their howl?

"How do I know?" James looked puzzled. "They just howled."

"What exactly did they do to the bear?

"They growled and flew at it like bullets from a shotgun. That's all I saw. Guess I fell then.

"Was Dog with them?"

"Yes." James said. "She led the pack."

They paused in the hall of the hospital to talk. James was relieved to unburden himself.

"Describe her."

James had already told Ben she was young and female, and she had distinct dark markings on her eyes. With each detail James gave, Ben nodded as if factoring an equation. Soon, Ben smiled broadly and started chuckling. What was so damn funny? Ben smiled and explained how it was James's good fortune to find a spirit wolf. "You will have the wolf's other-worldly protection bestowed on you," Ben explained. "You've earned it." Having a spirit guide is proof, he said, that James is a quester. To Ben, this was cause for joy.

Seeing Ben laughing so hard, his twisted face bunching up like that, James started laughing, too. And so it went: one would stop, then the other would chuckle, and they'd both start up all over again. James realized afterward that he had never before seen Ben cut loose and laugh.

Once they wound down, and James wiped his eyes, Ben said, "Now I will explain wolf medicine." He looked around, to be sure they were alone.

"Wolves are the true spirit of the wilderness, the free, wild spirit. They howl sometimes just for the fun of it. Yet wolves teach us that true freedom requires discipline, and loyalty demands responsibility. This is the medicine that you need, James."

"Think of Dog, the alpha wolf, who led her pack to save your life. They didn't kill the bear. They ran it off. Often a mere glance, a posture, or a growl is all that is necessary to determine dominance. Now, like the wolf, you don't have to prove yourself. You know who you are.

"The loyalty of wolves to their pack has no limits. They protect their own against every danger. They'll kill if they must. Of course, they must kill to live, to feed their young. Yet they show gentleness and respect to their females and cubs. They will never leave behind one of their own. They regularly sacrifice themselves for the good of the pack." Ben paused. "What can wolf medicine teach you?"

One word jumped out for James. *Sacrifice*. A wolf had saved his life. What must James now sacrifice? He would think about that.

"Dog will visit you in dreams and visions. Even if you live in a city, it doesn't matter, she'll be there to protect you your entire life. She will bring along a battalion of wolves, if necessary." Ben reached over and put his hand on James's arm. He smiled. His eyes were moist.

"You've brought the Ghost Wolves back to Spirit Lake."

77

After the doctor removed James's sutures, he was released from St. John's Hospital to the care of his aunt and uncle who promised to keep him still. Dizziness and headaches hobbled his every move. He recuperated at their small house in Longview. Uncle Hank shuttled back and forth from Spirit Lake until he closed up for the season, in late September. But he promised James they would have one last night at the lodge before he left.

In the first week of September, public schools reopened all around the country, but James was instead enrolled in an antibiotic limbo with an infection in the cut on his head. In his feverish mind, he had written his final version of the meaning of life. He was ready to go.

But apparently not. With time, his fever and headaches subsided. By the first of October, James announced to his aunt, who'd anticipated the day, "I'm ready for that campfire."

"I'll round up the crew," she said and hugged him gently.

Harmony Falls officially closed each year the last week of August, when the Portland families who owned the resort and cabins descended on Spirit Lake. Their Regatta was famous, as were the sailors who ran the finest, fastest rigs money could buy. By the first of September when the Portlanders departed, it was clean-up time for Marie and Hank.

They prepared the old lodge for winter, sealing windows, reinforcing cabins, and chopping an impressive wood supply for the mountaineers from Longview Ski Club who always happened by in winter's deepest snow.

It had been seven weeks since James had been back. He was eager to see Gloria and Ben, who shared an apartment in Portland. More than missing any one person, though, James was desperate to get back to Spirit Lake.

When Aunt Marie drove them all up from Longview that day, she picked up Ben and Gloria at Townie Diner, where they'd driven in from the city. After big hugs all around, the four piled back into Marie's car. Ben needed the whole back seat to keep his leg straight. Though the cast had been removed recently, he still wore a brace.

"How long before you can walk without crutches, Ben?"

"That, my young friend, remains to be seen."

Gloria jumped in. "His doctors are amazed at his recovery."

"It's all Charles Atlas, James. I can assure you." They shared a laugh as James remembered what a scold of a coach Ben had been.

Shifting in cramped quarters in the front seat, James smiled at Gloria. Once he'd thought Ben and Gloria were an unlikely couple. But, as with so many things that summer, he'd changed his mind. Turned out they were both outcasts at the game of love, with trust in short supply all around. Despite that, or because of it, they got along.

When James wrote June letters or funny postcards — and he tried to write every few days — he promised he'd see her soon. He knew that made her happy, and it did him, too. Some days, though, he wondered how he could possibly leave.

That first October day was surely one of them.

James was the first one out of the old lifeboat when it reached the dock. Delicious balsam fragrance filled his nose, and candy-colored autumn leaves pulled his gaze up to the lodge. The big cottonwood next to the kitchen shimmered bright yellow. James stopped moving. As the sun touched the canopy of heart-shaped leaves, each leaf gleamed like hammered gold. Poetry, James thought. So beautiful, yet each leaf was already dead. Beneath the canopy, a tangle of red-orange vine maple leaves flamed over cool green boulders sunk in umber moss.

"Hey you, stranger!" Tess yelled from the top of the diving tower. She had come up a day earlier with her dad. James waved at her like crazy. Tess had taken a job at the Portland animal shelter, which included a small apartment, so he hadn't seen her through his recuperation.

"Come on down, Cousin." He turned back to the boat. "Ben, hand me the crutches." James took them in one hand and with the other offered Ben his arm to help him get on the dock. Gloria tied the boat.

"Thanks, James. I'm losing patience with the need for them."

James shadowed Ben as he checked off completed cabin repairs and listed more for spring. The afternoon passed in tranquility. Later, James and Tess walked up to the bottom of the waterfall, where it became Harmony Creek. It was the steepest hike James could manage without getting dizzy. They sat on a felled tree by the bubbling water and gazed up.

Where frothy water cascaded over the high cataract of Harmony Falls, ice formed like fine lace over veiled cleavage. Chunks of speckled ice melded but did not melt, in the crooks of fallen trees that crossed the falls. Swim season long over, this time of the year was sweeter. Once the tourists left, autumn brought a sharper brilliance. The stalwart few who stayed on the lake through the winter must have hailed from the Langes's stock, the pioneering homesteaders who cut the first wagon road into Spirit Lake before the turn of the century. James's cheeks stung from arctic winds, and he too felt connected to the Langes.

"I wanted to tell you about Max." Tess brushed away a few orange leaves from her hair.

"There's more?" There was always more with Tess.

"He talked to me like he'd known me all my life. He said I was gifted, James, that I could find more children like I found June. He told me about a group of people who search for missing kids — parents, detectives, all kinds of people." She nodded. "Max searched for his daughter, Suzy. He never found her."

Tess looked away, sat up a little straighter, and turned to look James straight in the eye. "I have a confession to make." She paused. Then her crooked smile broke her face open. "I've been working with the missing kids' group. You thought I was at the animal shelter, right?" Tess smiled, her green eyes wide.

James slowly nodded, unconsciously peeling the bark off a log.

"I know. Everybody did. It was all on the quiet. But here's the news." Tess's eyes were bright. "We found three kids so far, and I'm getting more leads. They come to me in my dreams, James, just like you said. I can sort of see the child against a bit of background. It's the background that locates them. Like the eagle's nest with June. And the three girls at the carousel, remember? That's where we found them. In a warehouse under the carousel floor. They were kept in the control room. Look at these pictures, James."

James took the prints she'd been holding.

Oh man. Hard to look at. One tired little girl was dressed like a circus floozy. Unwittingly, James transposed June's face onto hers. His gut lurched. Stricken for those poor kids, James dropped the photos as he put his head in his hands.

"I don't know how you can do this, Tess. You're braver than I am." James looked away, never wanting to see another picture of her rescues again. Then he reminded himself that these girls were the lucky ones.

"Oh, nonsense. Be happy for me. I feel useful." Tess's face glowed pink.

"What about the ones you find too late? How will you handle that?"

Tess nodded, solemn. "I don't know…. but I won't let that stop me." Quiet then, she swirled a branch in figure eights in the frothy water.

"We wouldn't have found June," James said, "or the other kids, if it hadn't been for you." He nudged her, teasing. They laughed together sitting by the splashing creek. When they stood to go back to the lodge, James hugged Tess, ever so briefly. "Thanks."

James often imagined a new kind of family, his Northwest relatives, living in a cabin near Spirit Lake. It could work. Tess was like a sister to him, and Aunt Marie and Uncle Hank were cooler than his mother, by far. Ben and Gloria, well, they had become kin.

James sat on the deck while Tess went back inside. He tried not to think of how he would say goodbye. On a tall snag beside the golden cottonwood perched a belted kingfisher, the first he had ever seen, though he had heard the repetitive cackle in the trees when Ben identified its song. With a large crested head and prominent beak, the bird blinked down at James, a sort of 'hello', and flew off. James had learned the songs of most local birds, Vaux's Swifts and Townsend's Solitaires, even the soft *churring* of Lewis's Woodpecker, from his hikes with Ben. He was proud that he could also identify several species' scat, from bears to martens to coyotes. Funny thing to be proud of. But he was.

———————◆———————

By afternoon, Gloria and James had purple fingers from filling a three-gallon bucket with huckleberries for her jams. The nearest berry patch happened to be in the same sunny meadow that had been, earlier that summer, bright with rainbow lupines and paintbrush. It was the same meadow where James and Natalie rolled in cotton-tailed bear grass. For an instant, the sweet clean scent of her hair swirled around him. But where they had lain, bony stalks of browned bear grass replaced lavender and scarlet. All the blooms had gone to seed.

78

"Put that stuff on the table, guys." Gloria knelt on the floor in her Indian-print skirt, scrubbing the walls of white cabinets that lined the kitchen. The upper cabinets would be sparkling, too, when she finished.

Tess and James toted into the kitchen two cardboard boxes of supplies, salmon fillets and wild rice, for one last dinner, and eggs and bacon, coffee, and fresh sourdough for breakfast. Once everyone left the next day, Hank would close up the place and trailer the lifeboat to dry dock for seven months. After that, any day trips to Harmony Falls would have to be on snowshoes or alpine skis.

Preparing dinner, Gloria and Tess and James shared a hard-won optimism.

"How's June doing? Gloria asked.

"Better now than she was at Dan's." James could laugh about it now. "She's probably watching *Lassie*, maybe eating ketchup-covered meatloaf on TV tables with Mom."

Tess said, "I can see that." She laughed.

"I'll tell you one thing," James announced. "June'd better be there when I get home. Otherwise, if my mother can't get custody, I might just grab a transcontinental Greyhound right back."

"Here, here," Gloria lifted her ice tea. "'Course you'll have to move to Longview. We're all cut off from Spirit Lake after tonight. Until May, maybe. Depends on the weather.

"Hey, James. Let's head down to the pit. You pick the firewood." Ben waited for James.

"Deal."

The early evening passed in tranquility. After the meal, the others lingered over Gloria's poached salmon with mountain blueberry sauce. They guffawed in the dark burl-wood dining hall, a tavern of buddies riding each other as only close friends can do.

He could have been a part of that, he knew, but James preferred to be outside, to feel the clear cold night on his cheeks. He filled his lungs as deeply as he could and held it a moment then exhaled slowly.

It felt natural for James to slip beside Ben's left elbow while he walked, in case he needed support. Day by day, Ben was walking better, and maybe soon he wouldn't need the crutches. He'd already carved himself a cane of alder, sanding the handle buttery smooth. Ben would prevail.

They had built the fire in the late afternoon. Ben now set a match to it. He handed the fire pole to James. Really? This was an unexpected honor. James loved pushing together those throbbing coals, seeing the strength gather in the glowing blue center. This process now felt elemental to his nature. He had to watch the coals closely, looking for chances to intensify the flame. If he was distracted, the fire languished and perfectly good wood fumed, left unburned at the sides.

A good fire needed tending.

"I've been wanting to talk." James paused for Ben's eye. "About wolf medicine."

Ben pulled from his pocket a kerchief filled with dried sagebrush and he threw some small branches on the fire. With a crackle, the herbs caught fire and smoked. James inhaled deeply. The scent relaxed him into a memory of Dog, her soft warm coat, the way her eyes had said thank you, how good he had felt caring for her, having her company. Sage odors of family Thanksgivings blended with these wilder memories. Both were kin.

"You had to find your own path to this place of forgiveness, James." Ben leaned towards him to put his big arm on his shoulder.

James nodded. "A wolf would have done the same to save a cub," he said. James bent down to break off a sprig of sage and rolled it in his fingers. He said quietly, "I would have died for her."

Ben nodded.

"You know," James pulled back to face Ben. "The hardest medicine is saying goodbye. This is the sacrifice you spoke of."

"You'll be back," Ben said. "The Northwest runs in your dreams now, courses through your blood." Ben tapped the embers with a branch.

"I guess we'll have to see what happens."

"What do you *mean*? We won't have Dan's money now." James heard the whine creep into his voice. No. He shut his mouth and listened instead.

"You've come this far. Why don't you try believing in something you think is impossible." Ben stared at James, daring him.

A long howl rode on the wind. Then another. And another.

A pleasant familiar shiver danced up James's spine.

Dog and the Ghost Wolves.

79

Aunt Marie bolted outside, sprinting past James to the dock. He called to her.

"Hey, where're you going?"

"I left the fruit pie in my car," she yelled, "and Gloria will have my head if I don't get it." It took her about two seconds to untie, push off, and motor away into the darkness. James could still hear the purr of the engine, but the night had swallowed his Aunt Marie.

Exuberant laughter pulled his attention to the amber-lighted lodge, where Tess, Gloria, and Hank spilled out the front door, Tess bounding first to the fire to stand with James.

"What the heck were we doing inside? When we should be out here with you! It's our last night together." Her sentence faltered and dropped into a hole she rushed to fill. "But we'll make it fun." Tess sat on a seat-worn log, cradling her guitar as the other hooligans settled themselves around the fire.

"It was about time you guys came out." He teased them. "And don't give us any lame excuse about freezing your fingers off."

James tossed light sticks into the fire. His last night.

Gloria talked first, her eyes bright, looking at Ben.

"Tess has been telling us about the rescue operation. They're saving kids from trafficking. That's right. And Tess is finding them." Gloria beamed at her. "I want to help."

"Maybe we can all help." Uncle Hank was jumping in, too? Uh, oh. Hank was talking the language of lost causes, James's specialty. Ben must have noticed him slump. He nudged him.

"Wish you could help, too, do you?" Ben's gravelly voice touched James like soft fur.

James nodded. He looked away. Everything in the world that had been any good was bittersweet. Clearly, that was the way it would be from now on.

"James. How will you keep Spirit Lake alive when you leave?" Ben drew James out of his sadness. "Do you have some good places you can visit in your mind? The waterfall? The hideout? The bottom of Spirit Lake?" They all laughed.

"I've been thinking about that." James smiled. "Seems to me I left some of myself on the side of that volcano. Whenever I need peace I'll go sit on that ledge and face east. And just breathe.

Or into the lake, for submersion, where everything becomes clear.

Or lying on the diving tower touching the stars.

Your songs, Tess, and your dreams, too.

And stacking wood with you, Ben, when we had our best talks." James had learned so much from him. "When I recall your drumming, the whole summer will come back."

"I made something for you while we were in the hospital." Ben reached behind him and handed James a cloth sack.

Strange shape, thought James. He slipped his hand inside and eased out a dream catcher. James held it up to the firelight. The webbing Ben had spun in the center circle was finely woven with two owl feathers. Two long feathers hung off each end. James looked quizzically at Ben.

"I gave you two of my eagle feathers. The others were in your medicine bag."

The brook stone hung from a shorter string of rawhide. Most mysterious, though, a tuft of blond wolf fur danced on a rawhide string. James stared, not believing what he saw. This was Dog's talisman, her soft bunch of pale fur. James had no idea how it got into his medicine bag. She was gone long before he'd thought to keep a piece of her.

Ben smiled. "Hank found the fur in the cave. When he lifted you up, it was pressed beneath you."

"Thanks," James said. He shrugged. He didn't have to understand every mystery. When he hugged Ben, they held each other. James swallowed hard.

"Good grief, are those snow clouds forming?" Tess abruptly wrapped her arms around herself against the chill.

James gazed at the moon, dimmed now by low clouds floating in front of it. "Snow? How can that be? In October?"

Hank nodded his head and his grizzled beard shuddered. "Yup. We've had snow in July. Assume nothing when it comes to weather at Spirit Lake, James. That's how folks die on Loowit."

"Did you hear that?" Tess whispered. "A loon! Over there on the shore. James, look." She pointed. He located it by its laughing cry. He could make out its dots, tiny orbs against a black lake. Early autumn had brought the loons back, on their way south from their arctic breeding ground. Another loon's distinctive song answered from somewhere across the lake.

"That's good luck, you know," James said to Tess, and they smiled, remembering. "You'll have good dreams tonight."

"I believe you're right. Hey, that reminds me of an old Lead Belly song I want to sing for Max." Tess raised her Coke as a toast, and the others raised whatever they had.

"Here's to the brave old miner who saved June. And showed me my path. He asked only that I find his daughter and tell her his story, and I will. I promised him. Hey Gloria, sing along on the chorus. You, too, James and Dad. Come on. Do it for Max."

Tess paced the song like a slow waltz. She began to sing softly. After a few stanzas, they all sang louder and swayed back and forth in their seats. With conviction.

> Irene, goodnight, Irene goodnight
>
> Goodnight Irene, goodnight Irene
>
> I'll see you in my dreams.

James didn't sing or sway. He was too entranced by St. Helens, his fair Loowit, draped in gauze, still pulling him close. James whispered farewell. Loowit had been his lodestar through the summer. There was a vexing constancy about her as if day in and day out they each measured their mortal lives by her and came up poorer. Girdling her was a ripe wilderness so young and ruthless that James finally understood Uncle Hank's remark. Indeed. Here James had found his own wild heart. He sighed deeply, hearing again the hoot of the little spotted owl as if he knew James was leaving.

***

Stopping her song, Tess turned to the lake, where the pinpoint of a running light swelled with each second, and the faint hum of the motor grew. "Here comes the pie!"

Soon the old lifeboat glided up parallel to the dock. Aunt Marie hopped out and placed a foil-covered pie on the dock. She quickly tied up.

"What did I miss?" she said.

Right then, fat clouds blotted the moon's light. A silhouette stepped onto the dock and seemed to scan them at the fire. Clouds passed as her blond hair shined in the moonlight.

Could it be?

"James!" June screamed and ran straight at him. His heart blew apart with fireworks. He couldn't believe it! He opened his arms wide to catch her and pull her in close. Ben laughed heartily at the impossible turn of events.

Around the circle, all eyes were on them as June wrapped her arms around James's waist and commenced to jump up and down, screaming, "We're here, James! We're here to stay!"

Behind her, their mother stepped easily off the dock and walked toward James. Radiant, Kay placed her hand lightly on his arm and spoke just to him.

"Turns out you were right, honey. There was nothing for us back East."

James hugged his mother hard, still shaking his head. Impossibly, she had come through.

Just then, June squeezed herself into the circle of their embrace.

She was, after all, still June.

THE END

POSTSCRIPT

Mount St. Helens was mistakenly believed to be dormant for the first two-thirds of the 20ᵗʰ Century. In a violent eruption on May 18, 1980, most residents had been evacuated, but fifty-seven souls either chose to remain or couldn't get out fast enough. The atomic-force volcanic explosion caused an unprecedented landslide, displacing a third of St. Helens' mass into Spirit Lake. The attendant firestorm instantly leveled every tree and killed all living things within miles.

AUTHOR'S NOTES

LOSING JUNE is a story of spirits, of a lake inhabited by spirits and a tale told largely through my own family's spirits who, though long-dead, kept nudging me to write it. So I must first acknowledge them, now sixty years hence, remembering when we were all alive at glorious Spirit Lake. One summer. 1959.

Among them were my mother Catherine Maureen Sanders, a.k.a. Maureen Mitchell; my brother, James William Sanders; my Aunt Mary and Uncle Bob Gillis, and dear Cousin Cass, Mary Catherine Gillis (maiden name). None is entirely faithfully represented here. It is enough that they've come to the party. Becoming characters, they've come alive and chosen their own paths in the narrative, thankfully beyond litigation.

Among the living, of course, there can be no greater support than John, my partner, who has read every version, among them at least ten thousand pages of deleted junk, and given to each page not only his reason but his imagination. He has soared through the fantasy right along with me and the spirits. Thank you, John, for believing.

Early readers of fledgling first novels deserve a special gratitude as they are handed a bunch of pages of who-knows-what, and they take it on faith that somewhere in that mess of words there is a gem worth keeping.

I've been lucky to have quite a few of these encouraging souls who helped me find my way into writing a story that was already in my head and heart but not yet in my skill set. That kind of learning took a decade, but I wouldn't have persisted so doggedly without these first readers who, like me, felt the story before it was even manifest. They included Susan Brown, who dared me to enter a contest for Breakthrough Novels and helped to shape the early premise of LOSING JUNE – thanks, pal, we've come a long way. My sister Sue Labella has read nearly as many versions as John and has given months to the cause. Other readers include Peter Gunther, John Johansson, Bob Warren, Jessica Swift, Josef Woodman,

Peter Biello, Cynthia Ryalls, and Martha Dowhan -- they all suffered through early drafts. Thank you.

As LOSING JUNE began to take better shape, some of these folks patiently read many revisions and continued through the years to encourage finer versions. I found other readers, too, who dared to challenge me to more astute writing. These included Sally Linder, Ed Couch, Megan Mayhew Bergman, Jack Neuhauser, and Benjamin Squires, my 15-year-old great nephew.

My first year of the project was devoted entirely to research the places I'd been too young to remember. I was eight years old in 1959, so memories were spotty yet profound. To compensate, I read every book I could find on pre-eruption St. Helens, Spirit Lake legends and people, Native tribes -- the Cowlitz and the Klickitat, Fifties music and culture, volcanology, Portland crime and the McClelland Investigation, gray wolves' senseless extermination, prostitution and what used to be called 'white slavery' on the West Coast, as well as Old West legends and of course, ghost stories.

But the book that helped me remember the most about life at Harmony Falls was Christine Colasurdo's *Return to Spirit Lake*. Particularly for her details of Harmony Falls Lodge, the climb up St. Helen's, and the region's native plants, her book was invaluable. With a biologist's eye and a poet's ear, Ms. Colasurdo provides the facts that spark memories for those of us that have half forgotten the glory of pre-eruption St. Helens.

I include a full bibliography and blogs for LOSING JUNE in my website.

Special thanks go to our daughter Elektra Knight for tech support and to actor Ryan and Aura Paige for their audio book magic.

Gratitude goes to book designer Marian Willmott, who artfully used a 1959 family photograph of James, swimming in Spirit Lake, and to Rachel Fisher at Onion River Press. Thanks, too, to our family, who has believed in the story from the outset, a dozen years ago.

Finally, heartfelt hugs are bestowed upon my dear friends and beta readers, Rosemary Widman, Deborah Noland Witherington, Kit McGinnis, and Beverly Coe, who have gotten me over the finish line.

ABOUT THE AUTHOR

Former travel editor for GOURMET magazine, a travel writer for FOOD & WINE magazine, and a freelancer for other nationals, Catherine Bodnar is a retired professor who taught at two Vermont colleges with a Ph.D. in American Literature. *Losing June* is her first novel and is inspired in part by the time her family worked at Harmony Falls Lodge the summer of 1959 at Spirit Lake, WA. Catherine lives with her husband John in Vermont with their beloved dogs, birds and wildlife.

Photo: John Bodnar 2022

IN MEMORIAM

JAMES WILLIAM SANDERS

www.ingramcontent.com/pod-product-compliance
Lightning Source LLC
Chambersburg PA
CBHW030653190726
48286CB00008B/2795